In a Strange Land

The dramatic opening of Stanley Middleton's new novel will, perhaps, surprise his regular readers. James Murren, a promising young musician and composer, walking in the woods outside the proto-typical Midlands town of all Middleton's novels, finds a black, sodden corpse floating in a pond.

The body turns out to be the uncle of James's young mistress. He had committed suicide. And this ominous note is one that is sounded throughout this deeply felt, extraordinarily penetrating novel. For the dead man, life itself had been a strange land. For James, his work as a teacher, his unsatisfactory affairs, his relationships with pupils, acquaintances, chance encounters, never seem to add up to a significant whole. A Polish couple (the husband dying of cancer) typify quite literally the experience of life in a strange land.

Yet, this is by no means a gloomy book. For, while much of it is concerned with death, decay and the impermanence of human relationships, it is music that provides the contrapuntal note of hope and transcendent joy, and James learns that music 'could resume life after the most desperate of smashes'. Once again, in this subtle and complex book, Middleton explores human relationships with precision and understatement.

The novels of Stanley Middleton

A Short Answer
Harris's Requiem
A Serious Woman
The Just Exchange
Two's Company
Him They Compelled
Terms of Reference
The Golden Evening
Wages of Virtue
Apple of the Eye
Brazen Prison
Cold Gradations
A Man Made of Smoke
Holiday
Distractions
Still Waters
Ends and Means
Two Brothers

In a Strange Land

STANLEY MIDDLETON

Hutchinson of London

Hutchinson & Co. (Publishers) Ltd
3 Fitzroy Square, London W1P 6JD

London Melbourne Sydney Auckland
Wellington Johannesburg and agencies
throughout the world

First published 1979

Set in Linotype Plantin by
Input Typesetting Ltd

Printed in Great Britain by
The Anchor Press Ltd, and bound by
Wm Brendon & Son, both of
Tiptree, Essex

British Library CIP data

Middleton, Stanley
In a strange land.
I. Title
823'.9'1F PR6063.I25I/

ISBN 0 09 139230 5

To my friends in Carlton Ward,
Nottingham General Hospital
with gratitude.

1

The surface of the water gleamed coldly silver as the young man, hurrying, flicked with a rough stick at hawthorn bushes. From the other side of the pond he could hear, but not see at this moment, the schoolboys whom he had passed on the clay path between the two stretches of water. Their voices were clear; they had been arguing if this 'lake' (their name) ever froze completely and had been picking thin plates of ice from the bank, shouting, skimming. Now one sang, without energy, but in tune, choirboy-true.

> 'Ee-i, Topsy, will you go?
>   Topsy, will you go-o, Topsy, will you go-o?
> Ee-i, Topsy, will you go
>   Down to the ee-i-o?'

James Murren whistled his twig, then cast it, underhand and powerfully, to his right on to the deserted football pitches. He thrust his hands into his overcoat pockets, stopped, loosened with his toe a large pebble from the path, dribbled, kicked it dismissively towards his stick. The boys were talking excitedly.

He stared across the football pitches, with frost irregularly cleared by the sun, out to where the land rose in a gentle hummock hiding the ground behind which the hall once stood, though not high enough to mask the tops of lime trees lining the squire's avenue. Lost in thought, he saw nothing now; the park, empty as always on winter mornings, surrounded him, allowed him liberty to daze, to dream on his feet.

'Mester, mester.'

The two boys shouted, for him presumably. He heard one begin to run.

'Mester. Are you there, mester?'

'Here. What do you want?'

His voice sounded sharp, authoritative, since he was annoyed at the interruption of his solitude, his do-nothing. He paced round the water, was met by a trotting boy, face red, eyes disturbed.

'There's somebody in the lake,' the child gasped.

'Who?'

The idiotic question he barked out as he began to run. The second boy squatted on the edge where a black bundle floated by short-stemmed reeds. They could see the head, the hands.

'I can't reach it.'

James Murren knelt, stretched, was only inches short. Helplessly he tried again, found the distance unaltered. Pushing himself to his feet, he looked about. The second boy was dragging a branch along, cockily, knowing this was right action.

'How about this?'

Murren broke, tore off a few twigs, officiously, as if he needed to demonstrate his lack of panic to the youngsters. Now he knelt again, reached, hooked the thick end in the sodden rags and pulled. To his surprise he moved the body without difficulty. He dropped his branch, took a grip on the shoulder of the jacket.

'Right,' he ordered. 'Come on, lads. Let's have him out.'

They heaved, not easily, splashing icy water on

themselves, on the bank, before they manhandled the corpse awkwardly on to the path. Its eyes stared; thin hair divided itself in strands. He felt the dead heart, through the drenched clothes, the no-pulse. A grey face, old, chilled.

'Who's the runner?' he heard himself ask. The first boy stood ready. 'Get up to the golf house there,' he pointed, 'quick as you can. Nine-nine-nine, police and ambulance. Sharp.' The lad dashed off. They watched him. 'D'you know anything about resuscitation?' he demanded. The second boy turned his head away. 'No more do I.' He rolled the corpse face downward, lifted the saturated jacket, pushed vigorously at the ribs, strongly, in ignorance. Nothing happened. He changed his hold slightly, pressed, thumbed vigorously for no result. The runner had now crossed the rising field, had disappeared into the road by the thin line of trees, would make his destination inside two or three minutes. A light shone at the clubhouse; members turned up at crack of dawn in any weather. James Murren worked again at the body, until he panted.

'Is he dead?' The boy perched two yards away.

'I should think so.'

He pumped again, in a frenzy, as at a machine, feeling neither repulsion nor pity, only a fierce wish to be doing. Very soon he realized he wasted time, noticed the wetness of his cuffs, his trousers, the cold, heard a gust of wind rattle the black twigs. The steely surface of the lake rippled into movement.

'They do it the other way now,' the boy said.

'Other way?'

'They sit at the head, like. It's the Olga Nielsen, or some'at.'

'Show me.'

'I don't know. I don't go swimming.'

The boy, miserably pale, shrank inside his clothes. Over his right shoulder Murren could see two men running down diagonally across the field, and then, thirty yards behind them, his messenger.

The two arrived, panting, incapable of speech, staring at him on his knees. They knelt, turned the body in the wet, felt it, said that police and ambulance were on the way. Stiffly all got up, held themselves a yard or two from the corpse in a divided silence, men and boys, disheartened and shivering.

'Do you know him?' The question cracked accusatory. 'You lads?' They shook their heads.

'We were just walking round the lake. We seen this hump, bundle.'

A police siren shrilled.

'That'll be them,' one man said, turning, realigning his feet in satisfaction. 'They don't take long.' He spoke as if he were responsible for the improvement.

To James Murren it seemed long enough before the police car appeared to make a bumpy, leisurely way over the field. The party had been joined by a man with a walking-stick.

Two young constables looked at the body, conferred. Murren confessed he'd tried to revive the body. Heads were shaken. The questioning began. An ambulance trundled across and uniformed attendants confirmed death.

The next half-hour seemed haphazard, amateurish as the policeman took notes, names, addresses. They hardly knew what to ask, and repeated volunteered sentences as if triteness was not to be believed, or as if they had lost their grasp of the language. On the clay path, still wet with the corpse's drippings, the knotty branch athwart like some huge insect, the group stood, mumbling or writing in notebooks with purple fingers.

'That's about it, then,' one officer announced.

'Shall we hear from you?' James Murren, again surprising himself.

'Depends on the autopsy. What he died of.'

'Was he murdered?' One of the boys.

'Shouldn't think so.' The constable smiled with even teeth. 'We'll have to wait and see.'

James Murren pressed himself hard as he walked home, warming himself. His sleeves were sodden, his trouser knees daubed with clay, though the path had seemed frozen. He shuddered as he stepped, but would not pull gloves on to his polluted hands. For some minutes the boys kept up with him, but they turned off by the pavilion, not speaking as they left.

Back in Victoria Road he turned on the immersion heater and took a bath. He first swathed jacket and trousers with wads of newspaper, set them into the outside boiler house. At eleven-thirty he sat listlessly in his front room, warm but uncomfortable. When he took action, as for instance making a cup of coffee or fetching the biscuit tin, he flew at the job with violence, shouldering doors open, stepping strongly, cursing a splash from the tap. Otherwise he sat, crouched rather, energy drained as if he were an invalid.

He could not be bothered to cook his lunch, but made a sandwich which he ate as he listened to the radio. There was no mention of the corpse on the five to one Midland bulletin; he should have tuned to the local station. Making an effort he phoned Jessica, was answered gruffly by her father.

'She's out. In town. Gone shopping with her mother.'

'Have you any idea when she'll be back?'

'God knows.'

'Would you tell her that I rang?'

Mr Payne was less accommodating than usual, taking pleasure in his curtness. Perhaps he'd expected his womenfolk back to prepare a meal, but then he was rarely gracious. Payne by name, pain by nature. Murren shrugged his way back to his chair, slumped, found no comfort, dashed out to wash cup and plate, then perched himself at his piano.

Again he discovered himself staring at the music stand. Impatiently he rose, took down a volume of Mozart sonatas, propped it closed, gloomed at the faded gold lettering. A name, Winifred Peterson, on the first page; this had been his mother's. He looked at the composer's portrait, bright-eyed, with silver peruke, lace on his chest, handsome, sharp, idealized. After the portrait by C. Jäger. By permission of I. Bruckman, A.-G., Munich. Birthdate, date of death. Murren morosely noted the three buttons on the coat, the semicolon between '1756' and 'died', made nothing of them.

This would not do. He must look at the A minor, Köchel 310, for a pupil. That wasn't the truth, either, for the girl would make her weekly wooden hash of the performance whatever he said or did. Page 138, *allegro maestoso*. He cocked his elbows, set off heroically, did not approve, began again, keeping the left-hand chords beating steadily, and had completed the first page without noticing either music or himself. He stopped. 'Calando, Italian, falling off'. Did Mozart bother to write that? Or the editor?

He concluded the movement, sat for some minutes before he replaced his copy. The girl would bring her own. A burst of winter sunshine dazzled in the room, cutting shapes of the windows bright and square-angled on the white wall. He moved to the darker living-room, opened Edward Holmes's *Life*, which smelt still of the second-hand bookshop where he'd picked it up last week. 'Leopold Mozart, father of the great musician, was the son of a bookbinder at Augsburg.' James Murren read on without interest, eyes heavy. Inside a quarter of an hour, he had laid the book on the carpet at his feet and had gone to sleep.

When he woke it was nearly dark at four o'clock. He had wasted the day. At nine that morning he'd set off to walk through the park in frosty brightness, intending to be back soon after ten, get his lunch prepared and spend an hour or so writing down the setting of a Housman poem he'd been working on. He'd meant to telephone Jessica before she went out and arrange to meet her that evening; perhaps she'd rung him while he was napping. He pushed himself up on to his feet uncomfortably, walked to the window. The sky had clouded over, was rusty; in the house opposite the fairy lights of a Christmas tree glowed unduly cheerful. That damned girl, Sonia, would be here for her lesson at four-thirty. He could not think why he had arranged it on a Saturday afternoon, especially a day that was for once otherwise free.

He drew the curtains in the front room, drank a cup of tea. If he heard nothing from Jessica he'd cook his beef, eat it late as he watched 'Match of the Day'. Nothing went right. A corpse in a cold lake. At four-forty, ten minutes late, his pupil hurled herself at the doorbell, her only enthusiastic motion, he thought, until she put her coat on to go home, bounced her large breasts in the hall and was conducted to the piano.

At fifteen she had the body of a sexually mature woman, but the face and nail-bitten hands of a child. He demanded a scale of D major from her, congratulated her when she arrived back without too many fluffs. Relative minor. She tried; if she'd only exert herself to practise she wouldn't be too bad. Those red, ugly fingers were skilful, capable of training. He asked for A major. She obliged, repeated it more quickly, and again, flashed the fourth time with some panache, jutted her ample chest at him. Well done. She flushed, chewed harder on her spearmint. She chased through a Bach invention for him, not too clumsily, and he made her repeat one or two passages, playing with her at the top of the keyboard.

'I kept up with you,' Sonia said, breathlessly.

'Let's hear your Mozart.'

'I haven't had much time for practice,' she whined. 'My mum's been ill.'

She stumbled on, he correcting, and broke down on the second page, claiming that was all she had done.

'Start again,' he ordered angrily. Sonia glanced up, shrugged, plugged away. Murren stopped her, began to talk. Here was the composer in Paris, cut off from friends in Mannheim, separated from Aloysia Weber, heroic, putting a brave face on it. He'd show them. The teacher nudged her from the stool, opened the movement, clashing, fighting the piano in plangent protest, but balanced, the heart-pang set over against, under the convention of classical design.

'Great,' she said, chewing not caring.

'You try.'

She did better.

'Play with me again,' she urged, but he made her sound off the chords of the left hand.

'Make them as interesting as the right hand.'

Sonia, all incomprehension, did her best. And again. Again. Aloysia Weber, first love, deep love, parted, never to be won. He played with the girl until the half-hour was up, and he had scribbled her next assignment.

'You're not at school now,' he said. 'Get some practice in, and you'll be good.'

She shrugged again, daughter of the headmaster of the grammar school, muttered she'd come on the Friday before Christmas, perhaps expecting his denial. He stayed at the front door unseasonably, where Sonia was greeted by a boy, heard them clump off together. She could love like Mozart.

He rang Jessica, refusing to put the phone down. Payne, blowing, answered. Must have been upstairs, in the loo, top of the garden, bottom of the cellar.

'No. She's not in. Don't really know.'

'Did you tell her I rang this morning?'

'I told her. I also wrote it down.' Payne buzzed, but there was no sarcasm about branding-irons or long-playing records.

James Murren poured himself more tea and prepared a beef casserole, potatoes for boiling. There'd be no Jessica today, otherwise she would have called him. He swore, but now almost cheerfully he understood what was what. The evening paper clacked in the letter-box, late again. He unfolded the paper and prepared for ten minutes' bored pleasure.

He found no mention of his corpse; searched again; failed.

In the front room, he took out manuscript paper,

wrote down the piano flourish, a broken sweep, a hiccough of curve which introduced the Housman poem he was setting. His eye touched the clock: six. With satisfaction he settled to his work, knowing he'd eat early, have time to walk to the Framesmith's Arms.

From far, from eve and morning
　And yon twelve-winded sky
The stuff of life to knit me
　Blew hither: here am I.

2

At twenty minutes to eight the song was almost complete. Murren leaned back, querying one stretch of the piano-writing; the voice sang warmth, concern, while below the running hesitation of the hands suggested the random assembly of a human being, one who could care but was no part of divine providence. James was about to try the accompaniment over on the piano when the front door bell interrupted him. He rose stiffly, he'd been sitting almost without movement in his concentration, but was not sorry. Though he expected no visitors, he'd done enough to deserve one.

Mrs Patricia Payne.

She stepped in at his word, inspected the hall, and by her elevation of nose and chin rebuked him for not immediately showing her into a room. She needed efficiency from him, obvious capacity, for she was a headmistress. Famous locally for her licking into shape of the young misses misled for three or four years by teacher-training colleges, she instructed her underlings: ‘People want to know you’re there. Show them. Pleasantly, certainly, with an intention.’ No one had doubts about Madam Payne.

Murren indicated the door of the front room. Mrs Payne considered the sheets of music-paper, her expression implied they could be tidier. She sat; he walked round her unnecessarily and placed himself on the piano stool, where he hugged his right knee.

‘I’m sorry to burst in on you like this,’ she said. ‘I can see you’re busy.’

‘Yes.’

She bridled, a fine but crude performance. Subtlety was thrown away on impertinence. Jessica’s step-mother did not waste much, even facial expressions.

‘This is embarrassing for me,’ she began again. It did not appear so. Murren looked at her, was excited, troubled; surely she was not about to warn him off Jessica! ‘This morning you helped recover a body from the ponds in the Northern Park. I had this from the police.’ He nodded. She sucked in her lips. ‘It was my brother.’

Immediately he admired the candour, the blunt admission. This well-dressed, scented woman in her pride confessed a relationship with a sodden bag of rags he’d manhandled out of water.

‘I’m sorry.’ The truth.

‘It’s thought he committed suicide, though there’ll be a post mortem. He was not altogether satisfactory. His history was, well. . . .’ She waved a gently dismissive hand. Murren stared her straight in the eyes; she returned the look briefly and, opening her shining handbag, extracted a photograph. ‘I haven’t got my spectacles on,' she informed it, at arm's length, and passed it over.

A young man in a trilby hat, anybody's father.

Uncertain, Murren looked again, held it out. Mrs Payne, both hands on her bag, fingers straight, fastened her eyes on the corner of the room, disregarding him. The pose was histrionic, arthritic, incredible, but she did not budge, so that he was compelled to withdraw the card, glance hang-dog at it again.

He steeled himself, laid the photograph finally on the table near her elbow. The woman had presence, with good gold-buckled shoes, a dark fur coat, a rakish hat of two-toned pelt, excellent legs. Her nose seemed large, an edifice, and her eyes wrinkled at the corners, deeply, were brown as her sleeves, but velvet; the lipstick on her mouth was applied with no intention of disguising the thinness of the orifice, nor its formidable line. The third wife of Walter Payne, she had married at the age of thirty-nine, but had refused to relinquish her headship to look after the seven-year-old Jessica, though she had moved from her old bungalow to his older, inconvenient, ivy-covered house, which she described as 'damp, draughty and expensive'. She knew her mind, they said. Jessica said.

She returned to earth, inquired about the morning's events. He told her, briefly, ended by claiming it must have shocked her.

'I don't know,' she said. 'He drank.' She said nothing further about her brother but described the visit of a policeman just as they had settled to a late lunch. So Payne must have known when he rang earlier. Murren put the point.

'He did know. He didn't expect to hear from you. Nor did he want to speak about the matter without consulting me. He's a private man, has been all his life.'

'Jessica wasn't out, then?'

'What makes you think that? She was. She hardly knew my brother. Why should she? And she had an engagement, so she said.'

Mrs Payne asked one or two more questions about the park affair, but equitably, as if he'd played his part out of friendship, and then rose to go, thanking him.

'You live here on your own?' she asked. He bowed his head in acquiescence. 'Do you own the house?' He nodded again. 'This is a very convenient, well-built place. Do you have a home-help?' He admitted it. Now it was her turn to nod. Perhaps she was making up her mind to beg him to say nothing about her brother's death, but she wished him good evening and waited to be shown out. He heard her drive away, hung theatrically on to a hat-peg in the hall, heard the grandfather clock chime before he bustled in to lay the table. A warm, meaty smell encouraged him. Outside frost and rags of fog combined in discomfort. He lit the gas under the potato saucepan.

Once he had eaten the meal, he hurried the dishes out to the kitchen and washed them. He could not sit at ease with dirty crockery, even packed out of sight in the kitchen.

A phone-racket coincided with the disposal of the wet tea-towel. Jessica Payne, ringing from her friend Janet's, asked if the pair of them could call. He answered with exaggerated courtesy, so that she demanded to know if he was all right.

'Yes, thank you. Why?'

'You sound as if you'd got it on you.'

He smirked at the receiver, said that it was not so.

This meant, he concluded, that Jessica intended to stay the night with him, and had inveigled Janet Bruce into driving her round. Her parents would be told, would believe that she was spending the night with the Bruces. Thus Jessica had the best of all worlds, to the discomfort of her friends.

Taking out a book he adopted a position suitable to hospitality, largely wasted as his guests did not appear until an hour later.

'Come in, Janet,' Jessica called. 'He'll give us coffee.'

Jessica was neat and shapely with short, dark hair. Large green eyes, a tip-tilted nose, an ivory skin suggested slightly scared insouciance. She knew how attractive she was, made much of it. She removed a shaggy-collared coat which she handed over to Murren, instructing him to put it on a hanger, then she made for the largest chair closest to the gas-fire, stroking her tights, smiling privately. One expected her to be catchily humming, but she remained silent, hands at work asexually over the nylon, mouth marginally delighted. She had made herself at home before the other two had appeared in the room.

Janet Bruce hanging up her coat muttered that the weather was miserable. James, ecstatic over Jessica's advent, exchanged words on the cold and wet. When Jessica was about, he considered Miss Bruce the woman he liked most of all his acquaintance. In her early thirties, attractive in a sturdy way, she'd been brown-owl to the young Payne, then confidante, elder sister, job referee, junior partner in deception. She dabbed at her hair with surprisingly beautiful fingers, pulled at a mannish tweed skirt and made a womanly entrance into the room.

'We're a bit late,' she apologised.

Jessica had already turned on the television, and now watched, lips in a pout of surprise, a doughboy kiss a lady also in uniform.

'Coffee?' he asked. Wide eyes opened wider. Green, or blue? Light under the blue-black hair. No answer until Janet thanked him. Jessica tried all three television stations, switched off and laid the remote-control box on the table by her side. She said nothing, ravished with herself, did not speak when he returned. Janet asked what anthems his choir were doing next day, talked about Purcell and Sir Edward Bairstow, claimed her Scottish father had been a chorister in York Minster. Had Eva Cardale approached him about playing the harpsichord in 'Acis and Galatea' at the university? True, they'd plenty of continuo players, but nobody anything like as good as he was. He hoped Jessica listened, though she did not give that appearance. Janet said right things, for him, in season and out.

'Are we watching the football?' Jessica. 'I'm hungry.'

'I've a beef casserole I can warm up in a few minutes.'

'Good idea.'

'Janet? You?'

She smiled back at him, shaking her head. On his return she asked about Mrs Payne's brother. As he described the morning Jessica picked up, toyed with the control box, without switching on. He had the impression that had his narrative exceeded a certain limit, she would have flung in some Saturday night screenful of banality, but she listened, spoke first.

'She was upset.' Box to table. 'But more about you, finding him, than. . . .'

'Now, then,' Janet admonished.

'She talked about nothing but James. "Fancy Mr

Murren. I wonder what Mr Murren does. On Saturdays he gives private lessons, doesn't he?"

'When people are upset they don't always say the right thing.' Janet, pacifically.

'What did your father think?' he asked, when Jessica had left the last unanswered.

'Doesn't like anything that reflects on him. He pulled a face, sniffed, said it would be in the paper. As if it were her fault.'

That would be about right, he guessed.

Jessica's attention drifted; he and Janet talked about a visit of the reconstituted Allegri Quartet to the university. They continued the exchange when he went out to the kitchen to pour the stew.

'On a tray?' he asked. 'Or will you sit up?'

'Tray, please.'

He cut a thick white crust from a new loaf, poured a glass of red wine from an already opened bottle in the cold pantry. She was no expert. He and Janet drank coffee, discussed Mozart, Dvořák, Bartók, while Jessica tucked in. Janet's knowledge – she was a fine cellist as well as a singer – and Jessica's appetite pleased him so that he felt little need to impress. This was his idea of delight: an accomplished conversationalist on a subject he favoured whom he'd want to shoo away before long so that he and his mistress could enjoy their bodies, in bed and out. The clock struck ten. Jessica's plate lay on the carpet, wiped clean, though her wine was barely tasted. She looked so beautiful, rapt madonna, that one could not believe she opened her mouth for food, merely to gape at angels.

Murren grinned.

Janet made her farewells, having first cleared away. Jessica had now dismissed the wine as swank, so that he'd swilled it back, before walking the older woman to her car.

'Look after her,' she said, tentative, guilty.

'Do my best.'

'I'll collect her in the morning.'

She sounded so bad that he put an arm across her shoulder, but she shrugged this angrily off, very strongly, manners dismissed.

'Cheer up,' he said.

Recovering she wished him good night curtly.

He and Jessica made love as he kept half an eye on the television football. In bed she described her step-mother's embarrassed anger when the policeman arrived. Jessica had refused to accompany Mrs Payne to the mortuary.

'Why?' he asked. 'You wouldn't have to go in.'

'I know. I couldn't bring myself to do it. She'd been rude about you. "That organist. He'll spread it," She was furious it was you.'

'Who went in the end?'

'She did. In her own car.'

'She came up here. Just before eight.'

'God. I could have bumped into her on your front door-step.' She laughed, nuzzled him; they touched, forgot words in passion, slept warmly.

3

Walter Payne dried the last of the breakfast pots and, peering through the kitchen window at sombre Monday, wished he'd more to do. Once he'd vacuumed Sunday's crumbs from the dining- and sitting-room floors, he'd shop for the evening meal he'd have on the table at five-thirty. His wife did not allow him to wash clothes; he could not see why, resented the prohibition.

'It's no trouble to me,' Patricia said. 'There's no work attached with that machine.' She tapped the giant chrome and cream marvel she had brought with her.

'If it's so simple, let me have a try.'

'Then I'd have ironing to do on Monday evening. I do not want that.'

It was often Thursday before the chore was complete, on account of her committee meetings, parents' evenings, organizational round. Education took precedence over domestic duty for her. This afternoon she would attend a conference called for heads of primary schools by the director of education. There would be little conferring; he would announce what he wanted them to do; a few of them would praise his prescience, and all would be dismissed to carry out, or neglect, the diktat. And yet on Saturday, before the brother bother, and all day Sunday she'd fretted which hat and coat she'd wear, and once touching a nadir hinted that Frederick's suicide made her, in some unspecified way, unfit for the pure company of the director even though he was protected from contamination by some sixty or seventy other educational experts.

Payne, a cynic, did not expect reason from his wife. She won her arguments by vigour, emphasis, decibels. Patricia was ambitious and uncertain; joy dwelt for her in the presence of officials from the office. So her husband listened to the catalogue of advantage of one garment, to him indistinguishable from the other, and feigned not even a token show of interest.

They hit it off well enough. When they'd married thirteen years ago he'd been a bank manager in Mansfield fifteen miles off and glad to have a mother for the seven-year-old Jessica. Patricia, recently appointed to her second headship, continued to work, but extended herself to look after the child on the evenings she was at home. The two were not antagonistic; the step-mother thought the girl selfish and self-contained; Jessica judged the woman to be typical of adulthood, engaged in boring or alien transactions, but in this case superb with presents and good for a hand with homework. Jessica remembered her mother, her death, but did not speak often about that.

Walter Payne, first customer in the butcher's shop, sourly observed the sharpening of knife on steel; this was no time of morning for display. He paid, wished the man good-bye, but had earned himself a swear-word as soon as he was out of the glass door. He would have been pleased rather than otherwise, had he known. His Monday politeness was grudging, stiff-backed, won no affection either in the greengrocer's or the newsagent's, where he paid his bill. The way home led through terraces of small villas, bay-windowed behind five feet of garden and a Bulwell stone wall. Independence of idea had led to a garish variation in the colours of doors, frames, gates, from dull browns and greens to a pillar-box red and a princely purple with panels outlined in white. On a sunny day the effect was bearable, laudable, but in December, in spite of Christmas trees, Payne tongued his dentures critically. A Pakistani family, a mother and three small, trousered girls, followed his progress, wide-eyed, from their front room.

A door, original with its three narrow gothic panels,

was scraped back. From the top-step a man in flapping shirt sleeves beckoned, gibbered.

Payne stopped. In command.

'For Christ's sake,' the man gasped. 'Come in.' His trousers gaped wide; rent of belly, belly-button topped grey, wrinkled underpants. 'Come on in.'

'What's the trouble?' he barked, suddenly stiff, a military figure.

'M' wife. I've knocked her over.'

Payne did not shift from parade-ground attention, but bristled. For a minute he thought the man would stagger down the steps and into the street to drag him in. He was curious, unafraid, without wish to commit himself.

'Will she need a doctor?'

'Christ Jesus.' The man seemed about to launch himself back along the corridor, arms flailing. His accent struck lowland Scots, guttural; his pale eyes mad marbles. Payne swung his shopping bag, stepped through the gateless gap, mounted steps. In the passage the air, raw as that outside, reeked with cigarette smoke.

The man paused again as if surprised at the dapper shopper on his doorstep; Payne marched forward, caught him by the elbow. They floundered through a curtain and into the living room, into a sideboard littered with cups on newspaper. On an exclamation from the other, Payne wheeled. A tall, young woman stood back to the far wall, between window and scullery-door, stark naked. Her hands helplessly touched the discoloured paint. Her head hung as if her neck was broken under hair held just in equilibrium by pins and rollers.

'The dirty whore.' The husband, hardly audible.

She was too fleshy to be beautiful, but Payne stared

open-mouthed at breasts, dark-dug navel, lavish pubic triangle. Her thick-thighed legs, tapered to neat ankles, then scruffy slippers, her only covering.

'You whore, you.'

She sobbed, or perhaps mumbled in appeal, or reply, raising her dark eyes to fix on Payne's. Her face, pale, slap-reddened on the left, showed no shame for her condition, only a dizzy incomprehension, incurious, adenoidal.

'Look at her.'

The husband hunched his shoulders, slouched back, his mouth gaping. His breathing rasped. Payne bent, picked up, shook and pulled into order a dressing gown that had been bundled to the floor.

'Let's have your arm in,' he said, as to a child. She obeyed. 'Now the other.' It stretched tight across the shoulders. 'Button it up.' She fumbled, managed. The thing was as short as it was stained.

Sitting with knees naked, she seemed indecent now. Her husband had retired, muttering, allowing Payne to cover her, lead her to the chair where she obliquely eyed the gas-fire. As Payne backed towards the table, her husband advanced, thrust a cigarette into her mouth, one into his and brandished a match. Smoke eddied, acrid lungsful.

'Is there anything I can do for you?' Payne asked.

'We had a quarrel, like.' The man.

'I don't want to interfere. Are you all right?' The woman crossed her naked thighs, dragged hard at the ends of her gown to no effect. Flicking ash to the carpet she spoke.

'It's nothing.' Her voice was hoarse, faintly foreign in intonation. Now he looked at her he noticed broad Slavonic cheekbones. 'We had a row.'

'Ay, that's righ'.'

Payne waited for further explanation, went unenlightened. The couple drew competitively on their cigarettes. Both coughed with violence.

' "And the house was filled with smoke," ' Payne quoted.

That text was wasted. He looked from one to the other.

'Will you be all right?'

'Och. Ay.' A lung-searing hack.

'Are you sure?' This to the woman, who nodded. He looked over his shoulder on to the table, where the cups were clear of slops, plates of crumbs.

'If that's all, I'll make my way home.'

'Thank you, thank you.' Sincerely from the man. 'Sorry to. . . .'

'Thank you.' The woman, unclear.

Payne retrieved his shopping-bag, thrust his way to the door where he stopped. There should be more to it than this.

'I'll give you my address. If you like, when you've had a bath, come down for a cup of coffee.' He swung back to the room, biroed in the margin of a newspaper on the table, thrust it into the man's hand. 'If you like. About ten-fifteen.' He had surprised himself. He tapped the journal. 'It's only five minutes' walk away. Big house with iron railings.' He looked from man to woman, and back. 'Ten-fifteen.' A word of command. The man's nub hung from a wet lip. Payne picked up the bag a second time, made speed for the street.

He wondered what the pair were up to now. Laughing at him? Or the husband unbuckling his belt to his wife? Why had she thrown off her dressing gown? Presumably when her husband ran out, she was down, unconscious, but clothed? Payne remembered that belly, triangle, bobbing breasts, and walked excitedly. He arrived breathless at his front door, heart thumping, unchanged fingers bloodless from the leather of the handle. He leaned there, not himself, untidily challenged, with boots mud-splashed. At seventy he should go steadier.

He laid out three china cups and saucers, but no one came. At eleven, relieved rather than otherwise, he dropped the catch. They'd had their chance.

The evening meal was set for five-fifteen, and Mrs Payne's account of the director's conference took its pride of place. As the king-pin had been represented only by his third deputy, and the topic, vandalism, was one already settled in Patricia's mind, this was soon exhausted with a few cutting references to the unworldly vapouring of colleagues, so that Payne had leisure to describe his morning's activity. Jessica livened at once.

'What number was it?' she asked. He told her; he had not been too sure of their reception of the naked lady, was surprised to find it so easily assimilable that he sat back to hear his wife's rodomontade about what she'd do to work-shy loafers who were just staggering out of bed at nine-thirty in self-satisfaction. Jessica suggested that the man was on shift work, had just returned home.

'Did he say so?' Patricia.

'No. But he didn't say he'd just got up, either.'

The ladies argued, about appearances, prejudices, inference, with noisy ill-temper from step-mother, and quiet pleasure in her havoc from the girl. Father, unusually successful this evening as a raconteur, hummed as he changed the plates, invited comment on the quality of the custard.

'Will you call round?' Jessica asked, the meal over.

'I should think not.' Patricia.

'How shall we know whether. . . ?'

'You won't.'

'Unfair, unfair.' Jessica and her father laughed together. 'She might be in on her own next time.'

Payne was even more flattered when later his wife closed her book, turned down the television and inquired about his intentions. He had not had such a triumph since a bus had demolished the shop next to the one where he was buying boiled ham. She listened to his second retelling, and grim-lipped said,

'If I were you I'd keep out of their way.' He was given no chance of intervention. 'You don't know what such people are like. Or, rather, you do know.' There followed five minutes of assertion and anecdote. Her face had set in an expressionless mask, and her ugly hands jigged in nervous emphasis. Payne listened, but made no promises. If she were stubborn, he'd match her, but without noise. When she made her way upstairs, to her study, where she'd rattle notices and directives on her typewriter or nurse her disappointment at his lack of cooperation, he sat below smiling and rubbing his hands, comfortable. Thus it happened that Jessica beat him to the front door to answer the bell.

'A lady to see you,' she said. 'Mrs McKie.' A stout woman in a belted coat looked nervously about. Jessica came in, closing the door. A slam upstairs, too late, indicated the interest of Mrs Payne. 'You went in the house this morning,' Jessica elucidated.

'I'm sorry we did not come.' The woman's accent was slightly foreign. 'I had to see my father.'

Payne made correct social murmurs. Jessica smiled, the impressario, guided the visitor to a chair.

'He is very ill. Dying. It is worrying.'

'Is he in hospital?'

'No. While my mother is capable of looking after him, they will not see to him.' She spoke stiffly as if she did not think in the language, correctly, with even a suspicion of local vowels, but without fluency. 'He is suffering from cancer.'

This morning this woman stood stark naked in front of him; now she spoke like an applicant for public assistance, a shabby postulant, something like the photographs of D. H. Lawrence's Frieda, but without confidence. Jessica asked questions, was answered. He did his best. As far as he could make out Mrs McKie had merely come to apologise.

Her delivery was baffling. Though she spoke slowly, groping after words, never exceeding three or four shortish sentences, she let cats out of her bag with speed. She disliked her husband to whom she had been married seven years. He beat her. She would like to leave him, but now their daughter was at school; she might have taken a job, but she feared for her father. 'I could be needed at any time. But it means I cannot take the child to live there, or earn enough for independence.'

She had worked in the library for four years after leaving the girls' grammar school at sixteen. Then she had met her husband, a miner. 'I cannot tell you now how I came to marry him. I did not like him then. It is true.' She spoke without emphasis, pushing back her coat-sleeves, baring the golden down on her forearms. 'He is a pig.'

Payne asked what he, they, could do for relief. There was nothing. Mrs McKie was glad they had let her in, talked to her, shown her friendliness. She had nothing. Her daughter was in bed; her husband downstairs hogging the fire; her mother sighing in her own house; her father a skeleton. They detained her, but while Jessica was out, not a word was exchanged. They forced her to eat a chocolate biscuit before she looked guiltily at the clock, dashed down her cup, stood.

'I must go. I shall have only a quarter of an hour with my father. My husband must have his time in the pub.'

'Come and see us again.' Jessica.

'I shall tell my husband I have called in.' They accompanied her to the door where she turned, with a flash of white teeth. 'Will you come with me one evening to see my father?'

They showed surprise. Both shuffled; both acquiesced together, too loudly.

'He would like to see new faces.'

'Do you take your daughter across?'

'Christina? No. It would frighten her. Death is. . . .' She moved her hand, parallel to the ground, palm down, dismissing language. Suddenly she jerked down the steps, into the drive, was running along the street. Father and daughter, comically deserted, locked the front door, decided on more coffee.

Mrs Payne appeared, demanded. They explained.

'You won't go, of course.' Hoity-toity, censorious.

'We promised.'

'Isn't that morbid?'

4

James Murren heard the last of his choirboys, in a complaint. The nave of St Michael and All Angels towered in arched darkness over one smudge of light from the south porch away from the glare of the chancel. He listened standing by the upright piano dragged to the screen.

'I should think we'll manage that.'

The boy slouched off. Three of the men trundled the piano onto the south transept, noisy as devils, down three steps on its trolley, then metal on unyielding stone, echoing.

Murren carefully packed his music into a folder, donned his topcoat, put out the lights. The men followed him along the aisle, waited as he locked the doors of church and porch.

'Coming for a drink?' one asked.

'Thanks, no. I'm on my knees.'

'Good practice,' they flattered.

'Yes, it was. Have one for me.'

They walked the churchyard together, and he stood at the lych-gate. If they asked him once more, he'd go with them but they wished him good night, good men. His car was parked a few yards down the street, and he sat there for five minutes before driving home. Christmas tires housewives, publicans and choirmasters. He had a carol service on Sunday, two in the following week in outlying churches, sung eucharist on Christmas Eve, full choral matins on Christmas Day. The rector and his wife liked their choirs busy. A radio watch night service on New Year's Eve needed attention. The bishop had written in proleptically congratulatory terms. Murren had arranged to perform sacred music in the Roman Catholic cathedral.

He slipped sharply into his garage, banged the door into place. He'd hardly removed his scarf when the phone rang. Janet Bruce to ask if he could run her through a couple of songs.

'Now?' he asked.

'Now, if it's possible.'

Nine thirty-five. He made coffee, sucked noisily, shrugged.

Janet herself looked tired, a bad colour, dulled by a chalky navy beret and coat. She made grateful noises, refused a drink, said it was a case only of two Brahms songs that she had to sing tomorrow.

'I can't play the damned things and sing them.'

'My Brahms isn't anything to boast about this time of night.'

She explained that she was to perform at the opening ceremony of a new comprehensive school; the county music adviser had contacted her headmaster who had talked to the director of music at the new place, and, between them, they'd decided on Brahms, and in German. She'd hardly been consulted; she'd be ferried there, to sing to the discomfort of county councillors and officials, with no chance of rehearsal.

'I think Reg Barnwell can play 'em. He's not bad, is he?'

'He thinks he's good.'

Murren sat down to *Minnelied.* As soon as she began, he lost fatigue, tried to match the richness of her voice. She was a superb singer who would not make a living by it; her family had wealth. His fingers spoke romance to match the words, large eloquent chords moving easy as breathing, rare. He concluded; she nodded in thanks.

'Again?'

'If you don't mind. I wish you were playing for me tomorrow.'

'Not if Wet-Head's arranged it.' Barnwell, the adviser, two of whose choirs Murren's had thrashed in national festivals.

The second run-through was duller, neither exerting power, establishing the lyric.

'The other?'

'*Vergebliches Ständchen*. Same book.'

Now her voice played two parts: the swain, bright with lust then cringing wind-frozen, and the cheerful virgin, knowing a thing or two, not afraid to say so, '*geh' heim zu Bett, zur Ruh, gute Nacht*'. He ended impertinently, virtue cheekily rampant, seducer dismissed to his gutter *più animato* so that both laughed.

'Good enough,' she said. He looked at a shining forehead, peasant eyes, sage's beard, Brahms's delicate right hand in the photograph on the cover. He'd do something for Janet if he could. 'You're an angel.'

She was already slipping on her coat, building headscarf above the beret.

'Wish me luck.'

Janet, leaving, invariably spoke in cliché. She wrestled with tight gloves, a performance almost pornographic, snatched up her copy still thanking him to run out into the hall, let herself out into the street.

' 'Bye, Jan,' he said. She stopped on the flagstones of the path, saw he meant nothing by it, rattled the gate open. He returning to his cold half-cup of coffee hummed the *Minnelied*, to be interrupted by the phone.

'Are you in tomorrow?' Jessica.

'Yes.' His only free night this week.

'I'm bringing a woman round to see you.'

'About what?'

'She's Polish. We have to go and see her father. Yes, it is complicated, and I'm fagged out as well. I'll explain. Half-past seven.'

This did not sound like Jessica, who though sharp

enough on her own account was not usually found succouring others, but he was tired, loved her, agreed.

On the next evening the visitors had not arrived by quarter to eight, and Murren's temper snapped shorter. Jessica, noticing nothing, made rough introductions at seven-fifty, sat Mrs McKie down, pushed her man out to the kitchen. Laughing, excited, she explained her father's involvement. 'But my mother's interfered. She says he's not to go. Made him promise. Isn't it ridiculous? So it's you in his place.'

'Has she told you to keep away?'

'No. Not in so many words. I wouldn't pay any attention, anyhow. It's Mrs McKie's nakedness she's taken against.' She giggled.

'She'll have stripped off by the time we get back, will she?'

Jessica swiped him, exploded into a rigmarole about the necessity of visiting the sick man.

'Why, in God's name?'

'She wants it. She does. You can see that. Daddy should have seen it, and gone. He's dying, she thinks. But she must take somebody.'

'Let's smell your breath,' he said. She aimed another slap, which he dodged with grace. He did not like this febrile performance, instructed her to calm down. They returned, set off.

They walked sharply through the raw evening, past the Paynes' house, Mrs McKie keeping up with them. Jessica chattered, inconsequentially, about a man she had once heard playing a trumpet on the street corner, pointing out the house to which she had carried her guinea-pigs for pedicure.

'That's where you live?' Jessica's question instructed James.

Mrs McKie murmured.

Not fifty yards on they turned in at a semi-detached, small villa, with a cramped gothic porch. The woman, sidling to the front tapped with her nails on the glass, eased the door open, switched on a light. In the doorway at the end of the passage Mrs McKie's mother appeared, a sturdy, elderly woman, grey hair marked still with its earlier fairness. Her face was plain and rock-like; her mouth a line. In whispers she and her daughter spoke Polish, a gabble of syllables, but lightly touched, always in consideration of the father upstairs. About the rooms they smelt a dampness, not wholly uncomfortable or without warmth. The exchange ended with a sentence of translation.

'These are my friends. This gentleman is a musician.'

The older woman smiled thinly, inclined her head, but did not hint at trespassing. Further soft, flying sentences from the expressionless faces of the two. One could not tell whether they argued, questioned, offered information. Mrs McKie breaking off, not turning, said, 'We will go upstairs.' She fumbled for another switch. The landing above was now darkly illuminated. The three only went one behind the other. Murren could hear Jessica's breathing.

'Wait, please.'

Cautioned they stopped as their guide rapped, stroked one of the doors, and disappeared, closing it behind her. When he caught Jessica's eye she immediately looked away. They could hear nothing from the bedroom, but the stair creaked, and wind whacked about in the street. The doors were brown, comb-grained and highly varnished, the red and blue carpet a mere strip on dark-stained board floors. The pair stood in silence while the house fidgeted round them.

Mrs McKie reappeared, beckoned.

In a dry, hot room a huge bed sprawled and towards this they shuffled. The man who lay there watched them, propped on pillows, lighted from the side by an anglepoise lamp. He wore crumpled pyjamas, unbuttoned at the scraggy neck, but his hair glistened with life. It was iron-grey, thick, but cut short on the crown as in the neck, wiry, catching the light. Below it, the face disappointed, fleshless, yellow, sagging round the big, rather comical nose.

'This is my father,' Mrs McKie said. 'My friends.'

Jessica, with James Murren behind, advanced to shake a proffered hand. Suddenly he smelt the girl's perfume in the staleness of the sick room. The man's hand was warm, not moist, capable of gripping.

'I am glad you could come.' The foreign voice whispered huskily. Brown, liquid eyes fastened on Jessica. 'You are a musician, sir. It is a privilege.'

'Do you listen to music?' the girl asked.

'Here?' he said. 'Not in here.'

The quartet in silence, at a loss, was rearranged, when the daughter moved to the far side of the bed, where she sat.

'Place a chair for the young lady,' the man ordered gently. Murren obeyed, took a station behind it, palms on the carved ends.

'My father played the violin.'

'Years ago. And not well, you understand. For my own pleasure. I have lived in this country for nearly forty years. That seems no time.'

Jessica answered, with talk about piano lessons, her aversion to practice, her wish now that she had persevered. She did well, modestly light.

'It is not too late. You are young.' The voice was

clear and gentle, firmly belying the ravaged features, cracked lips. 'You play Bach?' to Murren.

'Yes.'

'He is satisfactory.' Murren wondered if he meant 'satisfying.' The formality of the conversation inhibited him, but he made a remark or two about Bach the contrapuntalist. The man listened, with a gravity that shamed them. Murren spoke of the 'Saint Matthew Passion'.

'I have heard it. I do not know it. We could have had a record, Elzbieta. We could have listened. We needed someone like you to instruct us. But it never happened. And perhaps we would not have bothered.'

'We could bring a player,' Jessica interrupted, breathlessly. 'Let you hear it.'

'Yes.' He seemed to answer, or wait for, some other question, and the rest sat silent, attentive to his re-emergence. 'It is windy in the street.'

They gabbled about the weather, as if it mattered.

To Murren there was an aura of culture around this house. He'd be pushed, of course, to cite evidence in support. Perhaps when Mrs McKie's miner-husband came, talk differed. The furniture was dark, solid, well cared-for, and the light-bulbs clear so that the shadow behind the dressing-table seemed itself substantial.

Jessica described the Christmas trees along the street, but the man could barely maintain a show of interest. His daughter stood, said they mustn't tire him, smoothed the bedclothes, eased one pillow from under him. He made no objection, but looked again at Jessica who held a hand out.

'Good night, Mr Wisniewski,' she said. Murren had not heard the name, leaned to shake. The sick man murmured, politely moved his head, foreign, courtly.

'Shall we leave the light?' Elzbieta asked, in English. She now spoke gently in Polish and he tried to smile, answered her. 'My father has enjoyed your visit. He hopes you will come again.' The brown eyes fastened on Jessica, who dipped her head. They tiptoed awkwardly out and downstairs.

Mrs Wisniewski heard them, questioned her daughter, who answered in English.

'No, I cannot stay. Jock will be getting restless. He wants oot.' She smiled. The mother put out her hand, and they made their farewells. It seemed un-English, formal, gracious. Murren would have liked to click his heels.

A few yards down the street Mrs McKie indicated that she must cross to her home. She thanked them, said she'd be in touch.

'Is he getting better?' Jessica's voice clear as glass.

The woman shrugged. 'No. It is only a matter of time. He enjoyed your company. He has only a few friends.'

As Murren walked away more quickly, he heard his companion gulp, found her crying.

'What's wrong?' He circled her shoulders, but she dashed his arm furiously away. 'What is it?' She stepped out, determined to keep ahead. They completed the two streets to her house in silence.

'I'm sorry.' She mopped her face, invited him in, but left him standing in the hall as she rushed upstairs. Her father put in an appearance.

'Hullo. You're back early. Where's her ladyship?' Murren pointed upwards. 'Come on in, then. Is it cold out?'

Payne had been sitting at the kitchen table, where a book lay open. This room was bright, with tiles, formica white surfaces, a chrome sink.

'I sit in here often enough now. Prefer a hard chair to a sofa.' Busy with coffee cups he talked back over his shoulder, impishly. His wife appeared, blocked the doorway, asked if she could have five minutes of Murren's time.

'Our coffee will wait,' Payne said.

Murren followed Madam's trousered legs upstairs to her study where she waved him to a seat.

'My brother,' she began. 'There seems no doubt it was suicide. He left notes. I wanted to ask you, this may sound odd, but did you see anything, well, er, wrong about him?' She wristed that question aside as inaccurate. 'What was the thing you most clearly remember?'

'He was dead.' She was affronted, touched her fringe. 'That was . . . right. He looked dead. And he was soaking wet. His clothes were saturated, inside and out.'

'Did he look desperate?'

'His face, you mean. I don't know. I haven't seen many bodies. He looked clean in a waxy way. But he must have been in despair, if he. . . .'

'He was only fifty-four. He appeared older.'

Murren shook his head, like a dazed boxer, asked if they'd had an inquest.

'Yesterday. Didn't Jessica tell you? There was a line or two in this evening's paper.'

'I didn't see anything,' he answered.

'It was a tragic case. He was intelligent. Started as a medical student but didn't stick it. He had no staying power. In the end he managed a shoe shop in Northampton. Then his daughter died, nineteen, a beautiful girl, and his wife left him. He gave up altogether, came to live over here, took a bit of a job in a tobacconist's in the city.'

'This isn't your part of the world, then?'

'No. Northamptonshire, originally. Near Wellingborough. I was the sole surviving relative. That's why he came. Or I like to think so. Not that he bothered us much. He's been living here for nearly ten years, but I didn't see him from one month's end to the other. I tried to get him to come for Sunday lunch, but he wouldn't. He had beautiful manners.'

'Where did he live?'

'He had a room in the town, on the Derby Road somewhere.'

'Didn't you go to see him?' Murren asked.

'You didn't know my brother. He was not to be intruded on.' A headmistress's phrase, for the first time. 'Walter once went into the shop where he worked. George, my brother, called him 'sir', as if he didn't. . . .'

The strain tugged the woman's face awry so that for the moment Murren thought she'd break down. He could not see reason for this confession. She muddied herself without relief.

'You loved your brother?' he said.

That wasn't sensible, but he needed to reply to her pathos. She showed immediate, surprised distaste.

'It's years since we were close. Only when we were young. Now he's. . . . I can't help wondering if I couldn't have done something for him. A man doesn't kill himself unless he's desperate.'

'I don't know. Some people have a predisposition for suicide.'

'Physiologically, do you mean?'

'I suppose so. Some weather appalling difficulties; others chuck their hand in at next to nothing.'

The conversation seemed to bend, to be without point, too bland, offering neither enlightenment nor sympathy. Both sat glumly until Patricia Payne stood up, and on his rising she rubbed a hand up and down his lapel. He did not back away from the contact, though it appeared overtly sexual. She grinned, showing her large, even, slightly yellowish teeth.

'I shan't eat you,' she said. 'Thanks for the talk. It's helped.'

'I'm sorry I can't do more. I didn't look closely. I tried to revive. . . .' He looked at his hands.

'It's no use saying anything to Walter, or Jessica for that matter. They've no idea.' Jessica who'd cried for the dying Pole? 'So I get hold of a personable young man, tell him all. It's sensible if boring for you. Thanks, anyhow.' Again the vulpine grin, the overpowering whiff of expensive, unattracting scent as a hand patted his bicep to expedite the exit.

Downstairs in the kitchen Jessica and her father nursed cups of coffee.

'Here he is,' Patricia said to her step-daughter. 'You can have him back.'

'You can keep him,' the girl said ungraciously. Father tutted. She seemed pale, her face set, unwilling to smile, relax. 'We went to see the Polish woman's father,' she said to Patricia.

'This family's dragging you through it tonight,' the elder woman said. 'You must love us.'

5

The organ pealed at the end of the last Christmas morning service, bouncing sound from the stonework. James Murren listened as he removed hood, surplice and cassock to his brilliant assistant-for-the-week whirling through the Fantasia and Fugue in G minor. The finger work rapped clear and agile; the pedals clubbed heavy as lead cut into neat, thin strips. Timothy Arnold Gelsthorpe, recitalist, was a marvellous technician; he gave the impression he could play standing on his hands on the organ stool, flicking stops out with strands of hair or coat buttons. He did not ruin Bach; he phrased the right notes sharp as glass, but he would not hang about. A big work was worth five minutes of his time, and that was all. He passed every examination with distinction, knocked off innumerable prizes at the Royal College, won an international competition. He had no nerves, and to see him open the swell box gradually in the middle of a solo pedal run was worth a day trip by any organists' society, but he played with the verve of a racing driver, cutting corners, tight-lipped. Now he zoomed on the fugue which danced and pinged as if it were on a harpsichord, not a Victorian Willis, updated with squealers. The result was unbelievable, clear and bell-like, but powerful and fast. The congregation talked its way out, without hurry, a church full, paying no attention to the virtuoso they could not see. If he had caved the roof in with a sudden crescendo they might have glanced up. Murren listened, appreciatively, as Bach's final dancing pedal entry crashed away among the pillars and made the stone floor shake.

'By God, he's in a hurry,' one of the basses mouthed, comically plugging his ears with his fingers. Echoes rumbled off.

'Lord's Prayer on a threepenny bit. That's him.' A tenor.

They laughed in affection. Murren waited for

Gelsthorpe, a local product who arrived in denims, cassock and surplice creased over one arm.

'Thanks, my man,' said Murren. 'Coming over for a Christmas tot?'

'Right.' Gelsthorpe wriggled into a cagoule, ran his hand through his hair, straightened his student's glasses, and blew into his fair moustache, disgusted. They set off for Murren's car.

'Have you got the programme out for your New Year recital?' Gelsthorpe nodded. 'Schönberg?'

'No. Humphrey Searle.'

'No Bach, Buxtehude?'

'Who said not?'

Gelsthorpe saluted a clergyman who raised his hat.

'Been to see the organ yet?'

'Never do. They send a specification. I'll have the afternoon to practise.'

Sitting in Murren's house, they drank gin and tonic.

'Is the turkey in?' Gelsthorpe on the piano stool.

'Beef sandwiches. Tinned Christmas pudding.'

Gelsthorpe didn't care, but rippled up Murren's piano keyboard prestissimo on double octaves. 'Blast,' he said at a fluff too fast to hear. 'Nice instrument.' He soured his face.

'When do you start?'

'Jan two. Lincoln. Then Ely, Cambridge, Portsmouth, Geneva, two in Zürich, one in Basle.'

'Do you like it?'

'I'd be furious if I weren't doing it.'

He lifted his elbows into a Rachmaninov prelude, nostrils flared like those of a Renaissance Italian grandee, skin pale, hair untidily flung back, or finger-combed untidily during rests. James Murren admired the immense drive of the man, his unnatural concentration, the will to excel that had outdistanced rivals, flogged into excellence. Since he'd won first place in an international competition in Germany last year, he travelled the world. Organ recitals were in again; people flocked in the States, in Canada to hear Bach and Flor Peeters, fancy French toccataists, duodecaphonal high seriousness, he said.

Gelsthorpe had come home this Christmas, played three services for Murren, borrowed his instrument for some hours of dedicated practice, and had winkled his father, who kept the town's music shop, out in the evenings for a drink. The young man looked wild, unbiddable, but his discipline was intense, mastering the great surges of energy, the talent that made all easy.

'Start recording when I get back.'

He left the piano, picked up his gin as if he'd drink glass and all, but took a half-sip, and dashed himself into a chair. Sometimes a maniac conversationalist, this evening he remained silent, unable to curb bodily exuberance, but failing to talk. Murren never knew what he wanted, watched the right leg cocked above the left kick at endless invisible targets.

'Better go for lunch. The old man's a stickler.' Murren knew otherwise, wondered how Gelsthorpe would pass the afternoon, did not bother to inquire. Here, in this room, sat a monster, a phenomenon, a prodigy, and yet he had ten fingers and two feet like the next man. Murren never quite came to terms with that, nor with the fact that this young man might at a quick glance have stepped down from driving a bread-van or a bus, but put him on the console with the 'Jig' Fugue, and he would baffle your ears with agility and yet wink and smile as he played.

Gelsthorpe rose. 'What are you doing this afternoon?'

'Christmas nod. Might read a book.'

'Is Jess Payne not appearing?'

'I think not.'

'Give her the sack.' Gelsthorpe had a reputation with women. 'She's no good to you.'

'How do you know that?'

Tim spread his arms, then flapped them pulling a face. He emerged from his cagoule, hair somewhat flattened.

'Shan't see you again. Going down to visit Howard Bowden. He thinks he's written some organ pieces.'

'Hasn't he, then?'

'He's a talented man, but he misses chances. Never do that, mate.'

Gelsthorpe glided out, into the damp air. As James Murren stood at his front door, a child rode by on a brand-new tricycle, father in the rear. A car started up; a party made a noisy beeline for the 'Quorn', uncertain of key in 'While Shepherds Watched'.

The gas-fire was warm; the beef delicious and the pudding eatable. Meticulously Murren cleared away so that he could sleep. He obliged himself immediately, but awoke half an hour later, stiff and uncomfortable. He poured himself a glass of port, deciding against going out. When the doorbell shrilled, he was pleased, he noted.

Mrs Payne in plastic mac with sou'wester, shaking her umbrella. It suited her style, nautical.

'I'm taking a walk,' she said. 'That's why I didn't phone.'

She removed the glistening covers, accepted port, overpowering. He admired her legs again in sheer, black tights.

'You'll think I've nothing else to do but call in here,' she began. He waved his glass combining wassail with understanding. 'It's my brother. As you might have guessed. I have to clear his rooms. There's no hurry; I am paying the rent. But I'd like to call on your help if that's possible.' She raised a hand, three fingers bright with heavy rings. 'You may wonder why I don't ask my husband. He's too close, if you understand me. I'm dreading the task, I'll tell you, and to have him round my neck, probing and digging, is more than I can stomach.' She frowned. 'You're not to take this as a criticism of my husband. He's admirable. But not for this. Now, Mr Murren, will you help me?'

'I don't see why not.'

'It won't be a big job. Two rooms. Three. But I can't bear the thought of being there on my own. I don't scare easily. But if you're about, I'll have to put on a public face, and that'll keep me cool. Set me in front of a crowd, and I'm steady. I shouldn't say this to you, should I? You don't see me like this?'

He made neutral sounds pleasantly, debating if it were the port which had affected her. She did not stay long, so that he was disappointed that she did not uncover further secrets. Formally, fully dressed, she shook hands, promising him a phone call. He outlined times when he could not oblige. When he returned to his room it smelt of her perfume. Clearing away the glasses, he wondered why he'd attracted favourable notice. The telephone blasted.

'Payne speaking. Have you got my wife there?'

'She's just left.'

'She's been talking about your sorting out G. O. Underwood's estate. I bet myself that she'd come round to you. That's why I rang. Many thanks. Good-bye.'

Murren laughed. He ought to have asked what Miss

Jessica was about. Glad that he hadn't, he took to the armchair again. At four Janet Bruce phoned.

'You're all on your own, aren't you? Come over and gorge. We've a few friends.'

'Thanks, but I like quiet.'

'Not on Christmas Day. I shall come to you like Porphyria.'

'And you know what happened to her.'

In the end she persuaded him.

The Bruces' house stretched huge and dark in spite of many lamps. Furniture towered; carpets were plush; tea from a huge table left guests bloated. Janet's parents were everywhere, he small and energetic, his wife statuesque, more beautiful than her daughter, polite in all matters, uncertain.

After the meal George McNair Bruce attached himself to Murren, made conversation about music as he flourished a neat cigar. His father had settled here from Scotland fifty years ago, set up his grocery stores, and his son, abstracted from the top stream of the high school immediately he'd finished matriculation exemption to learn the trade, had converted them into supermarkets just before the old man had died happy to see such profit. At fifty-five George looked older, but shrewd, natty, with a finger in every pie except politics.

'Janet looks flourishing,' Murren said, as the girl waltzed past, arms full of parcels.

'You know what her mother thinks.' There was a Scottishness about the statement, a sobriety, dourness. Mrs Bruce thought Murren would make her daughter a suitable husband.

'Well, yes.'

'Well, yes, what?' There was no speed about the question, nor ill-temper, mere ruthless clarity.

'These things can't be arranged, can they?' That sounded stupid.

'In some societies. . . .' Smoke lifted from mouth and nose, thick as cheese-cloth.

They did not continue. Both had made their point. These good, rich people wanted to present him with their only child, then load him with wealth, while all he could do was wince away, set his cap at Jessica Payne, accumulate trouble for himself. James, embarrassed, began to talk about the body in the pond, Pat Payne, the plan to clear her brother's room.

'Didn't know the man,' Bruce said, putting Murren in his place, as loose-tongued.

'Why should she ask me, not her husband?'

'Payne won't step outside his limits. He's made that clear. To her. To everybody.'

'Is she frightened of him?'

'I don't know. I shouldn't think so.'

Now the drinks were brought round by the women on silver trays, huge whiskies, great frosted gins, white wine. Soon the ceiling would undulate and the bunting snake. Mrs Bruce said they were not too old for a childish game, ordered them to musical chairs. Graciously she eased Murren to the piano stool, instructed him to play at length.

'Jan and I want to hear you play.'

Brahms waltzes, a Chopin study, Weber's 'Invitation', Liszt's 'La Campanella', Khatachurian's 'Sword Dance' were drowned in wild shouts, the laughter of an orgy. A handsome woman falling over kicked her legs shamelessly in the air. No sooner had they cheered the winner than they demanded another longer rowdier round. People mopped after that, men removing jackets.

'You look pale,' Janet told Murren.

'Alone and palely loitering.' He hollowed his voice to a ghost's as she stroked his upper arm.

They played Murder with staid enthusiasm. Lips and tits were thrust at him in the darkness of corridors and cupboards. This was, as Bruce explained apologetically, a party for the middle aged. They demanded seconds and thirds. The professor of archaeology grew red in the cheek alongside the director of leisure services. Two solicitors and a stockbroker swayed over their whisky. City councillors, members of the Chamber of Commerce, Masons, landowners, a radio personality puffed and blew, while their wives smiled broadly above low-cut dresses and below elaborate hair-helmets. The young people, there were a few couples, beamed, equally eager to make fools of themselves in such august company. The deputy director of the museum, early thirties, mopped his head and spectacles; a radio producer, equally youthful, shook his rough hair loose.

George Bruce came across again, mischief in his eye.

'You should have jumbled cities on the wall, and paper and pencils all round,' Murren chaffed him. Anagrams: Arpis to Dengibruh.

'And leave room for "Consequences".'

The whisky warmed both men, so that now the dark house glowed.

'This place,' said Murren, 'reminds me of the fairy castles in the annuals.'

'No turrets.'

'And no snow outside. Nor jesters with cap and bells.'

'Are you sober enough to play for Janet?'

'Depends. Depen's.'

She came across, put a hand on her father's shoulder, the only healthy, sober person in the room.

'Wants to know what you're going to sing, Jan.'

'What would you choose?'

' "All is fulfilled." ' Bruce looked into the liquid he held high at arm's length. 'The Lion of Judah fought the fight.'

'Is that suitable?'

They looked round the scarlet faces, the pointing fingers, the chins tucked in for listening, the handkerchiefs, the spilling of liquor under the yellow and red of the lamps, the multi-coloured clumps of balloons, the dipping and rising of Christmas trimmings, and were pleased.

Bruce clapped; the others composed their expressions, knowing what to expect. First she sang Schubert, *Auf dem Wasser zu Singen*, and Murren's fingers rippled with the richly pitching voice. A splutter of applause before Jan held both hands out to a minute man, beautifully dressed in a velvet smoking jacket and golden-buckled shoes.

'Your favourite.' she said, and found her accompanist's place. Balfe: 'The Arrow and the Song', words by H. W. Longfellow. Now she sang with simplicity, refusing to guy, as if reminiscing to the small man and no one else. Murren let the five concluding bars of A major tail away, climb and die like air, like morning sunlight in pinewoods. The quizzical frown on Janet's face seemed to try to recall what she had just performed, and why the audience were so noisily delighted. The small man, grey hair heavy across his pate, came forward took and kissed both her hands, bowing to her. She finished with the Bach, but it was too great; they needed sobriety, a church Lent not a pagan Yule for that. Jan brushed Murren's cheek with her lips, hurried off. The music lay opened still on the piano.

A blue-rinsed lady signalled attention from the accompanist returning to his glass.

'If she wanted to sing Bach, she should have sung, "Prepare Thyself Zion",' the woman informed him. He did not answer. ' "*Bereite dich, Zion.*" '

'Bach is like beer,' he began. It did not seem worth it. When he regained his seat, the small man approached and thanked him, praising his touch, in full admiration that he put both hands down together. They seemed lost in the space of the room, the conversation, the cigar smoke, the tang of spirits. Murren was lifted. Janet returned to sit on the arm of his chair.

'Who's this Polish fellow Jessica's so involved with? I hear of nothing else.' He said a word about the Wisniewskis, described his visit. Almost sitting in his lap she said pettishly, 'Isn't it morbid? He's dying, isn't he?'

He stroked her thigh.

'It will do her good,' he answered.

'You don't believe that.'

'Does she bother you with it, then?'

'No. The opposite.' Janet always appeared sober-sided when she discussed Jessica with him. 'She tells me, but keeps me away. She's morally superior, visiting the dying.'

'She can't have been very often.'

'She makes the most of it.'

A yard or two off a consultant surgeon's wife brayed loudly about a game of golf. A young woman listened, toe-ending the carpet.

'Who's the little man you sang for?'

'Did you like him? He's my godfather. Ralph Wilson. He's an engineer. From Scotland. His wife has died, a year ago. He's unhappy. I think he'd like to marry me.'

'How old is he?'

'Sixty.' It seemed ludicrous to match a puppet with a solid-fleshed girl, throwing her to waste in a doll's house.

'What do you think?'

'I'm unhappy. His children are my age. They're both married. Jenny was at school with me.'

'Would they mind?'

'Would anybody mind?' She pushed off from his chair, had nowhere to go but consulted with her parents and supervised the appearance of more food. Murren ate an apple with a piece of cheese, sufficiently drunk not to be disturbed, but certain of pain, about a diseased spot. Now he was isolated, in an armchair nobody approached. Trays and trolleys had silenced the crowd; they munched, glassy-eyed. The snack seemed interminable, though people changed places, always neglecting Murren.

In the end Janet Bruce and her father prised him from his chair. They were kind, led him round the room, forced him into words with chewing nonentities who did not know him. He did his best.

At eleven guests were dragooned into singing carols; the Bruces had printed sheets ready. Wilson, the diminutive engineer, acted master of ceremonies, demanded gusto from his singers, and achieved it so that the room rang with choirs of angels in exaltation, snow on snow, noel, noel. Murren thumped the piano absentmindedly, once worked himself into a counterpoint so remote in key and rhythm that he and Janet burst out laughing. The waits, not appearing to notice, bawled on.

At midnight he announced his departure, not the

first, but by no means the last of the guests, who talked with undiminished vigour in groups, heads wagging, glasses steady. Janet drove him back, serious and flushed.

'I'm glad to come out,' she said, at his gate.

'Do your parents enjoy giving parties?'

'I don't know. They've always had them. Mummy likes the preparation. They love the anticipation. I think about the washing-up.'

'You've got a machine.'

She flapped her arms about unable to argue, and he kissed her, inviting her in for a drink. Inside they drank coffee, miserably, weighed down, snuffling.

'Christmas ought to be wonderful,' he said.

'Something ought.'

She spoke about Ralph Wilson in terms of affection and despair. He was a good man, young for his age, well-to-do, a keen musician, genuinely fond of her. Every word of praise damned, but even that without enthusiasm. Janet seemed not far from tears, but polite. When he kissed her, she responded unaccommodatingly, out of good manners.

The church clock struck one bleakly, though the weather was not cold. Lights were still on in windows downstairs. Boxing Day had begun.

6

James Murren did not get round to helping Patricia Payne until the middle of January, when he telephoned hoping she had given him up, cleared her brother's rooms without his assistance. He made his excuses;

he had to start the Choral Society on the *Missa Solemnis,* his pupils at the training college had come back from holiday with work that needed marking, he'd been invited to adjudicate. Fluent as he was he did not convince himself. Mrs Payne bore no ill will; he was most kind; she realized how busy he was, like her, and this would be an excellent, most convenient time.

They fixed on a date. Willing to be propitiated, she gushed, not impressing him. She asked if he had seen much of her step-daughter. He had? She purred pleasure so that he was left stranded, hardly able to answer her euphoria with civility.

At high tea on the Friday night chosen, Mrs Payne acted out the importance of the mission. Her husband showed amusement while Jessica sulked, pretending uninterest.

'We wonder what you two are getting up to,' father said.

Jessica looked hard at her plate as one who had never seen boiled ham before.

Away at six-thirty, they drove through the centre of the town and out northwest, past fine, shabby residences and into a street of bow-windowed terraced houses in Edwardian brick, the pointing admirable still. A group of boys kicked a white ball in the road under a concrete lamp standard; the best dribbler and most vocal was a tall West Indian in a track suit. The players worked hard, every man's foot against every other's in a series of mad darts, shoves, shouts, sometimes a violent kick checked more often than not by an obstructing body. The corporate energy was immense, with flying elbows, skittling legs, loud obscenities, but pointless since the ball hardly moved more than a yard or two at a time. If a car passed, the footballers lined the pavement, without truce, inclined to wrestle for a punch at the ball one held.

Mrs Payne mounted six worn steps, used a Yale key, stalked in. This was not her first visit. A short, flag-tiled corridor led to formidably steep stairs under a narrow wooden arch. She led the way and on the first floor turned her second key. Once they were inside she did not switch on the lights but moved over to the windows, stared out. Now Murren could see the furniture of the room, wardrobe, table, sideboard, a bed, an armchair in the light from the street.

She dragged the curtains across, shouting at the last skirr, 'Switch on.'

He did as he was told, and was surprised. The chill of the room, the stale smell, had not prepared him for its brightness. The wooden furniture was old, unveneered, but marvellously polished; the carpet, yellow, orange and black, and the armchair were brand-new. The paintwork of the fireplace, skirting boards and doors struck white, while walls and ceiling shone more creamily, but finished not more than three months ago. Tankards, horse-brasses, a wall-plate were beginning to tarnish, but the one picture, a reproduction, the Bellini madonna and child, was framed in gleaming silver, the blue of her gown spotless. The effect under a strong bar-light contradicted expectation. He felt that Mrs Payne had been in every day with her duster, keeping up the good name of her brother. Could he smell polish? This dazzle did nothing to suggest the sodden scarecrow he'd dragged from the pond.

'What do you want me to do?'

She opened a wardrobe door, showed its contents, ties, shirts, suits, shoes.

'Would you get rid of them?'

'To charity?'

He explained what he could do, and she asked about the furniture. He named firms who'd clear the place, explained the finance, speaking expertly as he'd dealt with the house of a bachelor colleague not six months ago. She spoke a girlish admiration.

'Did he leave a will?' he asked.

'Yes. Everything is mine. He said his wife and daughter could, if they wished, choose one thing each, and I agreed. I wrote to them, but haven't heard.'

The landlord, an elegant Sikh, obsequiously reported that Mrs Payne was wanted on the phone. While she was away, Murren rapidly searched the room, the kitchen, the lavatory. George Underwood had either left no written records of himself or, more likely, his sister had removed them. Even clothes drawers were empty, though lined with moderately recent newspaper, 28 October, 2 November, both *Daily Telegraph.* The pigeon-holes of the bureau were empty and dusted; not a paper-clip, rubber or elastic band cluttered the bright surfaces. He'd been fetched in to decide whether one could make a pound or two for the furniture; perhaps Jessica, who'd accompanied him once or twice to Tom Singleton's ramshackle place, had enthused over his sharp eye for a bargain, and her step-mother had listened, delayed, paying rent for the non-existent profit on these sticks.

He could not guess from the room anything of its occupant's character. George O. Underwood, the corpse, had been wet, dirty, bedraggled past description. This room shone, cared for, with no trace of the slovenly habits of a grass-widower. There were no books, not a pack of cards, no television or radio. The medicine cupboard in the bathroom was empty;

surely a successful suicide would have his stand-by bottle of aspirin, if not Valium. Did the man not drink? There were no cups or glasses. Smoke, cut his nails, shave?

Patricia Payne banged back, flushed.

'You won't believe it,' she said.

He dragged himself back from the shell of a room.

'Do you know what that was? George's wife just turned up. She's just passing through. At this time of night. Walter and Jessica have invited her to stay. I'm not sure that's wise.' She frowned. 'But isn't it a coincidence?' She looked round. 'Will you please go through everything for me? Quickly you know. So we can see where we are.'

Murren dropped the lid of the bureau.

'Nothing here.'

'Oh, I cleared that. In the daytime. Mr Singh let me make a bonfire. I've been in and made a start. Several times.' This contradicted her first assertions of fear.

She disappeared again while he conducted his second search and on her return presented him with a typed list.

'That's just about correct,' she said. It appeared so.

'Why didn't you give me that in the first place?'

'I didn't want to interfere.'

'Why didn't you ask me to make my own list out? We could have compared.'

'It doesn't matter all that much.'

Patricia Payne smiled, evasively. There seemed no reason for his presence; neither a lack of confidence on her part nor a wish to dominate or use him accounted for her insistence that he helped, her acceptance of delay.

'I'll give you the addresses and telephone numbers you need,' he said.

'Would tomorrow . . . be possible? I'd like to get it cleared up now.'

He promised, not hiding his annoyance.

'Let's have a cup of coffee,' she argued. 'At home. Jessica will be pleased to see you. And I've got to deal with this woman. Mary. George's wife, widow.' She tried softening her voice as she dealt with fire, lights, lock. He watched her stiff movements; at one time she must have been somebody's little daughter. In her school-assembly voice she called out to the landlord, who appeared in white and pastel shades to agree with her, rocking his right hand in self-deprecation.

Outside there was crude silence. The football players had disappeared from the street, leaving shadows, house-bricks, stunted privet, threat of fog.

'We'd better not mention,' Mrs Payne straightened from her car door to stare over its roof, 'to Mary that you found George. That would be asking for trouble.'

He nodded.

'I've no idea what sort of woman she is, haven't seen her for years. I hope the other two have the sense to keep their mouths shut. You never know.'

Mrs Underwood sat with her thick legs together, a pretty woman of perhaps sixty, talkative on the subject of her nervous complaints, trying to make a good impression with repeated thanks for Mrs Payne's kindness in writing. They shunted Murren out to Jessica, and there was no mention in his presence of the sodden corpse.

Jessica, in front of a colour television, was not enthusiastic in welcome. She pressed her lips, offering no drinks.

'What's wrong with you?' he asked.

'I'm thinking.' Childish.

'I'd better go then.'

She flagged him back into his chair with a bored anger, and returned to the telly turned down nearly to soundlessness. Murren stuck his legs out, determined not to wait too long.

'What are you doing here?' Jessica, in the end. He explained about the visit to George Underwood's room. She repaid with a remark or two about George's wife and her stupidity. Mary had 'made eyes' at Mr Payne, grotesque female. Jessica had got out of the way. Murren quietly checked facetiousness, inquired why Patricia had dragged him out to Austin Road. As Jessica paid no attention, he explained again how little he had done, why there was no necessity for his presence.

'She likes a man at her beck and call,' Jessica snapped.

'Look, she could have cleared this place in December. She was on holiday. She's paying rent, a month's worth, for no reason that I can fathom.'

'She's perhaps not sure.'

'Of what?'

'How should I know? Ask her.' Jessica relented. 'I'll make us coffee.' He settled more comfortably. She brought cups in cheerfully, began talking immediately.

'Elzbieta McKie saw me on the street today. She wants us to visit her father.'

'How is he?'

'Better, she says. Miles better.'

'I thought he was dying?'

'He was. But there's been a recession, if that's what they call it, remission. He's eating quite a bit, and sits out of bed. He's been downstairs. She's pleased as Punch.'

'Is it likely to last?' As he put the chilling question, he mused on her last phrase.

'Nobody knows. It sometimes happens with cancer, the doctor told her. But he's so different. He seems stronger, and not wandering in his mind. He asked to see us, she said. The musician and the pretty lady.' Jessica laughed, eyes tearfully.

'When, do you suggest?'

'Tomorrow, Saturday. I'll have to let her know.'

'All right. You and this McKie woman aren't,' he slowed up, 'attributing this miracle to our,' he coughed, 'appearance there?'

'No. Should we?' She dumped herself on his knee, pinched his cheek painfully. 'Will you go round with me to the McKies', as well?'

They stood like schoolchildren outside the door next morning as Mr McKie, lipping that his wife was shopping, insisted they should come in. The living room was tidy, the table clear, though the air tanged with cigarette-smoke. The husband spoke through clenched teeth, as if to make his thick accent and his short sentences more cryptic. His pale face creased without warning into what he meant as a sociable smile, but was otherwise as expressionless as his brilliantined hair. The light blue eyes darted suspiciously.

'Sit down,' he ordered. Very rapidly Jessica explained that she would go with Murren to see the Wisniewskis that afternoon or evening. Their host hummed, ayed, shifted like a boxer from foot to foot. He'd no idea of his wife's plans; she could go to the phone box when she got back. Again the muttering died into sounds which presumably marked their presence and his favourable attention to it. Then the three sat in awkward silence.

'Mr Wisniewski's very much better?' Murren began. A short crescendo of argument. McKie did not seem to feel the need of further comment, but when they had given him up, he spoke, words chipped from granite.

'It's cheered Liz up.'

'There wasn't much hope?' Jessica. 'She was fond of her father?'

'I didna understand it. My father. . . .' He stopped, stumbled a step or two to sit on the edge of the table. 'She's a g'id woman. Knows wh'it . . . .'

'Your little girl is out with her?'

'Ay. She's her mother's child.' The sentence needed disentangling. 'Won't leave her side.'

'Have you lived here long, Mr McKie?'

'Since I was fifteen.'

'Your father worked down here?' Murren in sociability.

'Still does. Same pit.'

'On the coal-face?'

'No. No. He d'is not.' Why he needed to stress that they could not understand. 'He's no' a man like Liz's father.' Vowels were swallowed, or crunched between fierce consonants. 'He's had education. Me, my dad, we're nothing, colliers. She's a g'id woman, my wife.'

They left him, having arranged the time for Elzbieta's phone call.

'I wouldn't like to meet him on a dark night,' Jessica said, mouth champed together in a crude imitation.

'He was doing his best for us,' Murren answered. 'Praising his wife.'

'I wouldn't fancy his blame, then.'

'He'd be better at that. Suits the style.'

They laughed uncomfortably. At the Paynes' Murren had been invited for lunch; they noticed an air of subdued festivity, marked by grocer's red wine. Patricia spoke graciously, especially to Mrs Underwood, to whom, she revealed, she had been talking all the morning. The memento had been chosen, a couple of cheap reproductions of women's heads by Corot, pale, but nicely framed, which had once hung over his desk, according to his wife. They had been found by his sister at the bottom of a drawer wrapped in newspaper. Patricia did not want them, but Mary had shown taste in picking them, so that compliments abounded, non-existent links were re-welded, middle-aged people trotted about knowing they had done good. Father Payne presided, not without cynicism, but glad to be included in benevolence.

'You'd think,' he spoke in a low voice to Murren, 'she and Underwood had never parted, and my wife had been living next door. She upped and left him God knows how long ago. The propensity in human beings to self-deception is extraordinary.'

That fetched a laugh out of Murren.

'Polish it,' he said. 'You've got an epigram buried there.'

'You suffer from the delusion you're the world's only educated man.'

'Keep trying. That'll make number two.'

He liked Payne in this mood, a sharp chap. Oddly he never connected him with Jessica. This spruce, volatile, suspicious fellow had none of the attributes of a father, and was certainly never treated as such by his daughter, who claimed, when he had got across her, that you could never squeeze an answer out of him, only half a dozen contradictions, varying with the moon or his digestion.

'We're going to the Wisniewskis',' Murren tried him.

'So I understand,' He did not miss much.

'Jessica seems really interested. I'm surprised.'

'I'm not.' But he'd say no more, shamed, perhaps, by his wife's dominance.

McKie, in a garish light-blue tie crossed with a design of barbed wire black, brought his wife to the door. She perfunctorily kissed her daughter, who seemed content to stay with dad, but not her husband. On the short journey she spoke, soberly, of the improvement in her father's health. Again, as they stood in the passage, the mother waddled out to greet them, relapsed into Polish, peering apologetically, signalling her apologies with expressive hands. Elzbieta ran ahead upstairs. Mrs Wisniewski made some baffling statement about 'eating', at which they nodded and smiled, the three of them, as at an intellectual victory.

With the mother accompanying them the visitors crowded the bedroom, were pressed back against the wall. Wisniewski in a heavy tartan dressing-gown sat with his straight back to the window, one forearm projecting, the hand gaunt. To first impressions he showed no signs of a return to health, his lined face ghastly ill, with only the short-cut grey hair alive above livid skin.

He expressed polite, slow greeting, then ordered, 'Give the lady a chair.' Mother, daughter, Murren all moved to obey; James placed it for Jessica, who accepted proudly.

'We're so glad you're so much better,' she began.

'Yes. Yes.' The old head bowed; his women waited for him, but when he did not continue Elizbieta again outlined his improvement, his ability to keep his food down, to sit, talk, read. She was interrupted once with a garrulous burst of Polish from her mother, then what appeared as a question or contradiction from Mrs McKie, and an answer delivered from energy, pungency even. Wisniewski nodded at the end of the exchange and, smiling at Jessica said,

'Yes. It is so. I am better.'

Jessica asked about their Christmas celebrations, rousing the women, and then described her own with ingenuous simplicity. She still, at her age, hung up a stocking which her parents filled with chocolate, combs, an orange, felt-tip pens, tights, liquorice sticks, a sugar mouse with a string tail. She spoke slowly, as to Mrs Wisniewski, but a translation was necessary, with father intervening once. The women began to laugh; the old man's face cracked.

'Is that the mouse?' Jessica asked.

'She thinks it is beautiful.'

Offers of hospitality were made, tea, coffee, wine, and refused. The father pointed to his tray and bottle; his wife poured the yellow liquid, and he raised his full glass to them, and sipped. They watched, for this demonstrated the new man, the cancer at bay. The mother suggested, and they understood, that there were Polish customs, and the statement merited applause.

'You would have music?' the man said to Murren, replacing his glass, still two-thirds full on its tray. 'In the churches?'

Murren spoke his share, touched on Timothy Gelsthorpe's brilliance at the manuals, said the young man had given a recital in Warsaw last year.

'It is the king of instruments.' At Wisniewski's pronouncement they assumed serious faces.

'I shouldn't have thought they'd have been interested in a Communist country,' Jessica said, recovering first.

'Bach's *Thomaskirche* in Leipzig's in East Germany,' Murren answered her.

'I have been there,' the man said. 'You have?'

Murren had; they exchanged memories, he excitedly, the old man in sad agreement.

'I don't suppose you've been back to Poland?' Jessica.

Wisniewski translated this into Polish for his wife, and she immediately talked at him. They had no idea of her drift, whether it was warning, reminiscence, even anger. Neither face proffered clues, and the woman's energy tailed off. Only then did the father condescend to guest, and English.

'We have been,' he said. 'It was much changed. We stayed with relatives.'

'You didn't like it?' He shrugged at Jessica's question.

'There was much damage in the war. It is not a rich country.'

'You wouldn't like to go back to live there?'

He translated for his wife who was immediately voluble, but laughingly so, answering the fool perhaps according to folly. Again she faded, unsure of her role.

'They would not have us. We are of no use to them.'

'Did you try, then? To get back?'

'No.' A final word, heavy as oak, as hard. He picked up his glass.

'Did Elzbieta go with you?' Jessica asked. This brought smiles.

'She did. She was a girl. And our relatives used to laugh at her English accent when she spoke Polish.'

Mrs Wisniewski added another incomprehensible sentence or two, which the father had translated.

'They said she was the little Englishwoman.'

The room wrapped one in warmth, with no noise but the hissing of the gas-fire. A cat miauled at the door, and the daughter let the animal in, to murmurs of approbation. It settled at once on the hearth.

'When I think,' Wisniewski said, spacing out his words, 'of my youth in Poland, it is always spring and always sunny. That cannot be true, but it is how I remember it.'

'I'd imagined it as thick snow, and peasants.' Jessica.

They laughed, translating.

'I remember that, of course. And days of hot summer, but to the other my mind turns without will. That is what appears.'

The old man's English was formally beautiful, foreign, limpid. He sipped with similar care. The daughter disparaged Newstead Road in the winter, but her father seemed content.

'This is a temperate country.'

Jessica said they must leave; Wisniewski asked them to call again.

'You do me good.'

His wife tried out her creaking English, made her pleasure understood, delighted them all. There was a hand-shaking before the four trooped downstairs. Elzbieta did not immediately accompany them out, appeared ready to traipse upstairs again, perhaps to return her father to bed.

'He is better,' Jessica said, in the street. Murren could just believe it.

'Are you coming home with me?' he asked.

'No. I don't think so.'

'What are you doing?'

'Minding my own business, among other things.'

They quarrelled insipidly, he annoyed at his own feebleness, she perhaps concerned with what happened in the dark bedroom, that little Poland. They wished each other good afternoon like a tired brush salesman and a preoccupied housewife.

7

After evensong Murren, coming down from the organ on which he'd shepherded the congregation homewards with Purcell, was met by Janet Bruce. Pleased, he shook her hand.

'Madam?'

'Will you play for me in April? They're arranging a week-end school at the university, and they want me to do the Saturday evening recital.'

'What are you singing?'

'We could decide that. I could do a James Murren.'

They laughed; she'd sing one of his songs if she were accompanied by a left-handed monkey. Honesty decked out as temptation appealed to them.

'Let's have a drink on it.'

She insisted that they use her car, and this meant he had to drive his back home before they made for the Park Tavern.

'Have you heard from Jess?' she asked, slipping off fur coat immediately her martini arrived.

'Saw her yesterday afternoon. We went to see Mr . . . .'

'I know. But not since?'

'No.'

'There was a rumpus there last night.' He liked her word, matching the pleasure with a swig at his pint.

'At the Wisniewskis'?'

'No. The Paynes'.' Janet, enigmatic, waited, but he was in no hurry either. 'Patricia and this woman, Mary Underwood, the sister-in-law. Nearly came to blows. In the end Ma Payne kicked her out of the house. Seven-thirty at night. Father made Jess drive her to the station. Don't know if there were any trains on Saturday night. I don't suppose he did, either.'

'They were all over one another when I saw them.'

'So I understand. Until after the evening meal. Patricia wasn't pleased that Jess went off with you in the afternoon. And the old man skipped out as well. She seemed rattled, they said, but Mr Payne and Jess cleared away, washed up, took the old biddies a port and lemon in, and then, then. When dad got back there was our Patty raging, scarlet in the face, standing over the other woman, screaming at her, about to lay violent hands on her.'

'Tell me more.'

'It was frightening. She was accusing Mary of driving her husband to suicide. That was daft anyway, because she'd left the man years ago, and with good reason, as far as I can make out. But it was Pat. She was literally hopping, with her lips drawn back from her teeth as if she was having a fit. Jess thought she'd heard shouting when she was in the scullery, but it's a long way off.'

'Has she acted like this before?'

'Apparently not. She banged her fists on the table.'

'And the . . . Mary?'

'Scared out of her wits. Just sat there with her mouth open, crying.'

‘Does Jessica give any reason why all this happened?’

‘That’s what’s upsetting her. There is no real . . . . Not with this Mary Underwood. They think it’s Pat who’s gone . . . . Her school’s a strain these days, and she’s well into the menopause, and old Payne’s a bit of a funniosity . . . .’

‘I like him. I thought he was a clown, but I’ve come round. There’s something about him.’

‘You’re not married to him, my man.’

Murren watched Janet who was enjoying this. He’d always seen her as a balanced woman, right side up, but she relished this trouble.

‘Is there anything we can do?’ he asked.

‘I’d keep away. They won’t brook interference.’

A wobbling electronic organ smashed into favourities of the thirties, thumping bass through the floorboards. Nobody sang at this stage; glazed faces stiffened as at a sermon. Murren did not think highly of the beer; he and Janet drank up and left. Back at his house, with gin, they sorted out songs. It was warm in his music room, and the lights glowed down on to the marble mantelpiece, the black surface of his piano. They sang and played, not seriously, by snatches, though they did the whole of Bach’s ‘Sighing, weeping’, *Seufzer, Thränen, Kummer, Noth,* and once, but laughing, completed Sullivan’s ‘Will he Come?’ Janet was never slipshod, touched the high soprano notes of the Bach with ease and purity. He congratulated her.

‘I don’t trust your transposition,’ she said, punching him. The phone interrupted her horseplay. Jessica, rather short, said she’d tried twice before.

‘I’ve been out for a drink.’

‘Who with?’ No finesse.

‘Janet. She’s here now. We’re working on a recital.

We've just found an old Sullivan to words by Adelaide Anne Proctor. Come on round. Give yourself a treat. I'll fetch you.'

'No, thanks.'

'Did you want anything?'

'No.' She wished him good-bye, rang off.

When he reported the conversation to Janet she asked, 'Did you say anything about Patricia?'

'No.'

'Thank God for that. You'll be in trouble, anyway.'

He struck a chord, played six diplomatic bars of a Mozart aria, but she did not join him. Suddenly he wanted her out of the house, off his back. She, quite composed, leafed through an album of Handel, knees together, a red spot on each cheek; an attractive, well-dressed woman he did not want. The evening had spoilt itself.

'I'm tired,' he said, yawning.

'Oh, so she's coming round, is she?'

'She is not.'

'But you want me out of the way?'

He did not deny it, was relieved to notice she seemed almost eager to go. For the moment, he was sorry, wished he felt as strongly for her as a woman as he did as a singer. Her short fur coat with matching hat suited her; sturdily calved legs, high-heeled elegant shoes flashed with attraction as she walked along his hall. She was not Jessica Payne. That was her only fault.

As soon as she closed the door his heart sank, and he took out a batch of essays on Byrd's importance as a church composer. Red pen lifted, he was glad of work that killed time.

Though during the next week he heard nothing of the Paynes, he made no attempt to inquire. Jessica and her father, different as they were, were private people, not keen to be caught out, nor rushed into confidences. Mrs McKie called on him just as he set out for his Thursday choir practice to inquire how she had provoked the Paynes who had pretty well ordered her off the front step.

'Who did? Jessica?'

'And her father. My father would like you two to call again, wanted me to inquire. He was insistent. I went. Mr Payne answered the door, and then Jessica almost immediately after. He spoke politely at first but he was troubled. I could see that. As if somebody would jump out behind him. They did not ask me in. Jessica said she didn't know, she was busy. She snapped her mouth shut as if I'd insulted her, or she hated the sight of me.' Mrs McKie threw her own fierce glances round the shrubs in his front garden. 'I wondered what I'd done.'

'I don't know. Perhaps they'd just had a pipe burst, or something.'

'Both would not have come to the door.'

'No. Suppose not. I haven't seen them, or heard from them.'

'You have not quarrelled with her, then?' Murren could hear an English, more demotic version of Wisniewski's voice in these formal sentences, in which Slavonic propriety, not the miner's Doric, predominated. He shook his head. 'Would you call round? Perhaps they need help.'

'It's not likely.'

She made no attempt to hide her disgust. He half-promised, and she thanked him, this woman who'd stripped herself as her husband fetched help from the street. She knew what domestic crisis was. When he offered her a lift, she curtly refused; husband and child waited.

James Murren drove madly fast to his church, then sat outside. He seemed removed from these wrangles; he quarrelled, lost his cool often enough, but never at home, never with relatives. He had no brother or sister, and his father and mother were dead. The old man had lived the last part of his life abroad, in France, where he was partner in a light engineering concern which still provided James with a small income, and Mr Murren returned to England only on matters of business. This country was ruined, he'd often launch into the diatribe, and he'd work in a place where people had sense, knew the value of money, earned it. He'd started up soon after his demobilization from the Royal Engineers with two men he'd barely known. 'We hit it off,' he'd say. 'We had the same objectives.' He'd given up the position his firm had held for him through the war, and slaved grimly in England to make connections for his new venture. They'd done well, but after ten years he'd left the London office to a subordinate, had bought a house near the French factory, supervised extensions, watched growth.

The life of the elder Murren must have been uneasy in that he left his wife behind in England to bring up the four-year-old James, making it clear that as soon as the boy was old enough he'd be sent to preparatory school. Club friends chaffed him, demanding why he, the admirer of France, did not have his son educated on the continent where they organized properly. Murren, forty-five now and looking older, coughed his prejudices.

'James is an Englishman, and he'll go to the sort of school I went to. That's his right. Otherwise, he might hold it against me. I choose my way of life. He cannot, as yet.'

He'd bristled, friends said, perhaps because he felt guilty deserting his native country. Others said Winifred, his wife, had decided, and his bluster camouflaged the defeat. The old man worked, James remembered, spent long hours in the factory, or on his travels, but never relaxed, never enjoyed himself. His ulcers prevented indulgence in food and drink; his reticence made intercourse with wife and child little more than an exchange of barked questions and unheard answers, but he loved them.

Winifred Murren was a musician, a fine pianist, a violist in good amateur chamber music, a concert-goer, and at this time her younger sister, the cellist, Dorothea Peterson, lived with them in London, first while the girl studied at the Royal Academy, and then between her earliest recitals. It was Winifred who had started James at the piano, who removed him from a preparatory school where music made little showing to one where his training could continue.

'I don't want him to be a professional,' she said. 'Dotty's life's warning enough. But if he wants to develop his talent that way, then I'll see the groundwork's put in.'

James sang in the nearby Anglican choir when he could, not because, of his outstanding voice nor his mother's religion, but because the local organist had demonstrated flair and musicianship out of the ordinary. Winifred chose, consulting with Dorothea, his teachers, and had made it clear at his public school that she expected any musical gift to be nurtured.

'Why's your mother so keen to make a player of you?' the music master, 'Mutton' Lamb, used to ask him. 'I wouldn't put my worst enemy to it.'

'She'd have liked to be a professional herself, sir.'

'Yes. And you'll do it for her. Yes.'

And 'Mutton' would slip into a Bach trio as if the end of the world was four minutes away. 'Yes,' he'd break off. 'Yerrss. A not inconsiderable notion.' And his fingers and feet would scuttle into Bachian intricacies again, to prevent him thinking any longer about pretty singing boys or mothers' ambitions or whatever it was that troubled middle-aged bachelors.

Mother and son spent surprisingly little time in France, a month in the summer, a week at Easter, at Christmas, and Winifred did not settle permanently there until James was ready for Oxford. He remembered the ugly house and housekeeper, his father's fluent, bad French, the excursions into the countryside, the dinners with the partners' families, the occasional trip to Paris. He had not enjoyed himself, had spent much of his time practising, or mooching round dusty roads bored and expectant. Nothing untoward happened; he ate solid meals three times a day, played Bach now and again on the organ of the church, where he and the priest exchanged exploratory sentences in French; he thumped his anxieties and frustrations out of the keyboards and lanes, hating everybody.

Now he realized how much his father thought of him. The old man with his bad breath would stump in to listen to his son's Beethoven or Bartók. More often than not the boy would spot him and turn to the one or two Webern pieces he had bought, trying to tinkle and jab his father out of the room. But Thomas listened; Scriabin or Schönberg came alike. Only the inevitable telephone fetched him away. If James paused, the older man would nod, clear his throat and ask what that piece was. The young man would answer politely, dating the composition, adding information about the composer's age, life, sometimes an anecdote. Murren, senior, would listen, not smiling, as at some ceremony, and perhaps this was the case, that he felt himself unmoved or untouched in the presence of music that loomed importantly in the life of his wife and son, and saw himself as bound to register his recognition. So he'd nod, and twitch. As James thought the matter over now, he wondered if the old man weren't trying to express affection, for he'd lay a hand on his son's sleeve to ask if there was anything he wanted.

By the time James had finished his five years at Oxford, his father was preparing for retirement – he called it retiral – and began to sever his connection with the firm. He had bought a house in Brighton, near enough to London for his wife's concert-going; but, during the excitement, if that word could be applied to his grumpy expeditions to agents and lawyers and sites and board meetings, he was taken suddenly ill and died, in England, aged sixty-three at the beginning of his son's second year of teaching. Winifred seemed hardly hurt by the death and had set off for America where her sister Dorothea was now prosperously settled as recitalist and professor, and five months after the death of her husband had herself been killed in a car accident.

Murren in his first teaching post, at a large public school in London, had found himself thus bereft of family. Suddenly his rock-solid father and his energetic, organizing mother no longer existed. He could not believe it; it should not have happened.

It was difficult to recall anything now beyond the barest outline. He remembered the kind interest of colleagues and wives on the death of his father, and something of the pride he felt in containing his grief, which was real enough. He had not seen too much of the old man recently, but the impact of death was as substantial as his father's body in life. Somebody as real could not die unremarked. But Murren busied himself, co-operating and tangling with the brilliant head of his department, a man not ten years his senior, training choirs, orchestras, groups, playing the organ for two choral societies, and saw his first year out with élan and success, even making an admired television appearance. In the summer he travelled to Germany as accompanist to a small male group of singers, and returned for his last fortnight of holiday in Brighton where Dorothea Peterson was over persuading his mother to join her in New York later in the year. Winifred left like a whirlwind just before Christmas, three months after her husband's death.

At the end of February she was killed.

Stacey, the headmaster, had sent for him, ordered him to sit down.

'I've an awful task.' The head pulled his shirt-cuffs down, almost stammering out the choking cliché. The pang broke inside Murren, uncoordinated, not aligned, merely perhaps the echo in a sensitive man of the senior's terrifying inadequacy. Stacey's thin, handsome face hung palely on his cheekbones like dirty curtains. His hand, when not resting on the desk, shook. 'I have some very bad news for you.'

Murren forced his face upwards; the other waited, allowing settlement or imagination.

'It's your mother. In America.'

'Yes, sir?' Did he speak?

'She's been involved in a serious car accident.'

'Is she . . . is . . .?'

'The worst.'

'She's dead, do you mean?'

'Yes, James. I'm dreadfully sorry.'

Stacey stood, impressive grey hair flopping, by his desk, still wearing his gown. Perhaps he'd dressed for the ordeal. Murren saw that the master's eyes were full of tears, that one had slipped to his cheek where it hung unwiped. 'Your aunt rang just a few minutes ago. It's early morning there. She would like you to phone again at six this evening.' He handed over a paper with number, name, time. 'She did not seem to have much detailed knowledge,' he fumbled for words, 'herself. It happened last night. Your mother was staying with friends. She was brought back to hospital, where she died after two hours. I've put the phone number down if you felt you wanted to call them. She never recovered consciousness, did not suffer. Apparently the car ran off the road. The driver, a John Nathan,' he raised his eyes to see if the name registered, lowered them, 'was killed instantly. Just a few miles outside New York. I did not press for names. Your aunt was,' he waved a hand, 'cut up.' Stacey shuffled. 'But she does want you to ring at six.'

The head now sat down at Murren's side, quietly, breathing, immobile. This lacuna lasted for three or four minutes; Murren in a frenzy of thought, lounged incapably. Stacey patted his arm, fetched out two glasses like a conjuror, and unlocking a cupboard produced whisky, poured two small measures, locked the raw bottle away.

'Taste that,' he said. Murren wet his lips. 'Now what are we going to do? You will want to fly out for the funeral? I'll get Mrs Pickard on to the arrangements. I have a cousin at the American embassy, in case there are difficulties. Your passport's up to date? You'll need to ring your bank. They'll have to smarten themselves.'

Now Stacey was himself again, organizing, questioning. No need to worry about money, or time off. He himself harried Murren's bank manager, re-emerged satisfied, confident. Mrs Pickard in the outer office was already working.

'What are you going to do, James?' he asked. 'Now?'

Murren looked hopelessly round. He did not want to do anything; the wild posse in his head pillaged him. Stacey issued orders. The young man was to go over to the master's home; Mrs Stacey knew already and would be waiting. They'd talk together again, at lunch, and by that time tickets would be under way, a flight provisionally booked so that he could give hard information to his aunt. Murren obediently scuttled across to the school house where Mrs Stacey nursed him with coffee, subdued sympathy, tactful absence, the headmaster's two newspapers. When he now groped back, it seemed impossible to believe that he had behaved as he had, weeping as soon as she had opened the front door, crouching down like an animal on the huge sofa where she had abandoned him. He could not recall feeling sorrow.

The week in New York seemed fictional. His aunt loomed, large, in personality and figure, her husband huger, both in winter furs. They would not let him decide for himself. He must bide their time, so that when they thought fit they described the accident, and at their chosen moment he viewed the body. His mother seemed to smile, but he had never to the best of his knowledge seen her flat on her back. It ruptured nature. Highly made-up, she lay dressed to kill, he thought, and the inappropriate phrase squeaked like a fork on plate, not pleased with herself, a craftsmanlike dummy, but unfamiliar without voice or movement. She was dead, unmarked, but utterly dead. The snow on the afternoon of cremation, the familiar phrases of the English prayerbook delivered in a slow American accent, the over-heated rooms, the unknown sympathetic faces all remained, but vague, ill-defined, bobbing.

On his last night Dorothea and her husband took him to a concert. 'That's what your mother would want us to do,' his aunt said, and again he wept. Through the service at the funeral parlour, at the hundred warm handshakes and kisses, he had kept his face straight, but not now. Dorothea bundled him into her scented arms, cried with him, deserting her husband for grief. She had acted right.

The concert had been an anti-climax: *Egmont*, the Tschaikowsky violin concerto, superbly played by a young unknown, a fine Mahler fourth. He'd listened with a detached, connoisseur's ear, enjoying every popular note, remark, new face, but like some other man, some distant cousin.

When he arrived back, he seemed not to have been away, except that he had no mother. He struggled successfully through his work as he did through interviews with solicitors and bank managers, was grateful to occupy himself, but left on his own he staggered. Sometimes he shouted, screamed, windmilled his arms, walked out into the night streets punching the air, spitting an unbridled monologue. At other times, he lay so much limp flesh, on his bed, on the hearth-rug, half in, half out of a chair, broken with depression, every nerve flaccid and feeble, every fibre loose.

Stacey seemed to understand.

'I think you should move this year, James. In fact,

there's a very attractive job here for the taking.' Hardly a vice-chancellor or principal existed who was not begging Stacey to do him a favour by recommending somebody. 'You'll have done two years here. *Magna cum laude* as they say in the New World. But two years under Ashley's long enough. He's brilliant; he won't leave us; but I don't want you a carbon-copy of that lightning conductor. Possible, you know, possible. I shall miss your organ in assembly.'

Not a word about the distracted Murren who knocked his head on his bedroom wall, who one night had stumbled, jumped, he could not say himself, into an ornamental pond. Cold water had startled him into shame, so that he'd run, dripping for three miles through dark streets in a red fury of angry self-scorn. He'd managed the stairway to his flat without being seen; a dry-cleaners managed his suit; filthy water spotted his heart. He'd never be able to call on his mother for advice; a second set of death duties took toll before the first were clear; he hated lawyers and legality, signed documents with trepidation or insouciance, needed a drink to steady him after these sessions, but would dash out of the handy pub after two or three sips merely to be elsewhere.

Stacey put him in touch with a Beechnall solicitor; a house was found and paid for. All congratulated him on a bargain. He finished his year at school, and, after a visitation from clergy and churchwardens during the summer term, was appointed master of the choristers at the mother church in the city, duties to start in September. By the time he arrived, his name had gone before him and he found himself conductor of a long-established madrigal group. It seemed as if musicians had retired or moved to make way for him. He took his chance, worked long, vigorous hours, won golden opinions, was even hated. In the fifteen months he'd spent here, he had made his mark, fiercely.

Now sitting in his car, the great black wall of the churchyard above him, he took no pride. He had occupied himself, had met Jessica, considered himself lucky in love. He thought of his parents still, but without violence; he had set out to make his choirs outstanding, and succeeded. He raced competitively; his head of department, a nonentity, feared him; the adviser had met his master; the university music department viewed the prodigy with amused respect, stroking their doctoral gowns. Already he had begun to look for new jobs, having refused a cathedral post. He would be famous but he did not know for what. He could make men and women work for him, perform beyond themselves; that seemed his destiny, though he did not like it. This drilling of choirs and orchestras was menial compared with composition, but he knew that he could not excel there. He had not come to terms with himself; he had money, remarkable success for his age, able lieutenants, one of whom was already inside this grim castle of a building making absolutely certain that exactly at seven-thirty the rehearsal would begin; people liked, respected, feared him, but he did not care for himself.

Slamming the car door he raced up the seven steps, along the flagged path, in at the south porch. The choir were already seated, music stopped. His third assistant at the console quietly played a Bach chorale prelude until the master appeared. As Murren ran the aisle, he heard a rare wrong note from the organist.

'B natural, Roger,' he shouted. The choir laughed; they liked his drama. The deputy peered over the rail, goggling. 'Second line, second bar, third note.' The choirmen roared.

'Sorry, sir.'

'G minor, Roger,' He opened his first copy. Faces turned to him. They knew his method, were ready at his demand.

Practice began while the clock still chimed the half-hour.

8

Jessica phoned. Outside it snowed thickly, in exciting silence. Snow on the first day of February suggested long shudders of winter.

'I thought you'd have been round,' she complained. He made his excuses, an impressive list. 'Yes, anything before me.'

'What is it?'

'My mother's still off work. Nervous exhaustion.'

'I'm sorry.'

'I bet.' She laughed, giddily. 'She asked to see you.'

'What exactly is wrong?'

'Do you mean,' she asked, 'to tell me that Fat Janet didn't fall over herself to split?'

'Why should she?'

'Did she?'

'Janet said something about a flare-up with Mrs Underwood.'

'Flare-up? That's hardly the word. Are you coming to see us?'

'It's snowing.'

Jessica dashed the phone to its cradle; he put on his topcoat and Wellingtons. She grinned at him, fished out a pair of her father's slippers, led him to the kitchen where Payne watched a portable television.

'We heard those Monteverdi madrigals you broadcast,' father said. 'Very good, weren't they?' No one answered; Jessica rummaged for cups.

'We recorded them last November.'

'Beautiful singing.' He sighed through sentences of praise.

'How's your wife?'

'Well, there now, yes. Not well, I'm afraid, not well.'

He preferred talk of Monteverdi. 'I don't know what we shall do.'

'What's the doctor say?'

'What can he? Rest. Take the tablets. That's about it.'

Payne was frightened, fidgeting up and down, without a tie in an old-fashioned, collarless shirt. Jessica bustled in. 'Sometimes she's normal as tapwater. Listens to the radio, the TV, makes these little jokes. Then she'll plummet down. She is black, then; despairing.'

'About what?'

'She seems . . .' he searched his words, 'bothered. Beyond her wits, if you know what I mean. As if there's a catastrophe imminent.'

'Without reason?'

'As far as I can tell. You have to see to . . . .'

Jessica poured hot drinks, replenishing her father's cup. After she replaced the kettle she patted his biceps, as with a dog. Suddenly in this sad place, Murren felt cheered, in delight with the girl, in a small heaven. He could not account for this except perhaps that the pair of them, faced with this obscenity, kept up an appearance of modest decorum. The three drank.

'I'll run up to see if your mother wants one.'

'That's right.'

'Perhaps James will go up later. I'll say you're here.'

He trotted out, occupied in himself, patting his pockets.

'How's he taking it?' Murren asked, surprising himself.

'He has to look after her all day, and she leads him a dance. But he puts up with it. He's lively for his age.'

'I've no idea how . . . .'

'Sixty-six,' she said, curtly. 'It's good for him.'

'Is she showing signs of recovery?' He phrased the question awkwardly; it attracted crooked ways. Jessica shrugged, grimaced.

'How do we know? She's just normal sometimes; she does what she wants to do; if she can't she plays up.'

'You mean she's putting it on?'

'How would I know that? She doesn't want to work, so she lies in bed.'

'That's not like her.'

'Umm.' A thin, interrogative humming.

'What's that mean?'

'Nothing, nothing. Should it?'

Payne appeared; his slippers seemed next in importance after his face, new, tartan, high up the ankles.

'She doesn't want a drink. She'd like to see James.'

'Now?' Murren picked up his cup to ward off the immediacy of the summons.

'That's what she says. She looked quite pleased.'

Without hurry, nobody pressing, they finished their coffee, attempting to appear at ease.

'Well, then.' Payne rose, tartan slippers prominent. Jessica stood with him, but the father led the party out and up the stairs. They had more room than in the Polish house, but there was the same air of an official visitation as in Pan Wisniewski's bedroom. 'Here's the young man, then,' Payne called.

Patricia sat up in bed, in green silk pyjamas, wearing an ornate dressing gown, padded and crossed by trellis lines of dark red on cherry. Her face was rouged, haggard, but she had straightened her hair within the last five minutes; brush and comb lay on the bedside table.

'How are you?' Murren asked.

'I'm not so bad, thank you.' She smiled, large-toothed. 'A little better than I have been.'

'That's good.'

'I don't like to be ill at all. It's not me.' She sounded angry.

'You've got devoted nurses, I hear,' he said facetiously. The room was warmly scented.

'They'll tell you so.' She smiled again, like a sagging face. 'They're very kind.' She shifted, to put her hands on the duvet, where her chunky jewels flashed. 'Everyone has been most considerate. But I don't like illness. It's not me.'

'No,' he said, heavily. 'Are you able to get up at all? Will they allow it?'

'I'm to rest. I can go downstairs if I feel up to it. But I must not overdo things. That's been my trouble. I have not given my body a fair deal.' She opened her unbuttoned dressing gown wider as if to reveal the maltreated trunk. 'They were Dr Clower's words.'

She patted the quilt. 'Sit down for a minute, James. Here. On the bed.' He obeyed. 'Schools are places of stress,' she said, firmly. Her face was both lined and puffy, but the perfume rose sweet. 'Tell that to your students every time you see them. They must not be misled.'

'They'll be lucky to get jobs in the schools,' he answered. She frowned, affronted.

'Yes.' This word barely formed itself, and she stared ahead. The bedroom creaked as Payne moved his chair. Jessica still stood, excluding herself. 'Yes, I suppose so.' The sentence dismissed him; she did not want his polemics. 'I think I could do with a drink now, Walter. Lemon barley with ice. My mouth's parched.' She blamed somebody. Payne silently turned.

'I'll do it,' said Jessica, and was rewarded with the wide smile.

'Sometimes I become hot,' Mrs Payne said. 'Feel my hand.' She grabbed. 'Good grief, your fingers are frozen. Isn't your circulation good?' As she did not relinquish her grip, the question leapt awkwardly flirtatious. 'Are your feet cold in bed?'

Payne rescued Murren with an anecdote about low temperatures, in the Antarctic. Apparently one of his service colleagues had been there on a whaling expedition. The story was flatly delivered but restored normality; brothel becomes sick-room.

'I should have thought a musician needed warm hands.'

Now in his turn Murren obliged with the story of a distinguished concert pianist and his fur-muff. They listened, distantly, not interested. There is no place for eccentricity in intensive-care wards. When Patricia had drunk half her tumblerful, she demanded an account of Murren's choirs. He did his best, but as he talked she suddenly shrugged, a violent movement, and put her face down to the pillow. He stopped.

'Are you . . . are you all right?'

As she did not answer, he turned towards Payne, who smiled grimly, and looked away. Jessica's face petrified.

'Perhaps we're tiring her,' Murren said.

'Shall we go down, dear?' Payne asked, after a considerable, awkward pause. She did not move; her eyes were open and she held her hands together on the pillow under her cheek. Jessica pushed forward, heaved at and straightened the bedclothes.

'James is talking to you,' she said, tartly. 'He's telling you what happened in the Catholic cathedral.'

He could not see the invalid's face easily, but she made a noise, a sniff, that suggested she was crying. Her outline in the bed was awkward, a childish crouching. Jessica gave up, touched his arm to lead him away. Payne muttered a phrase about settling down for the night.

'Good night, then, Mrs Payne,' Murren said.

She turned on to her back; her eyes were distorted with tears, but her features scowled obstinately and mulish. She nodded, cracking her face into a smile. He wished her a second good-bye, and again clownish nods rewarded him. Jessica led the way from the room. Downstairs she slapped her hands on her skirt, sighed, said,

'Well, that got nowhere, fast.'

'She didn't seem too bad at first.'

'I think she packs in. It gets too much, and she . . . .'

'Do you mean deliberately?' he asked.

'How the hell would I know? She's been used to her own way, pushing people about . . . .'

'What's the cause?'

'She told you. Stress. She's found she can't cope. She's been self-sufficient. We discuss it, daddy and I and Dr Clower. That's what it seems. We don't know whether she's putting it on at all, or whether it's real.'

'Doesn't Clower know?'

'No. He's as much in the dark as we are. He's not very clever. Did you come in your car?' When he informed her he had walked, she fetched whisky and dry ginger out of the cupboard. 'Let's have some comfort.' She set out three glasses. Father came quietly in. 'Join us?' She filled, handed out glasses, drank from her own without gesture.

'I'll go back to tuck her up in a minute,' Payne said. 'She was really pleased to see you.' Unconvincing. At ten o'clock he went upstairs, reported that she was fast asleep, demanded a final glass.

At ten-thirty, Murren, slightly unsteady, was shown to the door by Jessica, who perfunctorily kissed him, repulsed further advances. Thoroughly disheartened, she tightened her lips; the skin of her face tautened, pale as candle-wax.

'I'll take you out for a meal,' he said.

'Think about it.'

'I don't like you like this.'

She opened the door, shooed him off without comment. Outside an east wind raked the streets, rattling windows, ripping snow like smoke in the gutters. Low in spirit, he decided on a bus, which would provide company, even if it saved little time. Shuddering, he wondered why request stops occupied such bleak positions. Immediately he boarded he stepped into trouble. The driver, a neatly bearded negro, allowed his fare to rattle into the machine, pressed the delivery button as he stared into the dark windscreen.

'Are you getting off?' the driver said, with a weary aplomb. Murren started.

'We're gooin' to Valley Road.' Two youths, scruffily jeaned, standing.

'Not on that ticket you're not. You paid twelve pence.'

Murren, the driver at his back, the young men half-crouching in front, felt menaced. Any time now the words would die, blows thud. Murren did not move, stood in the middle, afraid a step would spark conflict.

'Are you getting off?'

'Ah. At Valley Road.'

After a pause the bus jerked forward, so that the three standing passengers were toppled together.

'Yuh black goon.'

The bus stopped again, with equivalent violence. This time all three held on. The driver snapped open the gate of his partition, and without appearance of hurry made off through the outside doors which he had not closed, into the floodlit snow.

'Where the bleddy 'ell's he gone to?' asked one of the youths.

'You're a bloody nuisance,' a woman shouted. 'Some of us want to get home.'

'Bollocks.' He bawled with malice, nose becking.

The youths stood uncomfortably in the cold from the wind, peering out. The passengers sat silent. The deserted driving seat, the two gaping doors, the dead engine had a frightening, unnatural quality, as if God had intervened cruelly.

'They should get off.' The woman's voice, after a time. 'Or pay up.' Nobody answered; the passengers hunched shiftily, afraid to look about for support.

'Excuse me,' Murren said to the youth directly in front. The man stepped, shuffled grudgingly out of his way, allowing him to sit on the cross-seat opposite the luggage rack.

'You want to get off,' the woman said.

'Yo', knickers.' Bored, no time for repartee, the two stood, without bravado, big rough lads, but awkward, very unsure. Murren could smell the beer. A gust of wind whanged at the side of the bus; discarded tickets danced like confetti.

'It's co'd wi' them doors oppen,' the woman railed. One of the youths stepped forward, touched a button on the control panel. The doors whisked to. For some minutes nobody spoke.

'Do you reckon he's run off?' somebody ventured. A thin man in a trilby, answered by a spatter of conversation. The youths stood, leaned; one tapped a tattoo on the chrome upper bar of the luggage rack. Again the awkward silence. A voice from the upper deck called down for information; the few passengers above argued without energy. 'Has it broke down?' When no one replied, a schoolboy clattered downstairs, stared his surprise round the passengers, returned.

'He's gone and left us, that's what I think.' The woman again. Murren leaned forward to see her; thin, with tortoiseshell topped glasses and a plastic carrier bag on her knee.

'He's coming back.' A young married woman on the high seat at the back. 'He's bringing somebody with him.' All bent to the windows; the youths stooped. The driver rapped sharply on the door. A second time. Murren rose, went foward, leaned down to read the instructions. None. His breath came short, legs trembling.

'Which is it?' he asked. The driver knocked again.

'That. At th'end.' One of the miscreants.

He touched it. Nothing. Pressed harder and the doors swept open, startling him. As the driver stepped in, the youths jumped out of the exit, pelted away. The second man stood by the driver. His shirt was open at the throat, his hair slightly untidy, his jacket rucked at the collar. The face showed no emotion, pale and hard; eyes squinted small. With a movement of one strong index finger he straightened his coat, and then, without hurry, grasped the upright bar by the door. The hand was big, paw-like.

'Did anybody know them?' he asked down the bus.

'They ought to be locked up,' the woman said. He waited. Murren who had resumed his seat saw that the man carried a two-way radio in his left.

'That's it, then.' A deep, formidable voice, but not so frightening as the unmoving face. 'Report it when you get back. I'll do the same. How late are you?'

'Ten minutes.' The second nodded, walked away. 'Thank you,' the driver said, resuming his seat.

At the next stop the woman got up, and as she waited for the bus to stop said to Murren, 'Streets aren't safe this time o' night.' She shook her bag in anger. 'Who was the fellow he fetched?'

'I don't know.'

She looked affronted by his voice, as if he mocked her with his posh accent.

'A police inspector. That was a police house,' the driver said, over his shoulder. He spoke without heat, clipped, sing-song, educated. 'He was watching television.'

The woman drew herself up as if in resentment, held herself to attention until she left.

'They're a nuisance,' the driver said.

When three stops later Murren disembarked, he

called out, 'Good night. Thanks,' to the driver, who raised a left hand.

Elated, half-scared he made for his house which was thoroughly warm. As he drew the curtains he thought of his evening, a headmistress ruined, two beer-sodden lads asserting themselves over an official because he was black. Ought he to have left his address? As he sat in front of his roasting gas-fire Janet Bruce rang to see if they could practise.

'This is your night in,' she said. 'I didn't disturb you earlier, but this is the third time since nine.'

'Is it so important?' Past eleven o'clock.

'I think so.' Then, 'Have you seen Patricia Payne?'

'Tonight.'

'How is she?'

He explained, noncommittally, not pandering to her curiosity. She would not, he decided, get at the Paynes through him, but as he talked she answered aggressively determined, almost shouting that it served the woman right.

'What have you got against her, then?'

She slapped down the phone, rehearsal unarranged.

9

A few days later Murren was surprised as the deputy principal led Ernest Payne into the staff-common room. There James occupied a large black armchair and himself with *The Times*.

'A visitor,' Chorley, the deputy, said. 'Colonel Payne and I were in the army together.'

'Mister,' Payne said. They were provided with coffee

and Chorley's social graces, military to Payne, musical to Murren. Both kinds were wasted; the administrator moved himself off to important, half-mentioned paper filling.

'What's he like?' Payne asked, watching the retreating shoulders, held squarer, perhaps.

'Jim Chorley? Not bad. Useless fuss-pot. But he works.'

'He was a young warrant-officer.'

'Good?'

'Anxious to please.' Payne chuckled, rubbed his chin. 'I've met him a time or two since. He introduced himself. He'd be a Mason, wouldn't he?'

'God knows.'

They laughed, as Payne squinted at the door through which Chorley had sidled, as if it could add to his prejudiced reminiscences. Murren warmed to the old man; shrewd and enjoying it. When he asked about Patricia, father reported she was much better, up and about, lively as a cricket.

'We've got a small scheme on hand,' Payne said half laughing. 'Jessica has. She and that Polish woman want to take the father out for a car-ride. I hire the car, because it must be a big one, with a good heater, and you're down as the driver. That's what she decided. You, she, the mother and father, the daughter, perhaps her girl. Large car, see. I arrange that.'

'When?'

'That's it. We know you're busy. Is your diary handy?'

They decided, bantering, on a Saturday, made the entry, synchronizing words. Only when the books were returned to pockets, Murren exercised his right to question.

'This is February,' he said. 'Bloody cold at that.

I don't want to shove my nose out of doors, and I'm fit, not dying with cancer.'

'Well,' said Payne, 'well'. He stroked chin. 'The old fellow's a lot better, so they say. And one thing he wants is to see the airfield where he served.'

'He won't be able to get out of the car, in his condition?'

'He can lay the law down. It's what he wants. Mrs McKie passes it on to Jess. She orders you and me. But he must have, she says, a week's anticipation at least. She thinks she can cure him.' The voice drooped. 'She suffers from misconceived ideas.'

They paused, both uncertain. Murren asked again after Mrs Payne.

'Better. Miles better. You wouldn't believe. It's as if she'd decided she'd had enough of her bed, and upped with herself.'

'And gone back to work?'

'No, not yet. But it's a possibility.'

'Another miracle?'

A lecturer in psychology, long hair and dirty finger nails, looked up hungrily at the word, wishing to join in. Payne chewed his moustache with distaste, examined his own well-kept hands, muttering agreement.

'What do you mean by "miracle"?' Charming, brown-lipped smile from the pscychologist.

'People minding their own business.' Payne bristled; clerks and subalterns disciplined.

'Beg pardon, I'm sure,' said the lecturer, high-camp telly, but he moved away from this fierce little man in suit and pullover. Payne neither commented nor swore, sat stiff, well-shaven, lotion on his hair.

'Why did you come up?' Murren asked, put out. 'You could have phoned.' For a minute he feared Payne would round on him.

'It's a trip out. Retired people look forward to shopping or pubs. Like housewives. While Pat has been ill, I've scooted in and out, couldn't leave her for more than half an hour. Now, I can waste time round here.' He made a little, expansive, unsarcastic movement. 'It's a privilege.'

'Would you like to look round, then?'

They set off; it did not rain, but the gardens stretched bleak, the paths dented with wind-disturbed puddles. Payne admired light-blue cinema seats in the hall, saying at school he'd stood up. They looked through dripping limes out to farmland misted under wide, grubby sky, and further to where a modern colliery seemed neat, even prim. 'Nice situation, this. Are all these colleges? We were in one during the war, and it was magnificent. An old manor house.' Crossing from the main block, along the glass-roofed corridor, they met Chorley and the principal, a man of side-boards and wide-striped shirts. Chorley flashed an introduction; 'colonel' figured again; Murren compared Payne's suit, polished dark-brown shoes with prinny's three-piece and suede thick soles, while they exchanged banalities. They had time now; Mrs P. had risen to make leisure for man-to-man conversation. Murren smiled. The principal played with his thin fair hair, told the world that the college had been offered an organ from a defunct church. 'We'll talk,'he said, 'soon. We can afford it, mark you.'

Payne looked in at the art studios, the craft rooms, the laboratories, but only briefly, always from outside. In the practice cubicles a student dashed the opening bars of a Mozart sonata, and seeing the visitors through the open door said to Murren,

'What's wrong with that, then?'

'Three notes and a trill.'

'Hell, hell and hell'. He meant it.

Back amongst the pillars, the trophy cabinets and the signed photographs of royals in the foyer, Payne tapped his upper denture with a thumbnail, moving his head slowly round as if he must miss nothing.

'It doesn't seem very busy,' he said.

'Quite a lot of students are out on practice this term. We scatter them.'

'We used to like stew-pots,' Payne laughed at his childish word. 'We larked about, but one learnt. I often think back. I don't remember any rainy days, though. Fogs, when we had to walk home, but no rain. It seemed a place where plenty happened. If you looked in they were going at it hammer and tongs, explaining and answering. I remember being sent with a message to a young master who was teaching two or three big lads, sixth formers. There weren't many, then. Most left after matric as I did. He had round gold-rimmed glasses, like these mod hippy lads, but they were unusual then. And the blackboard was full of line after line of his neat writing, x and y, integral signs, sin and cosec, and he was talking in a nasal voice, very quiet, and then he said, 'Well, my young jockey?' to me and the prefects laughed. I'd recognize his writing again though he never taught me.'

'What happened to him?'

'No idea. The buildings were decrepit, but a lot went on.'

Payne looked about as if seeking significance for this memory, hoping perhaps that in this institution such conundrums were solved. The head of the arts faculty dodged past, trilby spattered with rain, briefcase tucked under armpit. He greeted Murren, dashed into the inquiry office, bustled out, his free hand full of mail. James described him, as the man twirled the revolving doors.

'He doesn't look like a musician,' Payne said.

'What does he look like, then?'

'Manager of the Co-op supermarket.'

'His name's Mosley. The students call his "Ossie".'

Cold rain gunned the windows. Payne upped his collar, said he'd push a note through the McKies' door, waddled to his old red Rover.

Within the next two days Murren received a surprisingly literate note from Elzbieta, and a phone call with instructions about the hired car from Payne, who said, at uncharacteristic length, that he'd have driven it himself, except that he felt, well, errh, y'know, uncomfortable, after that little, um, ugh, incident. 'Odd, how it's taken me. Don't understand myself, but there it is. Have to put up with it.' There was no smoking-room smut, no bravado; the old chap admirably described facts as they were.

Murren asked after Jessica, was told she'd gone out. Three months ago the girl had practically lived in his house on Saturdays, had called him or on him, stayed with him twice or three times a week. Now, since George's suicide, mother's back-tracking, she'd withdrawn. He ought to have chased her, but he was too busy. They'd fallen into a relationship, with sex from day three, too easily, physically attracted and attractive. He thought he had been in love, delighted to have so beautiful a girl on his arm at the junketings after concerts, but he knew now he had not thought at all. There was nothing to it, otherwise he would have worried about her evasions, her absences, her failure to cobble up adequate excuses. He was slightly annoyed as he listened to her father, but not enough to count. Perhaps he should shoulder the blame. He'd expected her at his beck and call, and she wasn't having it. He frowned as he returned to the interrupted lesson he was giving; Jessica was below standard, somehow. He twisted his mouth at the phrase. She was lively, marvellously vibrant, but they'd run parallel courses, each pursuing an ego that only vaguely recognized an outside world. Two selfish people had met; she'd outdone him in selfishness.

He listened to the Bach Book 2 E major fugue beautifully managed by a twelve-year-old who handled inner parts with style. To see those stubby, scrubbed fingers so accurately at work, untying this great contrapuntal knot, fascinated, delighted and appalled. He made a suggestion or two, then complimented the boy.

'You like that, don't you?'

'It's very good.'

'Is that all?'

'It's satisfying.' Mr Wisniewski had so described the Bach. The lad looked up through gold-rimmed glasses, grinning. They reported he excelled in football and cross-country.

Letting the pupil out to grey bleakness, Murren leaned on the door-post, depressed beyond reason, hearing exactly the clang of the iron garden-gate. That had no symbolic import, sounded the end of nothing, but it occupied his mind as the sole sensible element in unrelenting silent chaos. He did not wish to close his front door, though he knew he was cold. His sinuses burnt; a headache threatened; limbs pained as nausea hung limply about his guts. Something had ended, or he had realized this was so.

He shut the door, dropped to the piano stool, closed, then caressed the black lid. For the past months he had been busy, with choirs, church, pupils, a festival, his bouts of composition, and yet his energy was such that he'd not felt he'd overdone it. If he went to bed dog-tired in the small hours, he'd be up again at eight, raring to go, dynamism restored. He'd accomplished a great deal, and had yet had time to read, enjoy a drink, a walk.

Yet in those month's he'd lost Jessica without knowing it.

She had lost him, perhaps. That struck nearer, and yet she had not shattered his pride. That he had been too occupied to notice that their relationship had changed seemed incredible, and yet it was blunt truth. Their intermittent meetings, their sexual tumbles had sufficed him. Yet he would have expressed his satisfaction, looked forward in a year or two when he'd have become more settled to marriage, had anyone doubted. No one had, and he had not himself asked questions. And now he had put the poser, why was he convinced that all was over, smashed, and, worse, why had it unmanned him to the extent that he sat stroking the polished wood of a dumb piano? If he went round to Jessica, got his hands on her, what would he say?

He should start with some positive statement of his own.

'Look Jessica, let's get this straight for a start. I love you.' His lips sickly twisted into a grin. That was not his style. What in hell had style to do with it? What was the truth? 'Let's get this straight. I don't love you.' Straight? He was crooked as a bent pin. He walked round the rooms of his house, the music-room, the lounge, the dining-room, kitchen, hall, stairs, four bedrooms, bathroom. Once he knocked at a door as he came out, but it did no good. A man had learnt something of himself, and not liking it, tried to ease it out of his system by these physical actions, however slight. He could mock himself, but scorn cured nothing. That he could be content with so little dashed him, downed him. It hinted, plainly outlined a satisfaction with himself that contradicted his belief in the discontents, the romantic disturbances that made him what he thought he was. As soon as he, stamping round, cooled sufficiently to put this into words, to suggest that he was no more than an overworked commercial traveller, or till-bashing shopkeeper of the arts, it merely wasted a minute. His consciousness of wrong stayed with him, blackening the day. He could not philosophize himself out of that. Returning to his piano, he opened the lid, struck a note, G above middle C, followed with a thin major chord. Nothing doing. If he had any sense, he'd search out music that he'd never mastered, and practise, drill his fingers until everything else was forgotten. Liszt, now. The last Beethoven, the Webern pieces he'd bought promising himself to study, the Boulez sonata. He'd barely begun his list when his mind flogged back in grief. He closed the lid, poked at an itching left eye, remembered, forcing himself, his first meeting with Jessica.

He'd been fetched in late to accompany Myra Friedlander, the violinist.

Her usual man, Miles Hinton, had been rushed into hospital on the day of the recital, and agents either could not find or could not produce substitutes. At ten to eleven the secretary of the music club rang Murren at the college asking him to deputize.

'What's she doing?'

'A Handel, Tartini, Mozart A major, K 526, and the Brahms D minor. I heard you play that with

Peter Worth last month. That's why I thought of you.'

There were instructions. He had to drive straight into town when he would play through with her, and, and. . . . If she found him below standard, she'd cancel the recital.

'What's she like?' Murren asked.

'A bit of a firebrand.'

He put off his remaining lecture, drove to a studio over a piano emporium, where the secretary stood with his upper teeth over his lower lip in fright. He was glad Mr Murren could come, it was most kind of him to put his other engagements aside. They would be in real trouble if the recital were cancelled. He would phone Miss Friedlander's hotel.

'Have you got the music?' Murren asked.

'No. She'll bring that.'

'How long's she likely to be?'

'That I don't know.' The man backed away, embarrassed. The room was enormous, irregular, with three grand pianos, all covered, all locked. Racks lined one wall; five uprights crowded a corner, one a Steinway, one Görs and Kallmann. Sunshine blasted in through a rooflight, but the place stood free of dust. Murren made a move for the windows which overlooked the street; he glared down at the tops of buses, the heads of pedestrians four storeys below. Angry after two minutes' wait, he went downstairs and out to buy coffee in the Kardomah next door. He did not enjoy the scalding drink, found, breathless on his return, that the Friedlander had not arrived.

'She's in no hurry,' he complained to the shaking secretary.

'She might cancel. Perhaps that's what she wants.'

The man seemed near tears as he clumsily unlocked

the piano with the bunch of keys which he shook like a demented gaoler as he talked, then removed the dustcover.

'A Bechstein,' he said. 'If she's satisfied, they'll take that to the hall.'

'If she isn't?'

'We try the others. Or she cancels.'

From below the street noises were clear, brakings, hooting, once or twice a snatch of intelligible conversation. Murren poked out a chord or two. The room seemed airless and melancholy against the brightness of spring sunshine outside. The secretary chose one of a dozen chairs, sat with outstretched legs, his hands latched together. 'I shall be glad when this day's over,' he said. He appeared to talk to himself.

At twelve-thirty Myra Friedlander arrived with her husband, a bald ape of a man. She was small, Jewish, energetic, in early middle age with a matching hat and coat of fur. The secretary made a diffident introduction; she nodded, looked hard at Murren, lunged out of her coat, swung wild breasts under a light-blue sweater. She wore trousers, olive green, clashing with the azure above, the multi-coloured neckscarf.

'Let's make a start,' she said, snapping open the violin case her husband had laid on one of the tables. Murren sat down, watched her miniatures of violence, struck A. 'At least it's in tune,' she said. 'Is the piano any good? Music, Hugo.' The copies were battered. 'Handel first.' As Murren looked through his copy, the A major sonata, she scurried about a few feet of floor, deciding on a place to stand. 'Ready?' She faced him, bow raised, imperiously signalled.

Sound leapt, huge and sweet, from the violin.

The whole of the woman was concentrated round

the shining wood between her hand and chin; body swayed as bow swept, and incredibly massive tone, quite unforced, honey-liquid, struck, bounced from the many surfaces of the room. 'More sharply,' she called in the first allegro, but friendly, not stopping, to an equal. 'That's it. That's right.' Murren gained confidence, backing her will, underscoring Handel's marvellous few bars, the second slow movement, as she called impassioned out into the deep. They ended the final section with breadth, *allargando*, the flying rhythm enlarged, solidified into magnificence, proud as her eagle nose, her superbly tremendous elbow.

'Don't be afraid to let it go,' she said, 'at the end. You won't swamp me. We'll look at the Mozart. Have you done it before? No?' She came up to him, and briefly outlined what she intended. 'You've not done this before?' She clicked her teeth together. 'You've done the Brahms, though? Recently? Well, let's try this. You can practise on your own later.'

This time she stopped him twice, with suggestions; he argued once, made his own view known. She listened, tried the passage, said, 'Good idea.' At the end of the work she expressed satisfaction. 'I liked that. We must do one or two bits again, but it was good.' They tackled awkward spots; though she played the teacher, she was not afraid to correct herself, standing at his shoulder, peering. 'That was not what I wanted,' she instructed herself, and set matters right. In the end she applauded him, and joked. 'You play Mozart with feeling. You have the right face for Mozart. We'll do Brahms, now, eh? Before Tartini? Before I wear you out?'

He knew the sonata well, it lay mastered under his fingers, and perhaps because she realized this, she demanded more. 'Make me work', she said. 'Play me off the ground.' Sometimes she stopped him. 'You are too nice, too polite. Mount it.' Often she sang phrases, made him repeat, singing, calling, angry. 'Big fingers here. Big hands.' She sounded foreign, then, exotic, and sweat gleamed on her brown skin. Once when she was pleased she called out to her husband, 'What do you think of that, Hugo? This boy can play.'

'I'll need to go over this,' he said.

They did the Tartini, and two short encores. She laughed, relieved.

'This is a very classical concert,' she said, mocking the secretary. 'They are pure, here, in this town. Now, what do we do again?'

They finished at one minute to three; she must have her rest. 'Do not overdo it, and wear yourself out. Leave something for the concert. But you are young. I don't want you shy. You must be big, like me.' He smiled at the little woman with her dancing beads, fierce eyes, marvellous hands. 'He is laughing at us, Hugo,' she said. 'Get this piano over, and tuned,' she ordered the secretary. 'Get a good tuner for him.'

James Murren rushed home in exhilaration, practised almost to frenzy, cooling himself with swigs from the tap. His white tie, thank God, was in good order. He forced himself to eat, toast and marmite, to drink China tea. He could not deny himself a last ten minutes at the keyboard before he left in denim for the hall.

The concert went magnificently.

She said little, seemed nervous as she stalked about, her long dress peacock-bright, wide skirted, so that she no longer seemed short; now size matched talent. She shook hands limply with officials of the Music Society who came in to be introduced, disappeared ten minutes before starting time to the cloakroom, and returned in a wave of perfume. Her husband opened the case this time, but she removed the bow, then the violin, flicking the strings with her thumb. Five minutes later the secretary, shifting his feet, announced they should make an appearance. He, with Hugo and some understrapper, attended them to the stage door. Murren trailed, bowed discreetly from behind his piano stool. There was no one to turn over; he had forgotten. He touched A, glanced at the crowded, rising tier of seats, checked his pages. Ready, she turned, lifted scroll and bow. They were away.

Once they had begun on the second movement he knew hc could cope. He listened to her, glanced from time to time, made no show himself. People had not come to see him. When she made a slight alteration in tempo from the afternoon, he aligned himself exactly. On the second repeat he even decorated mildly, allowing his fingers the chance to improvise. He was not moved by the short slow movement, though she played with grandeur, high and lifted up. He had no time for anything but his own superior task. The last *allegro* danced; now she forced him so that they reached the final line in a broad plain of delight, rich, with the hall full, awash with the brightness, the huge splendour of their sounds. He reached for his handkerchief, and stood. Myra, fiddle and bow in left, reached out her right hand to call him forwards. He took it; they bowed together before he stepped back, followed her safely off stage, the clapping enthusiastically battering them still.

No one in the artists' quarters. She left for her cloakroom; he sank to a chair, clutching his handkerchief. Hugo, his second, the secretary all appeared.

'That was good,' the husband said, in a heavily

foreign accent. The Friedlander appeared, held a whispered colloquoy with her husband, then spoke loudly.

'Don't worry this young man,' she warned. 'You rest. Out, you men. Out.'

She played the Bach unaccompanied *Partita* in D minor, and though Murren, in solitude, could hear it plainly, for all the sense it made it might have been wind in telegraph wires. He sat, exhausted until he began to finger the Mozart and the Tartini, and missed the great concluding Chaconne. He sat up guiltily at the crack of applause, but it seemed an age before she came down, returned her violin to the case. He clapped softly. She made for the cloakroom. When she reappeared she ordered him to carry both copies. 'We are not coming off between Mozart and Tartini, you see.' Hugo and company kept away; she strode a few steps very rapidly, golden high heels clacking, then snatched for her violin. This time she smiled at him, touched the four strings with the point of her bow, then stood upright. Her breasts were held in disciplined roundness now. Head in air, she made for the stage.

That little joking touch on the strings with the tip encouraged him. She wasted no time tuning. They played with brilliance, man and wife in music. Between the sonatas she came across, ostensibly to tune, and said, 'They like us. We will make them like Mozart now,' and laughed at her whisphered quip.

In the interval the artists' room was crowded; everybody talked high on the sherry provided. All delighted in speaking to Murren. Myra Friedlander laughed a great deal, but cagily, as if she could change behaviour the minute it suited her. She did not drink at all, and disappeared before the twenty minutes were up. When she emerged, the effect electrified; now she wore blood-red velvet which left her shoulders bare. Murren, amazed that so consummate an artist, so powerful, demeaned herself with show-biz tricks, could not help being impressed. He should not; no choice. She told her husband to get the room clear. He issued a harsh order; the notabilities knocked back their schooners, gruffly wished good luck, went into the outside world. Five were left; Myra ran fingers up Murren's arm. 'Brahms,' she said. He dodged for the loo, afraid now, bowels churning, shivers combing his back.

The audience settled.

He fixed his copy, this one his own, with his own marks, and they struck out. Her tone rang against the shifting chords of his piano, three ran against four in ardour, focussed in power. This needed no aleatoric inspiration; he knew this well enough, in fingers and brain, to match her huge breadth of tune, to push her, to show his own gigantic prowess. Between movements she did not look at him, turning only to signal a beginning. She had accepted him as she accepted Brahms, a consort for her talent, a fit partner. They ended in power, superlatively interpreting, a man and woman, rather a woman and man beyond themselves. The audience clapped, stamped, shouted; she called him forward, extending a hand which he, excited out of everyday calm, kissed. People joined in his ecstasy. He followed her three, four, five times off the platform. They did their encores; added one for good measure. The audience thundered.

Finally, she put her violin away. 'That is enough,' she said, though in fact they made one more appearance when she held up her hands for silence, said in a little girl's voice, 'I think we should go home now. We are tired.'

Again the green room crowded itself; cigar-smoke hung. Myra, back in trousers, thanked, praised him, said her agent would collect and forward his fee, of proper proportion. She seemed now merely smart, middle aged, ready for bed or the motorway. He remembered that tomorrow or the day after she'd be performing again, in Paris, Edinburgh, Berne or Düsseldorf. A Scottish lady with white hair and pearls asked him home for a drink. When he said he must change from his jeans, she insisted that she followed him to his house with her Mercedes, and carted him in comfort in hers. He had not met Mrs Bruce before. Myra kissed him before she left; Hugo shook his hand.

Already guests were noisily drinking in the Bruces' drawing room as he arrived. Janet, he knew her by sight, introduced herself, and a young, dark, neat, large-eyed girl. He asked if they had liked the concert. The dark girl, Jessica, said that she had not been there.

'You came in for the Brahms,' Janet corrected her.

Jessica agreed, but offered no further explanations. She seemed pleased to meet him, but calmly, in a friendly, smiling ease. Janet kept a line of guests shaking his hand. One stout lady did not immediately recognize him as the evening's pianist, but showed no embarrassment. 'Tailcoats utterly change you,' she said. Some asked what Myra Friedlander was like, or questioned him about his own work. They all wanted to know him, and he, tired and exhilarated, talked foolishly, he thought, too glib by half. He returned to Jessica's side, made conversation, found her natural, unimpressed by his reputation, glad to see him for his cheekbones, hair, voice, not his music. She drank bitter lemon, and allowed him to find ice for her. She would have preferred to have done the errand for herself, but he insisted. Janet played assiduous hostess; at midnight asked if he wished to go. Now he was fagged, though the other guests sparkled or shouted. She fetched his coat, drove him and Jessica home. As they two sat in the back of her car, they held hands; the girl pressed her leg on his.

'I shall see you again,' he said. She hoped so. He wrote his phone number on a piece of paper Janet provided.

He did not sleep well that night; he had accompanied one of the five best violinists in Europe, had excelled himself. Of course the programme suited him, but now he could boast he had played for Myra Friedlander. And there, in the back of the car, he had quietly sat with his, yes, his Jessica, in warmth.

She rang before the week was out.

10

Murren collected the Daimler from a garage, drove it to the Paynes', where the family inspected it, and then with Jessica at his side picked up the Wisniewskis.

Elzbieta met them at the front door, her husband behind her.

'How many can you take?'

'Four or five more.'

She shrugged as her husband grinned, muttered victory to himself.

'Jock thinks he should come.'

'In case anything happened to the auld man.' He modified his accent acceptably.

'It's enormous, with two spare seats,' Jessica said. On the short journey here she and Murren had barely exchanged a dozen words. 'How is your father?'

'He's much better.'

Elzbieta showed them into the front room, where Mr Wisniewski watched from an armchair by a strong gas-fire. He sat straight, propped by cushions, but his face was deeply wrinkled, cut almost, under the short grey hair. He looked thin, his hands claw-like, although his colour was pleasantly healthy, perhaps because of the heat of the room.

His wife leapt up, tried out her English, burst into a frenzy of Polish in the direction of her husband.

'She wonders if it will be warm enough,' the old man said patiently.

'If you wrap up well,' his daughter said.

'The weather is not good.' Spits of rain from louring grey scarred the windowpanes. He returned to Polish, which had, in his mouth, something of the melancholy, gentlemanly flavour of his English. Ill as he was, he concerned himself with his wife until Murren inquired about his health.

'I have made some improvement. You perhaps think that this trip, this jaunt is a foolish notion for a sick man. It is perhaps so. But I tell myself that if I get worse I shall never see the place again, and if I get better. . . .' He shrugged. 'It is romantic, if that is the word.' He smiled apologies, appeared not to notice that now his wife and daughter hovered with overcoat, scarves, a hat, half excited. Almost he talked to himself, rapt, foreign, with a deep whisper of a voice. 'I cannot return to my own country. I do not know if I would wish to do so. But this aerodrome, this village I recall. I was young, vigorous man.' The voice tailed away. The furniture towered, a sideboard, a glass-fronted cabinet, large chairs, dark curtains, all English, but solid, unveneered, heavy, frowning. Comfort did not count for much here, Murren decided, where one sort of local furniture was as unacceptable as another. Had not Madame lived thirty-odd of her sixty years in England without acquiring more than a smattering of the language? James said gravely that he'd go outside to start up the car heater.

Ten minutes later the party emerged, the father between his daughter and her husband, the mother behind with a cushion ludicrously in her hand. Wisniewski, grey trilby straight above gaunt Slavonic features, took his seat and looked neither to the right nor the left. He did not wish to see this street. In spite of the icy drizzle, two housewives, returning from the shops, stopped on the opposite pavement to observe under pretence of talk, limousine, faces, arrangements. Mrs McKie rushed back in for handbags, and a case. A small argument developed in Polish between mother and daughter as the old man stared stonily ahead.

When they were settled, the doors luxuriously shut, Murren turned and, sliding the partition between front and rear compartments, outlined the way he proposed following, and asked if they had any last-minute instructions. The women waited for Wisniewski, who did not speak. It was as if the few steps out into the open air had sapped his will.

'Any other place you'd like to see?' Murren persisted.

Again the women clashed into Polish. Elzbieta sat between her parents on the capacious back seat: William McKie just in front of the mother. Chin down to two scarves, Wisniewski did not move; he might have been praying. One hand held, though feebly, the door-strap.

'No. Just a steady run there,' Elzbieta said, in the end.

As the car slipped ahead, Murren found pleasure in holding the automobile, the rain fell more heavily, so that roads gleamed. They drove in silence through the outskirts of the city, amongst the pleasant ribbon-building, dull as cold ditchwater under the dark sky.

'Are they warm enough?' he asked Jessica, who inquired through the glass panel. They were, but the question inspired a further spate of fussing from the back-seat women. Mr Wisniewski sat unmoved through it, stiff as cardboard, colourless under his sombre trilby.

'We'll be passing over the Trent soon,' Murren called.

He slowed, above the river which lapped thickly, leadenly unattractive high on its banks, pitted with rain. The fields on either side were flooded, but the water reflecting the sober skies shone lighter than the sodden vegetation of higher land.

'Rain and frost,' he told Jessica. 'The water can't get away.'

She ignored him. He left his partition open so that he'd be ready for appeals from his passengers. None came. The four sat staring forward, only glancing out of the window, guiltily. His announcement that they were on the Fosse Way, a Roman road, brought no response. Perhaps they were afraid to assert themselves and so over-exert the father. He accelerated, sedately.

'It's like a funeral,' Jessica whispered.

'Cheer us up, then,' he said. She shrugged back into her large seat, furiously, so that he realized that the silence, the absence of even token jollity snagged her nerves. She looked pithered and miserable. 'We've picked a rotten day,' he said. He wondered who'd thought up the outing. The old man took responsibility earlier this morning, but that meant little. Did the daughter, or the monoglot mother, imagine that a trip to this place which he'd described often enough years ago would do him good? Or did Wisniewski know he was going to die, and in his weakness had let out this demand like a whimper or bleat, once, only once, to have it snatched up, embroidered on, organized by his family? They were obstructed temporarily by a line of agricultural tractors and carts in Newark, bright-new in the beating rain.

'The forecast wasn't too bad,' he told Jessica.

'They're never right.' She snuggled deeper into her coat. Now they were out in the country, the outlines of leafless trees, the green of the fields seemed less oppressive; the sky, though grey, was not uniformly so; one could see rain clouds flying more brokenly against smudged white. Murren pulled up by the side of the road so that he and Jessica could consult the map. When they had chosen their B roads, he announced the way, and guessed the duration of the journey.

'I remember one of those names,' Wisniewski said. 'Swarby.'

'Did you stay there?'

'No, no. It is only the name. The name.'

The intervention mildly excited the passengers; Willie McKie turned and talked gutturally to his wife in an accent incomprehensible as Polish. But they did not persevere as the car rolled between hedges and the enormous sky silvered slightly, as the rain eased.

'We shall approach Bardney aerodrome from the

south-west,' Murren told them, 'provided Jessica does her map-reading properly.'

'Is it still in use?' Jessica, brightly, everybody's friend.

'I don't know.' Wisniewski's answer seemed wrung out of him.

'You have never been back, then?' Murren asked.

'No.' Infinitely sad.

'I'll run alongside, that's a good mile and a half, and then we'll turn off into Bardney itself. There's an inn marked, for those interested.' The remark triggered McKie into a violence of speech, which Murren in the front seat could not understand. Whatever the gist, the voice seemed argumentative, until it ended in a chuckle.

'That's not right, Jock,' his wife said.

'It is so, I tell y'. It is so.'

McKie laughed the louder to convince so that his wife between the corpse-figures herself smiled: generously, as at a child. The husband straightened his tie and looked out of the window, satisfied.

'This must be the aerodrome,' Jessica announced. Murren pulled up, under a dripping elm, so that they could stare over the fence into a grassy space. In the distance they could see the hangers and an orange sleeve. 'The main entrance must be on this road.' Since no one spoke Murren drove slowly on. No activity took place in the area; one part of the field was very like another. It seemed not to be raining when they reached the gates, which towered, ungainly with rusty barbed wire, in bad repair. An administrative hut or guard-room just inside was dilapidated, dirty, though its windows were unbroken. Paint had peeled from the notice board outside, and on the tarmac road, wide enough for big lorries to pass, clumps of grass sprouted. Neglect ruled.

'Was this the main entrance in your day?' Jessica asked, and the rest waited on Wisniewski's answer. He smiled, thinly, only because a pretty girl had made the inquiry.

'I am not sure. Perhaps it was. One camp, and another. . .? I do not know.'

'It looks deserted.'

McKie intervened now, pointing out that the sleeve indicated use. He spoke very clearly.

'Amateurs, perhaps,' Murren guessed. 'Week-end gliders. ATC.' He got out and McKie followed him. Though the gate was padlocked they slipped through the fence without difficulty to peer through the windows of the hut. In the gloom they could see no furniture, no scrap of paper, only bare floorboards. Rain had run down, staining the wall behind the stove. McKie said that his father had blackleaded such stoves, and scraped such boards with a razor-blade during his army service. He cursed his father and his officers for shared stupidity.

'Have we come to the right place?' Murren asked.

'Oh, ay. Bu' it's thirty years ago. More. How w'd he remember?'

'Is he getting better?'

McKie yielded a foot or two at the question.

'I don't think so. They try to tell him he is. With these Poles, the father is something. If he told them to kiss his arse, they would.' He did not smile. Rain dripped from the verandah, though puddles shone unruffled. 'He's a fine man. Educated, if you know what I mean.' They walked round the back, keeping to cracked concrete, and found nothing.

Murren and Jessica consulted the map again.

'I'll drive further round the field, and then come back into Bardney.' They received this, as McKie's report, in silence. The tour revealed nothing, though at one point they were within a 150 yards of the hangars. Rectangles of concrete, partly overgrown, marked the site of huts, and a larger expanse the parade ground. Brambles sprouted, but only intermittently, as if the flat, soggy land lacked nutriment.

'Do you think this is it?' Murren asked.

'It must be. But I cannot say. Perhaps I shall remember the village. The aerodrome was a crowded and busy place, with hundreds of airmen, and workshops, offices.' His voice trailed off. 'It could be. With these few trees.'

Murren turned the long car, purred towards the village.

They passed new bungalows, one substantial house with a brick wall, spiked iron chains; trees were planted more closely on the twisting road. Suddenly they found themselves on the main village street, short, fairly straight. Four semi-detached cottages, then a terrace of three, very ancient, and then the pub, King's Head, painted buff, flag-decorated, with a gravelled car-park. Murren drew up.

They waited for Wisniewski. He did not speak.

'That's the name y' said. King's Head.' William McKie. The old man clenched teeth, nodded unemphatically. A shake could not have denoted more puzzlement.

After awkward silence, Elzbieta ventured, 'If you could find somewhere to park we could eat our sandwiches.' She translated. They edged along the street.

'That house,' the old man said. 'That house. I remember that.' Murren pulled up at once, backed in front of the gate of a largish detached place, with heavy wooden eaves, small sash windows upstairs. The lower storey was hidden by untrimmed privet. 'We were invited there from time to time.' The rest stared, at blue-painted woodwork, dull brick, one smoking chimney. 'The lady was called Mrs Marsh. We nicknamed her The Merry Widow.' The remark seemed out of place for the unsmiling mouth, the wrinkled features. 'I wonder if she lives there still. She will be getting on for eighty, but that is no age these days.' He breathed heavily, coughed.

'Would you like me to go and ask?' Murren surprised himself.

'Would it be impolite? I would like to know.'

'I'll come with you,' Jessica said.

The sodden garden stretched untidy as the hedge; withered haulm straggled round bean-sticks; a barrow rusted near the unweeded path. The young woman who answered the door had a smartly frilled apron, recently tinted hair.

'Marsh? No I've never heard of anybody of that name. We bought it from some people called Watson. Peter,' she called. Her husband, in fancy roll-neck, couldn't help. 'Yes, the name might have been on the deeds.'

'Would anybody be likely to know?' Jessica asked.

The couple frowned; they had little idea. 'We've only been here three months.'

The people at the shop were relative newcomers. They thought the publican hadn't been here long, either. They were sorry. They hardly knew anybody, really; they both worked in Lincoln. As the group pondered, the householders were in no hurry to shut their door, Murren thought of the Polish officers swinging up the path, bomber-pilots, half crazed with death, to meet the merry widow.

They reported sadly back to Wisniewski who expected that answer.

'It was a long time ago,' he said.

'Was there a Mr Marsh?' Jessica asked.

'Well, yes, I assume there was.' A note of speed, animation. 'But he was in the army. A major, I think. I never saw him. The house was called 'The Limes'. It had a notice, is that the word? on the gate. A name-plate.'

His wife asked a question of Elzbieta. Both laughed; father's face did not change.

'We were invited down. It was different from the mess; it was a home. Of course, there was black-out at the time, and rationing. And men died; many good friends were posted missing over Hamburg and Berlin. This Mrs Marsh was interested in Poland. I don't know why, because she was English, but she had a course of gramophone records. To learn Polish. She liked us to say little phrases, or we had to correct her pronunciation. I do not know why.'

'Perhaps she had a Polish lover,' Elzbieta suggested.

'It is possible. But it was warm, with a fire, and we would take a bottle of spirits. Sometimes we would sing, or play cards, or dance to the old gramophone.' The cast of his face pictured his pleasure; his voice did not echo the excitement, level but insistent.

As Murren eyed the blue paint, the cold sky behind, he wondered if Wisniewski told the truth, whether the old man had been the lover in this solid house in a dark land. They all looked left, up the garden path at the closed door. The father, leaning forward slightly to see across his womenfolk, breathed harshly. On the verge of Jordan, he chose to visit this. Murren moved the car sixty yards along the street.

'Will this do?' he asked. Looking through the back window, he could see the roof of the widow's house, pinkish tiles and blue woodwork. He reached down for his sandwiches; Jessica pulled her neat packet from the shopping bag at her feet. They discovered their mistake; the women in the back had prepared enough food for the whole party. He was so hungry that the sense of his gaffe did not diminish his pleasure in eating and his companion smiled, almost wickedly, at the undignified hurry he'd made to fish out his lunch. Jessica nibbled as she stared ahead. McKie ate in tearing mouthfuls, praising his wife's cooking, asking his mother-in-law the name of this or that delicacy. The car engine ran gently to maintain heat. Wisniewski took his food, very little, with seriousness, his face set against pain, growing grey with fatigue. Elzbieta talked to her mother after a time, and they, blessedly, laughed, searched in their boxes, folded greaseproof paper neatly. McKie spoke with guttural joviality, one of them, not locked out by language. The old man, straight-backed still, paid no attention.

William suggested the pub. His wife demurred.

'Only if Mr Murren wants to go,' she said. 'Father's getting tired.'

'No, no, no.' Beautiful politeness.

'This is hardly the day for cold beer,' Murren said.

'Any day's the day for that.' McKie rocked in his seat at his witticism, consoled against enforced sobriety. The two in front accepted scalding coffee through the partition, mum about their unopened flasks.

'This is the way we like it,' Wisniewski said. He held his tiny glass in front of his nose as if in a toast. Over his left shoulder, utterly without significance, the two triangles of roof, the blue eaves, appeared smirched in the dirty light. The couple in front tried to respond, but without encouragement. Mr and Mrs McKie still ate, and with speed; the old lady played hostess in bursts of Polish. When they had shaken crumbs clear and bags were packed, stowed away, Murren asked for instructions. Elzbieta waited for her parents, and on their silence, said, 'I think we should go straight home. My father's very tired.' Wisniewski nodded, allowing himself to be tucked again into his shawls, his hat to be straightened.

'I'll go slowly through the village again,' Murren said. 'Shout if you see anything.' He drove to the end of the street, turned the car, sidled back at hearse-pace. As soon as he was beyond the King's Head, he speeded up, and off the B roads he went as quickly as lorries allowed him. The return journey was short for rain clouds darkened the afternoon.

Mr Wisniewski had to be helped indoors, by his son-in-law and Murren. Sitting in front of the gas-fire, still in his overcoat, eyes closed with pain, he thanked the driver. Elzbieta made a speech in the passage; her husband hung uselessly about. Jessica had not moved from her seat.

'That didn't do much good,' she said sourly.

'I'll take you home, then drive this chariot back.'

'Have you left your car at the garage?'

'Outside.'

'I'll come with you then.' Large drops of rain spooned on to the windscreen. He drove off. 'We shouldn't have bothered.'

'We tried,' he answered. Saturday shoppers, hooded and hunched, stepped carelessly.

'He's really ill. They said. . . .' Her voice trailed listlessly away.

‘I haven’t seen much of you lately,’ he interrupted. The smoothness of the limousine made the opening easier.

‘No.’

‘What’s wrong then?’ She said nothing. ‘Have we fallen out?’ Silence. ‘What’s the trouble?’

‘I’ve met somebody else.’

‘Oh.’ His turn for pauses. ‘Do I know him?’

‘No. He works at the same branch that I do.’

‘Why didn’t you say anything?’

Her small, gloved hands were clasped between her knees. Her face, beautifully waxy, was held steady. She looked down.

‘What could I? I’ve been out with him for a time or two. You never asked me, recently. I didn’t want to make a thing of it.’

‘That’s not quite true,’ he intervened, sternly. ‘You’re never in when I ring, and you don’t call back.’

‘Is my job to chase you, then?’

‘No, but you could reply. Are you serious about this. . . ? What’s his name?’ Bullying.

‘Nigel. I don’t know. I’d sooner be with him than with anybody else, but that may not mean anything much.’

‘You’re willing to drag me out on this, this expedition.’

‘That was my father, not me. Besides when first arrangements were made, I hardly knew Nigel.’

‘It’s happened in a rush?’ he asked.

‘Yes. It has. At least. . . . Yes, it has.’

‘I love you,’ he said, at traffic lights.

‘I’m sorry.’

Now she looked what she was, barely above teenage, scarcely out of school, and caught in indiscretion.

The gloved fingers moved, writhed. She bent foward even more abjectly.

'I shan't be seeing you again?' he demanded.

'No, not if you don't want to.'

'What do you want?'

She paused, as if there was an answer to be won. All they heard was the swish of tyres on wet streets.

'I don't know,' she said, finally, looking diagonally away from him. 'You're somebody. You'll be something. Everybody says so. A conductor. Or at the BBC.'

'What's that got to do with it? I'm a human being, girl, just as you are.'

'Yes.'

'I love you. Did you hear me say that? I love you. Do you understand that?'

'You're angry.'

'Of course I'm bloody angry. With your sniffs and don't knows. Doesn't it mean anything to you that I love you?'

'Should it?' That gathered spirit, quietened him. She'd broken off an affair with a married man when they'd taken up together. She was no innocent; sexually she was the more experienced. He'd felt proud and degraded when she'd rushed into his bed, confessing with a fetching simplicity how she had dropped her lover, though he was a dish, because he, James Murren, had knocked her off her feet. Besides, Harry's wife was having another baby, and she must act fair. Oh, Henry Parkes was a lecher, no doubt, a seducer, but he worried, swallowed on his ulcer, squinted over his shoulder all the time. It was great to have a proper young man, not a hole-and-corner hypocrite. Her father, yes, would have gone mad, because he was old-fashioned, didn't approve of sex outside marriage. No, he wouldn't murder her, he'd creep away and sulk for a fortnight before he got over it.

She let all this out in the long talks they'd had, sitting, lying side by side on settees, beds, floors, armchairs. Dizzied with physical love for her, unable to keep himself off her body, he'd listened to her words, tempting her to talk as he fondled her breasts, thighs, belly, wetness of her sex, so that flat sentences describing adventures in the back of Harry's car, quick lunch-time gropings, one wilful day by the seaside in winter when she and her adulterer acted man and wife as they'd walked the deserted promenade, had laughed at snow-flurries, both excited and numbed him. Her naivety was almost incredible; she came out with these indecent banalities as though she did him a favour, blasted him between kisses. It was not even that she demonstrated a fierce sexuality; she had enjoyed herself, and Harry, however reprehensible or pained by guilt, had instructed her broadly, but Murren, caught between the blood-beat in his genitals and his orderly life, his average of social belief, imagined that she might just as well have taken up tennis or librarianship under an equally skilled mentor and gained an equal pleasure. His own love, attraction, give it what name one could, and he dared not joke about nomenclature, made it impossible to feel straight. Thus work, his music, became a long distraction from his affair.

'Yes. I think so. I may be mistaken, but I think so.' He kept his voice cold.

'I can't help it. I've changed.'

'Is it my fault?' he pressed. 'Do you blame me?'

'No. It's me. I've said I'm sorry.'

What she offered him was inexcusable, and a sad,

a soiled sawdust. They reached the garage on the far edge of the ring road, where they stood together waiting for the proprietor. Inside the high ramshackle building, light-bulbs failed to dispel the darkness of afternoon, and the cold matched in unpleasantness a floor messy with oil and water. Every sound echoed, magnified; rain dripped in by corrugated iron sheets; a transistor radio blared in the office, a wooden signal box, in the middle of the vast floorspace, and the shouts of men down an inspection pit bawled quarrelsome.

The proprietor smiled in spite of this.

'Satisfactory, was it, squire? Lovely jobs.' He'd kept them waiting, Murren guessed, while somebody inspected the car for superficial damage. 'You'd be surprised how many people want to hire them. It's like driving a coach. No, nothing to pay. That's all sealed, signed and delivered.' He pulled a sheet of paper from the pocket of his overalls as if to demonstrate his knowledge of contracts. 'Enjoy the run, lady?'

Jessica looked up, and smilingly thanked him. In this draughty place of greasy litter, dropped tools, metallic row, she represented neatness, order.

As they made their way to her home in Murren's car, he said, 'Is there nothing I can do that will make any difference?' This sentence trundled awkwardly enough after terse exchanges.

'No. It's not you. I can't help it.'

'You aren't sorry for me, then?'

'You'll get over it. You've plenty to occupy you.'

Back again, with sentences expressing nothing. These did not communicate much beyond her basic, obstinate belief that she wanted nothing from him.

'Doesn't what happened between us mean anything?' he asked.

She shook her head. He was relegated, with dyspeptic Harry, to a limbo. Nigel would hear about his performance, if Nigel had sufficient wit or sophistication to ask. What tore him, in its seeming wrongness, was that the neat, beautiful, demure child next to him, knees together, gloved hands on lap, acted with such cruelty. In his distress he debated with himself how much she knew. Sullen, she could guess his hurt, did nothing to assuage the smart. Outside her house, and now in half-dark the familiar outlines of wall, hedge, gate, windows were strange, inimical, she, she-devil, lived in that place, twisted its friendly ordinariness.

'We shan't be seeing anything of each other?' he said. He held out his hand, but she ignored the formal gesture, unanswering. 'Good-bye then.'

Suddenly her eyes, large blue, very beautiful, met his. '*A naked thinking heart that makes no show/Is to a woman but a kind of ghost.*' That's the way of comfort; Fine words, fine music, pageants and palaver. Her eyes locked with his most briefly before she turned, felt with assurance for the door handle, let herself out. She crossed the pavement, walked up the drive as she had done hundreds of times, without hurry, well and soberly dressed, dark hair bobbing. A passing dog-walker wished her good afternoon; she replied. This was no tragedy. His car jerked away.

11

The weather turned bitingly cold.

For three days snow-showers dipped blackly, cleared, leaving sheets of frozen residue in corners; on the fourth the snow began to float down thickly in the evening, and Murren's choirboys dodged out for the lavatory to report back on the weather. Even the men were excited, hurrying home when he closed the practice early. Since his break with Jessica he had spent an hour after rehearsal with his choristers in the Three Bells where he drank two pints, talked little, but laughed with them, and left on the stroke of ten as if he'd a strict engagement. It passed the evening for him; they liked his presence. Once or twice they'd tried to pull his leg, but desisted at his distant inability to see any point. He did not listen, based his behaviour on the extremes of theirs, smiling when they were boisterously amused, mouth grim as they grew sentimental or lugubrious. For the rest he waited for the bitter beer to dull his pain. 'He's about as much sense of humour as a water-closet,' they decided. 'Doesn't even flush.' But that did not count against him; they expected a difference, and as long as he fulfilled musical expectation did not much mind.

Snow swirled, in huge flakes, big as roses.

'Coming in?' they invited.

'Not tonight. I don't want to be snowed up.'

'Where better?'

The roads were white already, in spite of grit-wagons. Twice he skidded, was relieved to lock his car away in the garage. In the unusual conditions of the journey, he had not thought of Jessica. Now misery revived in the warmth, and he took to his piano for an hour's hard labour before librium and bed. The wind whipped fallen dry snow like smoke off the hedges and walls; he stood for a quarter of an hour at his bedroom window watching the weird clouds of snow particles ride familiar pavements, leap from roofs, whirl in maddened lamp-light.

For three weeks the piles at the roadside hardened to ice, were augmented, changing their humped contours. Main highways had been cleared, but side streets preserved unthawing, filthy ruts, grey-black and treacherous. Murren managed to reach college or practice rooms, but absenteeism in class or choir depressed him.

One evening after a day of frost, cold fog, unnatural stillness, with branches white and roofs prettified, after a flounder over the lumbered streets, Murren had eaten tea with the Bruces, a huge meal, and had worked for an hour and a half with Janet before declining an invitation to stay to dinner. He felt stodgy two hours after the first meal. They'd take their time, wash small courses down with wine or bitter fruit-juice, but he wanted no more. As soon as he was outside the house in the murk of the streets, he knew he'd chosen wrongly. He'd be at home, too fagged for work, with no demanding Janet to goad him, nothing to say to himself.

He had just closed his garage door when he heard his front gate clang, heard the peal of his doorbell. A woman in dark clothes stood shadowed in the cleared patch.

'Mr Murren?' she asked, after initial fright. 'I wondered if I could have a word with you?'

He let her in, did not invite her to remove her coat, but dragging the curtains to, motioned her to an uncomfortable chair, asked what she wanted. She was young, thirty at most, good looking. Fair hair burst from under her dark cap, he so designated the object, but her eyes were dark blue. Even teeth, a rounded chin, high cheekbones; he liked what he saw.

'Mr Murren?' she asked again. 'You are the organist

at St Michael's?' When he nodded, she said, 'I expected someone rather older.'

Her teacher, a Mr Maynard Clarke, unknown to Murren, had recommended this visit, and as she lived only ten minutes' walk away she had called on the off-chance of catching him in. Murren, taken aback, mentioned the weather, the icy streets, but she smiled these hazards vaguely away, offered her talents to his inspection. Maynard had said that her ear would be tested, and she would be asked to play. She had pieces with her. Murren signalled her to the stool.

'Do you play scales?' he asked. She lifted her face in willingness. 'D major, then. Four octaves.' She played with rapid efficiency. 'Again, please.' Improvement. He demanded one or two more, did not catch her out.

'What do you play?' he queried. 'Chopin?' He had no idea why he said that.

'Yes. What would you like?'

'You choose.'

She chose a waltz, flashing the notes, though the page was unsullied, showing no sign of finger marks. He listened, questioned her about phrasing. She answered well, but ascribed her knowledge to Maynard. She now offered Brahms *intermezzi*, Rachmaninov preludes, John Ireland, Frank Bridge. Whatever he selected, she performed, adequately, with taste, as she sat upright at the piano, still in her outdoor coat.

'Take that off,' he ordered. She complied. He took from his cupboard a book of Bach arias, and asked her to accompany him. She had no trouble. He tested her with a chord and she named the notes. Perfect pitch.

'Now, what exactly is it you want?'

'Lessons.'

'Aren't you satisfied with Mr Clarke?'

'Yes. He said I should move.'

'He can't teach you any more? Is that it?' Her face twisted.

'He's very good. He played in the proms when he was a young man.'

'Is he giving up?'

She burst into tears, a controlled, sad performance, in no way noisy, pointed with frequent dabs from a minute lace-edged handkerchief. After a time she staunched the weeping, and said, 'Don't ask me any more.' She snatched up her coat, dragging it up her right arm.

'Don't upset yourself,' he murmured.

'It's an inquisition,' she said. 'You men are all alike.'

Murren waited; all this cold night needed was a stranded madwoman. She buttoned her coat, though the collar needed adjustment, and stood with her back to the piano tugging her gloves on and off.

'I'm wasting your time?' she asked fiercely. 'That's what you think.'

Murren sat down, arm across the table, trousers hitched, his face composed into judicial middle age.

'You don't care. You go on your own way. At least there's some excuse for my husband. He isn't sane.'

'Is Maynard your husband?' he asked.

Immediately she began to laugh, almost cheerfully, brightly, though tears gathered in her eyes.

'Maynard's old, and a bachelor. He lived with his mother. He wouldn't marry me or anybody else.'

'I see. Is your husband interested in music?'

'Christ. He's only interested in himself. He used to play the violin. You accompanied Myra Friedlander, didn't you? I went to that concert. That's where I've seen you before. Was she hard to play with?'

'Sit down.' She did, and he talked sensibly while she fidgeted with her gloves. In the end she apologized for the outburst, outlined her ideas, her wish to sit a diploma. Now she was no more than a beautiful, calm young woman talking business. Only a slight breathlessness betrayed anxiety. He learnt, a fortnight later, that she had grown angry at her husband's late arrival, and had snatched up her music to venture out on that icy night.

Within that fortnight she became Murren's mistress. He made the advances, expecting rebuff, and had been taken aback by the violence of the response. In his own distress at his dismissal by Jessica he could not believe that he was responsible for this attraction, and, guiltily pleased, saw her merely reacting against her husband's indifference, cruelty, failure. She, Prudence Mark, barely mentioned what happened at her home; that was nothing. During her lessons she sat attentive, quick to learn, and went back to practise hard, but once instruction was done, she fell on him like a tearing hawk. He was terrified, shivering at her passion, delighted only during the mad climaxes of their love, but aghast at her careless, riotous turbulence. He tried to ascribe it to desperation, but her whole being concentrated on her sexuality, so that she burnt so much mad flesh, fair lines howling for a devastation, an obliteration of his personality and hers. What happened in sexuality between them had no connection with the world of earning a living, or food, or houses, not even with the black ice clogging the gutters. She appeared on his return from rehearsals; he could not think she had been waiting about in the streets during this bitter weather, but he did not put it past her.

He wasted no more time in pubs, but drove home, fearful, dominated, on edge.

Once he asked her if she still made love with her husband.

Her small nostrils snarled in delicate disdain; her blue eyes dismissed him. He saw her shaven eyebrows and the exquisite, waxen ears, the blonde, upthrust hair.

'Yes,' she said. They had finished a bout; he felt shattered; she calm after her bucking gross violence. 'Do you mind, then?' She scorned him, her husband. 'What's it matter to you? Anyway, if you make me pregnant, he'll appear on the birth certificate.' Her choice of words appalled.

'That's not what you want?' he asked weakly enough.

'No. L.R.A.M.'

He trembled.

Janet Bruce knew her, expressed no surprise that Mrs Mark had come for lessons.

'She was at school with me. Prue Fairhead, she was. Quite a good pianist then. And had perfect pitch.' She told some story about train whistles.

'Who taught her?'

'Miss Wheatley, the music mistress, I think. Not sure. The Fairheads lived near us in Mapperley, before we moved here. But we weren't very friendly.'

'And her husband?'

'Don't know anything about him. He wasn't one of the boys we knew at local schools.'

He asked Janet about Jessica. She did not know that they had broken it up, expressed a gruff concern.

'I haven't seen her. This happens. Then we get pally for a month or two. She goes her own way, but this weather's stopped me going round. I'll ring her up.'

She questioned him about the quarrel, learnt about Nigel, of whom she had never heard before, made disparaging comments on Jessica.

'She's mediocre. And dull.' He felt grateful for her effort, but it did nothing to sort him out. He took to work, filled in spare hours composing a movement for string quartet and contralto, this time to words by a local poet who had stumbled tipsily into a courting couple, and then been robbed. Murren did not know what he did, used classical forms, canon, chaconne with outrageous modernity and sometimes the voice as a fifth, low, wailing hooting instrument. He grew immersed in the scrawl, but warned himself one could be equally dedicated to a crossword or a jigsaw. If Prudence Mark interrupted him, he put down his pen, shrugging. Thus he went late to bed, woke tired, hating the weather but paradoxically energetic set about making himself more weary. He did not need alcohol. Winter lay unconsumed inside and out.

Janet reported that she had telephoned Jessica.

'She wasn't going to say a word about you. "How's James?" I asked. "Oh, all right." And that would have been it, if I hadn't pressed her. "We don't see each other much," she said in the end. "Why not?" "You know how it is." '

Janet had been blunt, then, though she did not report this to Murren: 'No, I don't know how it is. That's what I'm asking. Has he given you up?'

'Well.'

'What do you mean? "Well"? That it's not my business?'

'There's somebody I like better.'

'Who's that?' A pause lengthened: the worm considered turning, decided on lassitude.

'Nigel Brockless. He works with me.'

Janet drummed up questions, then laid it down that James Murren was a talented young man, with a distinguished future. Jessica said she knew it; she wasn't good enough for him. Janet, angry now at the indifference of the answering voice, shouted. People of his grade were rare, couldn't be ditched without thought of consequence.

'Ordinary people feel as hurt as geniuses,' Jessica muttered.

'I don't think so.'

'Have him yourself then, if you're so keen.' And Jessica had put the phone back.

Murren thanked Janet; he could not understand how his wild passages with Prudence left him desolate for Jessica. He took punishment both ways: longing with guilt. Sexual delight and puritan sophistication. Stripped naked under his paramour, stultified into breathless satisfaction, he wished he could walk the cold streets with Jessica, gloved hand holding gloved hand.

One evening, he had returned from a rehearsal of opera by Blow and Purcell, a practice he had had to take over as the London-based conductor had rammed the gatepost of his drive and ruined his car. He sat down worn out but pleased. On the way to college this morning he had decided that his quartet movement needed a slow prelude, introduction, initial *largo*. Immediately the idea had presented itself he had chased its form, had even spent an hour locked away inside the stockroom scribbling in a sketch-book preliminary notions. Now he'd look again, but he could not decide whether to work at his table, or improvise round the drafts at his piano. Both methods had advantages; anyway, the work didn't matter; it was fill-in material, a pastime. He did not believe that either, but found it impossible to make up his mind. He staggered out to the piano, drew the blinds, set his notebook on the stand.

The doorbell tore his ears. He had not touched a note. Ten-fifteen at bloody night, and they wouldn't leave you alone. Mrs Mark, again. Blood beat.

Elzbieta McKie primly faced him; wrapped up beyond recognition, she revealed herself by her voice.

'I'm sorry to trouble you at this time of night. I called earlier. Twice. You were not in.' Grudgingly he invited her in. She removed a foreign camphor-scented, face-muffling fur. 'I have never thanked you for taking my father to the aerodrome.'

'How is he?' he asked.

'Ill. Very ill.'

'I thought he was better?'

She shook her head. 'He talks about you. The musician, he calls you.' She smiled, trying perhaps to attract him. 'He would like to see you. I know you are busy and it's not fair to bother you. It's not about anything. But he feels in contact with culture. He is a lonely man. And he is dying.'

'I'll come and see him.'

'Thank you.' She seemed Slavonic, not so much in the cast of her features, but in the care of her speech. She talked as one crossed a river by stepping stones. 'I went to see the Paynes again, Jessica, but the mother ordered me out. She was rude and unsympathetic. As if I was begging for money.'

'She's suffering from nervous trouble,' Murren said.

'It did not seem. . . . Perhaps that is right. She said they had difficulties, but she told me to go. She was rude. She shouts at her schoolchildren like that. I felt ashamed.'

'I haven't seen her recently. I'd heard she was better.'

'Yes. My father's illness is affecting my mother. She can't make her mind up; she dithers. And she moans all day.' The demotic word, she meant 'complains', touched him. Her workmates, her husband, the neighbours were represented there washed up between the *ancien régime* of her father's Poland and Murren's alleged learning. 'She is worried how she will live. When he dies. She will have an old-age pension, but it is not much. She will have to take lodgers again.' Mrs McKie smiled, suddenly, broadly. 'They scratch the furniture and make a noise. It does not suit.'

'She could live with you?'

'That's what Jock, Willy, says. I say "No". It would not work out.'

She sat straight-faced, but uncharacteristically put one hand on his table and played with the corner of a sheet of manuscript paper. He inquired about his visit, consulted his diary, fixed a day.

'Can you bring Jessica with you?'

'I don't see much of her these days.'

'Oh. I thought you were engaged. You seemed so . . . suited.'

'We didn't think so.' The pronoun betrayed him. 'But I'll ask her.'

'My father would like that. He associates the two of you.' Murren wondered at the word, and, staggering himself, puzzled what the five-minute appearance of a couple of young people could make to a man as near the grave as this. It was mere myth on the part of Mrs McKie, an opportunity to go out of the house and talk to somebody else, a poor bitch's chance of doing something in the face of death. 'He is a strange man, my father. He was a Polish officer. But you know that.'

'It's dreadful, the way he's. . . .' Murren stumbled, but made the effort.

'Yes. I don't know how much pain there is. But it is the weakness, the inability to do things for himself. He says so. He even smiles. It is heartbreaking.'

'You must admire your father,' he said.

'I love him.' Her voice sank. 'He was important to me. More so than my mother. He helped me with my mathematics at the grammar school. And the French and Latin. What use is French and Latin to him now? I am his only child, and a disappointment. But if I had millions it would do him no good. I couldn't buy his health.' She stopped, and again her fingers reached, fondled, rustled the corner of paper. 'If I had to die I'd sooner do it in a dark, poky place. Not sitting out in a park.'

'Not in this weather,' he said, foolishly because he understood. She beamed again as he promised to contact Jessica, and fur-muffed held out a formal hand. Twenty minutes to eleven. God-a-mercy. Out to the bitter weather.

He met Patricia Payne by chance the next day.

'I haven't seen you lately,' she said, cheerfully enough. She piled the back seat of her car with bulging shopping bags. He made requisite noises, asked if Jessica would be in that night, explained why he wanted to speak to her. Mrs Payne bridled, standing up straight in the car park. 'I don't approve of this running round to the Wisniewskis'. It's morbid. What good can it do?'

'The old chap seems to want it.'

'The old chap. The old chap. That's no way to talk of him for a start, is it?'

'He's dying,' Murren said mildly, abashed at her pugnacity. 'If I can please him like this, it seems precious little. Do you think it harms Jessica, then?'

'How could it? She's tough as old boots. And selfish. You should know that. Besides, I thought she was having nothing to do with you now. That's what she says. That Brockless boy is always hanging round the house.'

'Mr Wisniewski associates us together. It pleases him.'

'Well, he's wrong, isn't he?' She spoke in a hoarse, harsh whisper. 'He's misleading himself.'

'But not for long.'

'There's enough trouble in the world without going searching for it. When I look at my husband I see he's going downhill. Just a few months ago, he was an energetic, well-organized man. Now. . . .'

'It's this weather.' They grimaced at frost still on the ground, on the tops of walls, on the branches of a car-park tree, withering the earth.

'When it's somebody near, dear, you don't deceive yourself. Make no mistake. When I watch Walter and he doesn't know, it terrifies me. He's old.'

'So you don't want me to ask Jessica.'

'You please yourself. She'll be in with her Nigel, I expect.' She slammed into her car with angry pleasure, dwarfing the machine.

When he rang Jessica, she said her mother had already mentioned the matter and that she was willing to pay the visit the next evening.

'Are you all right?' he asked.

'Yes. Are you?'

The streets darkened treacherous and uncomfortable. Mounds of heaped ice humped black as shadows under the lamp-standards; cold shuddered through the thickness of clothes. The two called first on Mrs McKie after a silent walk, Murren behind on the cleared, icy foot-width of pavement. Both had brought flowers, his bunch more ostentatious. Both concentrated on walking safely. He would not have recognized the hooded, slightly bent figure in front of him, and once when he'd called out about a magnificent display of icicles from a leaking overflow pipe, she'd not answered, not heard under the scarves and anorak. The cold deafened, deadened.

Elzbieta waited for them in outdoor clothes. She spoke cheerfully enough, led them immediately up the street. Once inside her mother's front door, with the trickle of English, torrent of Polish dried up, she invited them to remove coats, which were hung in the hall.

'You'll feel the benefit,' she said.

It was cold in the house. Warmth had hit them as soon as they entered, but died. Now draughts shivered. The two endured a brief hiatus on the landing, chillier than before; frost had greyed the small window. Floorboards groaned to their fidgeting. Presumably the women tidied Wisniewski, propped him on his pillows, prepared him for the living.

The old man's face had shrunk, so that it seemed impossibly small, like an axe-head, but yellow, deeply scored. His claws, when they shook hands, were warm. As well as the gas-fire, in one corner of the room a paraffin-heater burned, thickening the air. This time Mrs Wisniewski produced the chair for Jessica; father, though perfectly immobile, looked likely to topple from his supports, uncaring.

When he said it was kind of them of call, he whispered like crackling paper. His accent seemed more bizarre; the whites of his eyes had discoloured, but he watched. The two presented their flowers, and as he thanked them, his wife expanded into a rapidity of Polish before rushing away to find vases. Nodding, Wisniewski said that he felt very weak, but it was no use complaining. People had been most kind.

He mentioned the trip to Lincolnshire; he had found it 'interesting'.

'I'm sorry that we couldn't recognize any of your old haunts,' Murren said.

'Things change. I have thought about it. I was there in days of winter. The huts had stoves which sometimes grew almost red-hot at the top.'

'You spoke mostly Polish?'

'Oh, yes; There were English lessons, of course. I had studied the language before, in school and in the university. I did not finish.'

Elzbieta spoke of her father's legal studies, and his disappointment. He had worked in England in the offices of a factory and then a hospital, not testing his ability.

'I have met interesting people,' he rebuked her, and his tongue flickered on thin lips.

The visitors did not stay long, but exhausted the old man; they engineered short-winded conversations in which he did not join, though his eyes darted from speaker to speaker. His wife placed the flowers, badly arranged. He nodded thanks. They rose to leave; all stood for a moment, as at a memorial service. Murren had convinced himself, without reason, that the old man would die within hours. Hands were shaken. Wisniewski placed both his over Jessica's. Elzbieta did not kiss him.

As Murren waited at the door for the woman to pass him, the dying man asked, 'You still play and conduct Bach?' The man smiled; that wisp of face smiled.

'And Penderecki.' It meant nothing, went unheard.

'Yes, Bach is good.'

The visitors left together, while Elzbieta stayed with her mother, who whimpered, wet-eyed, unable to stand still.

The cold in the street knuckled them, since they could not walk quickly. They walked in a sullen file of two, and once Murren slipped, hit a rough stone wall with his elbow, hung ridiculously. Jessica turned, did not speak, trudged on when she saw he was not hurt.

Outside her gate he said, 'Thank you for coming.'

She nodded, wide-eyed, serious. 'I don't know what good it did. But he seems a decent man.'

'He won't recover?' Childish question she did not answer. Silence and ice.

'Shall I see you again?' he asked.

'It isn't any use, is it?' Misery stripped him to its extremes of cold. Dark houses towered; no voices stirred. He did not move nor she. He wanted her to get off, turned her back on him, but she held her ground prolonging his discomfort, perhaps deliberately. He would not shift; she must weaken by defying him, rejecting him.

That happened.

'Good night, then.' She had opened the gate. He did not answer.

12

Murren enjoyed a conversation with a colleague about travelling on buses, which the man had begun to use in the vile weather.

'You see the world. Punk rockers with chains of safety-pins,' Bates said.

'I could do without that.'

'But it's in comparative comfort. A travelling exhibition. If you can afford the fares.'

Murren was called to the telephone, where Alan Mark spoke to him. He had ferreted the number out of one of the St Michael's choirmen, with whom he played cricket. This weather? He wanted to talk about his wife, Prue, because it worried him.

The man sounded sensible, and dull. He had been pleased that she'd taken up her music again; she was talented. She'd put in hours of practice this last few weeks, and it was this that troubled her husband. He did not want her to go too far. No, he did not suggest that she was off her head, but she exaggerated, if he could use the word, in both what she said and how she behaved. 'If I can put it like this: she'd sooner walk on a tightrope than a pavement.' He sounded an earnest schoolmaster, though he managed a large timber-yard. What he really wanted to know was. . . . The man had difficulty. Was his wife any good? Was it worth while her studying? Was the intensity necessary? The questions suggested mere preliminaries, or so Murren feared. Soon he'd out with the real poser: Why are you committing adultery with my wife? So he answered with a dry caginess, and that awkwardness was never broached. He agreed, in the end, to meet the man in a pub for half an hour at opening time that evening.

Alan Mark stood a broad six feet with ginger-gold hair and darker moustache and sideburns. He swaggered, like a sailor, but spoke quietly, undogmatically from beneath a big, high-bridged nose. He insisted on buying the drinks. 'You are here at my invitation,' and surprised Murren when he confessed he was just returning from business. 'Yes, eight-thirty to six are my usual hours; sometimes I work later.' The few remarks that he made about his job showed that he did not expect Murren to be interested. A large, unemphatic man, he seemed in no hurry, pulling at the cuffs of a faintly striped shirt. Murren consulted his watch, urged speed because he dreaded the message.

Mark, 'my friends call me "Saint" ', went woodenly through the same rigmarole as on the phone, that he did not want his wife overstrained, that one had to be careful. Murren, convinced now, described the course he intended for Prudence, with its implications of study and practice, and the value of its end, a diploma.

'It will occupy her, and though she'll easily manage, I shall have to press her here and there. It's no use blinking the fact. If you think she can't stand that sort of treatment, the best thing would be to talk it over with her.'

'She might think I was interfering.'

'It would be the right thing to do.'

Mark nodded, sipping cold beer.

'You think she's good enough?' Reassured, he wetted his mouth again. 'She's a fine woman. We've been married ten years now. It's not always easy.' They exchanged banalities, the one about marriage, the other about pupils and success. Murren fetched second half-pints neither wanted. 'We have a good relationship, sexually, you know.' He put an innocent hand on Murren's sleeve, large fingered, capable, would give bowlers some hammer on the cricket field. Now for the plea, or warning? Mark dropped fair eyelashes over the china-blue eyes. 'She went off the rails once.' He waited; Murren looked away. 'I don't want that again. She left me. I don't claim I'm a saint,' he smiled, as if the verbal play spelt both seriousness and sanity, 'but it nearly finished me. She just told me, plain as you like, that she was going away with this, this man. I didn't know him. Nothing about him I could see. Nothing. I thought we were, well, all right, getting on well, you know.' Mark's face was pink, unlined; he himself might have been calculating the cost of planks. 'We'd been married four years.'

'She came back?'

'Not till after three months. Four. She'd lived in London. He was married. I had to lie like hell to cover for her. I didn't want people to know. I wrote, and begged. Then she sent a letter. Was I serious? She came back. They'd lived in lodgings. She said what a treat it was to have a decent bath.'

'Had she had a job?'

'Yes. In an office. She didn't say much about it. And I didn't. Shook me, I can tell, and I don't panic.'

'It hasn't happened again?' As Murren asked the question he remembered Prudence's feckless, headlong intensity, as if one pulling a light-switch triggered a thunderstorm. Mark did not immediately answer.

'Not that I know. But I didn't know before.'

'Does she go to work?'

'Sometimes. Sometimes not. She'll start, then get fed up. I don't blame her. There's no need for her to, money-wise. And she had lessons from this Clarke. He was a funny old woman, if you like. But it kept her occupied. I appreciate that. But then she takes up with you. And I wonder if the balance isn't getting upset. I'm not blaming you in any way. She's just a pupil to you; I see that. But it would be a sort of sign; it's possible.'

'You think she'd do better to stop?'

'What do you say?' Mark might have been talking to one of his foremen.

'The fact that you've asked the question means that you do. She's talented, but if she's going to take a diploma, she'll have to discipline herself. She could walk the exams, in my view, but whether she'll think so is another matter.'

Mark muttered once more through his difficulties, grew lavish and lucid in thanks; they drained dregs at six-thirty-five. The pub seemed chilly and inhospitable as they left it. Walking back, Murren felt no guilt, even a small delight that the cuckold had been so deluded. He did not take to him, a sportsman with his gold cuff-links and expensive shoes, and could not help wondering why the interview had been arranged at all. The marriage tottered; that was certain. Behaviour like Prudence Mark's could only mean a number of affairs, serious or not. But their gravity to her did not count; she might look on sex as lightly as on swigging gin, but her husband did not, clearly, like his property invaded. And yet. There were his letters which begged her, his own confessional word, to return. Was the man infatuated still after ten years? In the wintry streets Murren hoped puritanically that

Alan Mark would order, or persuade, beg even, his wife to suffer no more lessons.

At the same time he exercised himself over a letter from Bill Ashley, his old head of department, who had been offered a lucrative professorship of music in the United States. Ashley, knowing exactly what he'd do, said he was undecided, but indicated that if he went both he and Stacey, the head, agreed that Murren was the only possible replacement. He listed the public engagements for the next three years, the festivals, the prom appearances, the broadcasts. Murren was to think seriously; Ashley would make his mind up within the next fortnight; thus the warning.

This would be Murren's chance. He'd had enough of this city, with its cold, its death-beds, its broken loves, its crook-back lives. He would have spent two years, made his little mark, learnt something, hardened himself before launching himself in Ashley's wake in metropolitan culture. But there, up there, in Stacey's study, he'd heard of his mother's death. There was no escape, only the savagery of work or love. He wondered why he'd made no friends: neither at college, nor among the ale-sipping choirmen, nor with the Paynes, the Bruces and their like. He grinned at the conceit that he'd been thrown up here amongst the Saxons, or Danes, cold, rough, hot-headed men and lecherous, meat-tearing women. That spoke nowhere near the truth. His break with Jessica had hurt, and it connected itself with the dark house of the Wisniewskis. Only connect. No thanks. That old man died in an alien place, after a life of non-achievement, leaving a widow badly provided, who could barely make herself understood. In his pain, his debility, the sense of the imminence of his end, what talent could he offer, what prayer of thanksgiving? What connection?

In his letter Ashley had enclosed a typewritten copy of Spenser's Easter sonnet, with a laconic introduction. 'I want you to set this for me, four parts and huge organ. Lung-bursting, double-pedalling, nine-notes each hand. You can do it on your head. And don't hang about. Sooner, better.'

> Most glorious Lord of Lyfe! that, on this day,
> Didst make Thy triumph over death and sin;
> And, having harrowed hell, didst bring away
> Captivity thence captive, us to win:
> This joyous day, deare Lord, with joy begin.

Murren had set about it, lifting himself in a resplendent victory in and over the words. His sketches shouted success; he sat up all one night, excited at his own skill, dashing down a brilliance and simplicity that matched Spenser's. He photocopied his sheets, sent them off to Ashley, and found himself next day feverish with influenza. In bed, he shivered; his head banged with pain; he crawled downstairs for hot drinks and phone calls to cancel engagements. Janet Bruce appeared each night, forced him to eat, laundered his drenched pyjamas. At the end of three days his temperature had dropped to normal, but his body shrank, as if every muscle had flabbed, every nerve tuned in to pain. Forbidden by his doctor to leave the house, he dragged his aching legs because he could not sit in comfort, his eyes weak, his neck aching with mammoth depression. Once, reaching up in his kitchen, he knocked down a jar of instant coffee which exploded on the floor; he had burst into tears, sobbing as he dabbed with dustpan and brush.

A week later he hardly felt better.

The doctor prescribed a tonic although he cheerfully denied its effect. Murren could start work in two days' time if he felt up to it. Dr Brook twinkled; a lot of it around; see about an injection next year; the college would survive even if Murren had a month off. A young man, much of his patient's age, he'd no time for pangs of death or sepulchre.

A jubilant note from Ashley had as little effect.

Never mind about first draft. It's superb. We've started practising it for this year. Your pal Timothy Gelsthorpe looked at the organ part. Made a suggestion or two, but I'll get your OK. It's magnificent.

It did not feel so here; Murren could only just force himself to think drearily of the anthem, and reject.

> So let us love, deare Love, lyke as we ought,
> Love is the lesson which the Lord us taught.

He went back to work without enthusiasm, but delegated all evening rehearsals to his deputies. A cheerful letter from Stacey described Ashley's duckings and writhings at the American proposition. He hadn't decided yet, but he'd go. The 'unpaid secretary', Ashley's childless wife who wrote his letters and made up his diary but rarely saw him for more than an hour at a time, had decided she wanted a change, and the salary was far too large for foolery or idealism. So Murren had to gird his loins; as soon as Bill moved, he would step in. Stacey did not expect that proposition to be disputed. Murren wrote brief thanks; he would come.

Janet phoned, called now and then.

Their recital was three weeks ahead, and clearly she wanted him on his feet for it, though he refused to rehearse with her. He put in a few minutes for difficult passages, but found it as impossible to concentrate on the piano as on reading. All he wanted was to hunch in warmth, a hot drink in hand, and turn over in dull reverie his weakness, an ache in his shoulders, the listlessness. The door-bell on one such evening jangled his nerves so that he spilt his milk, and he shuffled to the door, expecting, half dreading Janet and her cheerful sense.

Mrs Payne towered, muffled and broad-shouldered. She sat down, refusing coffee, and he shivered from his one-minute exposure to hall and door.

'You have heard, I expect,' Patricia Payne began.

Her face seemed deeply lined and sagging as if the wrinkles had undermined the structure. Hat, scarves, large tweed coat were bright as usual, but she seemed shrunken, mere bones. A big woman, she'd become insubstantial and twisted.

'About what?' He could not raise politeness.

The lifted head, a large nose, bags that bulged solid under the eyes. Mouth gaped.

'Jessica,' she said, and moaned, a short unmistakable sound.

'No.' He froze; minor discomforts were terrorized. 'I've been ill.'

'Her young man. Nigel Brockless. He's been killed. In an accident.'

'When?'

'Over a week now. Tuesday evening. On his motorscooter.'

Murren pushed himself up, as if he could bear no more, went out to the kitchen where efficiently he put on his kettle. He had not spoken, but had walked out, leaving her, not understanding why he had acted so. Back with mugs of coffee, he stumbled into apologies. She pointed her stricken face into a corner of the room, unanswering.

'Would you like a spoonful of brandy in it?'

She smiled, shaking her head, and clasped hands round the mug. He took his time settling himself back into his chair.

'How is she taking it?' he asked in the end, steadily enough.

Again the mother shook her head, sighing loudly. They sat. Patricia tried again.

'It's awful,' she said. 'To see her.' Each moved coffee facewards. Withdrawal. 'We, we. . . . I can't tell you. At first, first, his brother came round. The same evening. It happened soon after seven. On the main Watnall Road. A car. Then a lorry. The boy, brother, didn't know he was dead. He died soon after. Daddy took Jessica, and Tommy, the brother y'know, straight down to the hospital. He was dead then.'

Unbalancing silence toppled, held.

'She was brave that night. When she went to the General. She was pale. And when she came back. She hardly cried. Bottled it up inside her. Daddy cried, when we'd put her to bed. It was for her. She looked such a waif. She didn't fill her clothes. She'd forgotten how to walk properly. It upset Walter, I can tell you. We went to the funeral service, and that was awful, people crying out loud in the crematorium, but not Jessica. But not Jessica. She just sat there, pulling at her gloves and biting her lips. And it was so cold.'

Mrs Payne seemed to make comfort for herself as she talked. She hit words as if to keep herself awake to reality.

'There's something I want you to do,' she said, in the end. He didn't answer, grimaced up at her. 'I want you to visit Jessica.'

'Would that be, do any good?'

'Why not?' She snapped as if at a child fidgeting during prayers.

'She threw me over for Nigel.' He had to fight to force out the words. 'Now when she sees me alive she'll resent it, I should think.'

'Nothing could be worse than she is now.'

'Has she gone back to work?'

'She's not had any time off. It would have been better if she had. She insisted. She's been brave in a way I never suspected. But she should start to get over it now. Somehow.'

He agreed to come round the next evening. Patricia talked of Nigel Brockless's parents, and let it out that neither she nor Walter had much approved of Jessica's choice. The boy had nothing about him; he was bank clerk personified.

'Perhaps that was what she wanted,' Murren said. 'He wasn't a kind of cultural examination.'

Mrs Payne's face, misshapen as a baked apple, gaped, but recovered quickly enough when he inquired about her health.

Murren slept badly, felt so ill next day that he feared his flu had returned in some new, more virulent form. He shuddered after his bath, snatched off and changed his tie twice, wore a dark suit. Arriving ten minutes late, he parked and spread newspaper under his windscreen wipers.

Every light in the house blazed downstairs; the stove in the sitting-room glowed redly; radiators thrummed with heat; the stereo played cheerful Handelian music; all three Paynes had taken to

Sunday-best. The older pair spoke effusively, shook hands, sat him alongside Jessica on the settee. At least he did not need to stare in the poor girl's face. She had not stood up, but had smiled, quite normally he'd have said, and when he'd mumbled his sorrow at her she had placed a hand on his sleeve, as if either to thank him or to prevent further embarrassment. Payne toddled round asking what the others would drink, commenting facetiously, staggering as if he'd been all day on the bottle. While he was out, it was Jessica who asked why Murren was not at his Friday choir practice. When he explained that he had been ill, that John Pendleton, his assistant, had temporarily taken over, she asked what had been wrong, if he were better, whether he'd started back to work.

The ordinary steadiness of her voice unnerved him as if she accused him of having time off for his three-day flu while she, in tragedy, slogged on. He gave an account of his symptoms, mentioned Janet had looked after him.

'And she said nothing about Nigel?' Patricia asked, determined to face Jessica with the worst.

'Would she know?' He defended her, mildly.

'It was in the papers.'

When Payne returned with the drinks, making out that he had forgotten the orders, his wife told him that Murren had been off-colour, and forced him to repeat his boring account.

'Your health,' Payne said, standing straight. 'Now you've got it back. That is, if you have.' He raised his glass; the others made embarrassed gestures in return, sadly inappropriate, but whatever they did, or failed to do, would have been equally wounding, inapt, cruel. They needed, Murren decided, pithered inside his thickest pullover, a miracle, a resurrection, not a glass of gin. Payne talked of illness, and they stared at the red windows of the fire, as the clock ticked in slow time. The silences protracted themselves into awkwardness, so that the lifting of drink to lips became an event. The father jumped up to fill glasses; Jessica laid her hand across the top of hers; his encouragement sounded desperate. Patricia, standing, then walking as if in need of occupation, left the room to return with oatcakes and sweet biscuits. Each grudgingly accepted a small token of hospitality;

'Can you play bridge?' Payne asked. Murren, so miserably wrapped up in himself that he did not realize he was being addressed, admitted he had at university. This led to further activity: the production of a card table, two packs, the rearrangement of furniture so that they could sit in front of the fire. Their rising to the feet, getting out of the way brought relief.

'Who's playing with who?' Payne called. They still stood.

'Are you any good?' Jessica asked Murren.

'It's years since I. . . .'

'We'll be partners, then.'

'You sit with your back to the fire,' her father instructed.

'No. Mum's always freezing. She should be there.'

Payne still acted as master of ceremonies when they had sat down. He had forgotten paper and pencil; then followed a search for a card detailing scores; finally he opened and shuffled a pack, at inordinate length, saying that at least they'd start with a random distribution. The cards looked stiff, brand new, purchased, Murren decided, for this evening. Having dealt, Payne pushed back his chair.

'Now before the serious business of the evening

begins, ladies and sir, does any one want further liquid refreshment?'

'Oh, for heaven's sake, sit down, Walter.' His wife's exasperation seemed almost normal.

There was no hurry about the play; much interrupting cross-talk about conventions. Murren, who disliked games, found that his interest had been caught in that now everyone had to speak, or shuffle, cut, deal. Jessica saying 'no bid' or 'two clubs' bettered Jessica silent, and once, when after a slowly played game she made three no-trumps to win game and rubber, she sounded excited, said she didn't think it had been on, argued a little with her father about the alternative bidding. Murren forgot his aches, thought hard to beat his opponents, even felt a thrust of anger when Jessica failed to return a lead, though he said nothing. Father Payne became more loquacious, commenting comically, ribbing his wife, congratulating Murren, openly triumphing over Jessica. Time passed; at half past nine the women went out to make coffee.

Payne who a moment before had brandished and played a hand with appropriate, bland catch-phrases, 'Pick the bones out of that', 'A little rain must fall', 'And that should make thirteen', now sat quietly, though with a flushed face, a small smile twisting under his moustache.

'It's very kind of you to come,' he said. 'We're most grateful. We really are.'

'How's she taking it?'

'Hard to say. No fuss. You can't tell. She doesn't go out in the evenings. Just to work and back. Still, every day passed is a day won.' He shook his head, unbelieving. 'This has been a success, really.' He pointed to the cards scattered on baize. 'We've not known what to do for the best.'

'And her mother?'

'She's desperate, desperate.' He blew his lips out, unaware of the action.

'In herself, do you mean?'

'In herself, and in what's happened. God.'

Jessica rattled in with a trolley; someone had been at enormous trouble with pâté, cheeses, rolls, a huge trifle, crisp brandysnaps oozing roses of cream. The coffee appeared separately, almost majestically on a copper-cornered tray the size of a table-top. One was expected to eat, drink as Payne bombarded with badinage. Jessica politely handed round plates.

After the meal, the stacking of dishes, the refusal to clean them there and then, they settled for a final hour of cards. This had no success; hands were unbalanced, made or marred themselves. Payne, who had pushed himself as joker for three hours, was silent and, unwatched, grim. Jessica played with composure; a casual observer would have seen a beautiful, pale girl, slightly dark under the eyes, joining in a game in which she had no interest.

Patricia called the halt. 'We shall never finish this rubber,' she said. 'And some of us have to be up tomorrow.'

'Saturday tomorrow,' her husband answered, but he collected, reboxed the cards, and hopping round with some of his former fervour, helped Murren into his topcoat. Murren thanked them, shook hands, even with Jessica, who stood staring off, not troubled one would say, merely preoccupied with something inside her head or outside the room. She wished him good night, and as the door closed on him did not bustle with her parents.

'You go to bed, then,' Patricia said, donning her apron.

The girl walked upstairs, hand on banister.

13

Mid-March. A thaw dirtily cleared the streets.

Murren returned to his full duty, which included two recitals with Janet Bruce. As the first approached, the singer lost her composure, complained, could not make up her mind about points they had settled early in rehearsal. Murren, not over-patient at practice, lost his temper.

'For God's sake, sing the bloody thing and stop thinking about it.'

'How can I if I don't . . . .?'

'Right notes and clear words.'

She burst into tears. He let her cry the mood through.

He had not in the past fortnight seen anything either of Prudence Mark, who had been ill with a double bout of flu. Oddly, her husband telephoned more often than necessary to cancel lessons, to offer bulletins. His wife seemed very down, went to bed most afternoons, did not enjoy her convalescence; the doctor had suggested a holiday, but she'd have to go on her own, or take her mother with her. Alan Mark did not convey information, merely wished to stay on the phone, to protract the exchange, though Murren could not guess why.

Nothing at all from the Paynes' house.

That did surprise him, in that he was pleased with himself about the visit, hinting in his head that Jessica's recovery dated from the evening at the card table. He expected thanks, communiqués, got none. Perhaps influenza had kept them all indoors, as weather brightened outside; he made no inquiries.

The first of the Bruce recitals was in Lincoln, and went well in spite of cold rain. Janet became very quiet on the day before the recital, refused a run-through, discussed nothing, but sang with eloquence on the night. Quite unimpressed by the clamorously enthusiastic reception, she thanked him, shook hands and left with her father and mother. Murren, pleased with the performance, was dashed at this off-hand dismissal, and surprised at a curt note through the post congratulating him and making two or three sensible suggestions. He had deeply hurt the girl, he felt, when she could fail so coldly to celebrate with him.

The second recital, in the hall where he had played with Friedlander, was well attended. The Bruces had influence, could drum up an audience; a contingent from the university occupied two rows; the music club had arrived in force with the educational fraternity, while the reporter from the local press, an enemy of Janet's, was present to air his pretensions. Janet, statuesque in gold, then deep blue, sang with a marvellous, fluid skill. She seemed affable enough, and after her first group, Purcell songs, thanked him. He knew they had done well, and had used a decorated accompaniment he had prepared in the final piece that had lifted her to a strength and delicacy of eloquence that he found unexpectedly moving so that he had to concentrate on mere notes. Her next groups, Mozart, Schubert, Schumann, Brahms and Wolf, seemed to gain in power, convincing Murren, who doubted her stamina. The last group of modern songs, Berg, Granados, Britten, R. R. Bennett, she ended with an added item, 'From Far, from Eve and Morning', by James Murren. He'd given her a copy as soon as it was finished before Christmas, and forgotten about it. They'd hummed it through together the night he'd handed it over, but had not sung, or mentioned it, since. Now, smiling in the barrage of applause, the deserved shouts, she had crossed to the piano and, from the back of one of the Schubert volumes, had taken a beautifully handwritten copy, and propped it on his stand. 'A Housman poem,' she said, 'from "A Shropshire Lad", set by' – hand extended backwards – 'James Murren'. He could have done with some practice on the thing.

'Speak now, and I will answer;
  How shall I help you, say;
Ere to the wind's twelve quarters
  I take my endless way.'

and the piano trailed upward into the bleak spaces of unbeing, undoing the warmth of the voice, the generous offer, sketching the transitions of life, the cold and blank skies, the bravery of one small human talking to, touching another, among the icy, eternal unconscious enmity of the vast universe. Locked in a chain of canons, the art of strict counterpoint sketched the gaping, cold cave of uncare round Housman's insect voice.

The audience sat momentarily silenced, the greatest compliment, before crackling into applause. She sang a second encore, Handel, and a third, Schubert, and left it. Murren had been made to stand with her at the front of the platform where she had kissed him. In these celebratory moments he'd looked about him for the Paynes, but they were not to be seen. The

Bruce parents led him off to a party, not at their own house, but at a larger mansion in the next road where he had sat bemused with admiration, questions and alcohol. At some time after eleven Janet, who had hardly exchanged a word with him, sat on his chair arm, a hand proprietorially on his shoulder. She seemed drunk with praise, slurring her words, a quite different being from the competent artiste, the nervous student; now she sat, lounged, like some perfumed houri, kif-drugged, in an exotic other-world. At twelve, guests showed no inclination to leave this mid-week junket, the pair were dragged from the chair and Janet gave them, 'I Attempt from Love's Sickness to Fly'. Murren could barely sit on the seat, or see the music, but she sang with the power she had commanded at the concert. To him it all took place distantly, outside, having nothing to say about love, or Purcell's approaching death, or James Murren's winter-world; a cream of ectoplasm writhed and fell among whisky-fumes.

'I'm going back.' Janet took his arm, expecting him to accompany. Nobody objected; the party created its own momentum. They were helped into coats, and shown out. They staggered the five-minute walk. Murren, elated but frowning, muttered Housman lines to himself, to the stone walls he brushed against, the lamp-standards, the high stars. Janet crushed her mouth to his.

'Now – for a breath I tarry
 Nor yet disperse apart –
Take my hand quick and tell me
 What have you in your heart.'

He clasped her, and they zigzagged on, the words

saddening from his lips in a hazy gratification that lifted him from reality. Here was nothing for tomorrow, for dark mornings, for the slush still under garden hedges. Slightly drunk, seeing the world as the world's not, he armed his companion deliciously through her front door, into the huge silent hall, and then, treading stairs as water, into a small, bright room where he collapsed across a chair, vaguely to watch her wave at bottles. He refused more drink.

'I'm going to,' she said. 'Just a small one.' She made ludicrous gestures of measurement with thumb and fingers, an eighth to three inches, 'Don't spoil the sport.' She laughed mildly, but seriously.

' "Speak now and I will answer; How shall I help you, say." ' She sang it to him, richly, a barmaid of culture, in white and refined gold. He wet his lips with the whisky she handed him; she moved about the room, threw a cushion at his feet and squatting on it took his left hand to fondle, to kiss. He stroked her hair absently.

'This is good,' she said. He did not have to answer that, but continued the movement of his fingers. 'I love you. You know that.' This time he covered his silence by conveying his glass to his lips. 'Do you hear what I say?'

'Yes,' he answered.

'Well? Doesn't it mean anything?' His hand touched the flesh of her cheek. Her lips found his fingers. She flicked both arms behind her head to unhook, unzip her dress, and stood stepping from it. She discarded the dark tights, pants and bra, posed modestly naked before him, beautiful in a heavy sculpture of flesh. Her mouth slightly open, she lifted her arms which raised the full breasts and at stretch looked down at him. She parked on his knee, and the warm weight crushed him, stultified him. Before he embraced her, he got rid of his glass; her mouth fastened itself to his, pinned his head with violence into the back of the chair so that he choked. Now her hand groped, found his sex blatantly, but he was flaccid, even under her urgent stroking.

'I'm tired out, and drunk,' he said.

'It doesn't matter; it doesn't matter,' Enthusiastic as the gym-mistress, she pulled him straighter in his chair. 'I love you. Stand up.' On his feet he staggered, caught sight of her naked, creamy back in the mirror, found it no more erotic than the naked woman touching, stripping, loving him.

They lay side by side on a thick rug; he had tried, had failed.

'I'm sorry,' he said, uncaring.

'It doesn't matter. It will be good because I love you. Do you love me?' He did not answer. She kissed him, like a powerful, boring machine, holding his head to the floor as in a vice. 'You love me, a little bit, don't you?' The voice wheedled, almost childishly, thinly arch. 'Just a scrap?'

'Just a scrap.' He repeated her phrase without embarrassment, surrendering in ashen, arid defeat. His sexual incapacity added a kind of martydom, a saving grace of boredom, a promise of further nothings. She battered him with kisses, mouth wide, tongue hugely penetrative, then laughing dragged him upwards.

'Home time,' she said. She spoke this naked white hottentot, like a schoolma'am, and her smile had switched from rabid lust to a sweetness of reason, teacher encouraging favourite to do what he already wanted. Murren pulled on his trousers, straightened his clothes with his back to her, his glance to the floor. His eye was caught by the gloss of his shoes.

He reeled towards the mirror, beaten, patted at his hair.

'Are your parents back?' he asked, though he did not care.

'Not yet. They'll stay in bed tomorrow. I'll drive you home.'

'I'll walk, thanks. We're too drunk.'

She did not argue, and her last kisses were sisterly. He welcomed the air of the street, found himself steady, able to think, progress, to make for bed. The overcoat he had not buttoned flapped in a wind that was not cold. Next morning he began his first lecture on time.

The sun shone, but as a neighbour shouted it was 'warm behind windows'. He had heard nothing about the London post from either Ashley or Stacey, and their silence galled him; something had gone wrong, or they had changed their minds. The importance of a move from this place made itself more evident. As his choir beautifully sang a *Magnificat* and *Nunc Dimittis* he had written for them, he lacked all interest; it might have been music for an electronic tape, equally to be reproduced anywhere, not dependent on effort or will, merely on physical laws. He would not miss these men; he'd be presented with better, and that was what mattered. He lived inside himself, because of his fear.

Janet rang each day, found out his free time, visited him, but seemed subdued, embarrassed, unwilling to push her luck. They kissed, she made a discreet fuss of him; once they made sexual love, but half heartedly, with the removal of a minimum of clothes, as if expecting an interruption, a knock on the door. She spoke her gratification but, he thought, with suspicion, expecting something different, but again, his own uncertainties probably suggested this. His difficulties increased.

He telephoned the Paynes to ask if they would like a return bridge party at his house, thanking them effusively for their hospitality. Patricia cut him short. It would not be possible. They were very busy at this time of the year. He was most kind, but no. The woman answered bluntly, adding to his unease. No, they were not coming. No.

Within half an hour Walter Payne rang to ask if they, he and his wife, could come round.

They appeared smiling, but refused all hospitality, removed their coats reluctantly, not intending to stay. Payne began with trivialities about the weather and football, but his wife, mouth thin, had none of it.

'We owe you an explanation,' she said. She kept it succinct, even tactful, but he could imagine the details. The day after the game of bridge Jessica had suddenly become furiously red at table as they ate their five-thirty meal, and ordered them to stop interference. As fierce, with as little introduction, as that. Payne asked what she meant, and the girl burst into tears.

'You know,' she said. 'You know what I'm talking about.'

'I don't.' Her father's sentence stopped her outburst momentarily.

'James Murren.' She had choked on the name, sobbed more nakedly. 'Because Nigel's gone, you can't shove him down my throat every minute. I don't want him. You want me to have him. You didn't want Nigel. You hated him'.

'That's unfair, Jessica,' Patricia said, countering hysteria with acid tone, 'and silly. Your father and I love you. We don't want to see you unhappy. That's what we hate. And we know how you must feel. We invited Mr Murren because we don't want to see you sitting there all on your own, in your room, never going out. He's somebody you know, and about your age. You can't spend the rest of your life grieving.'

'You hate me.'

'Why should I do that?' Patricia's vinegary reason stung.

'Because you are not my mother.'

The silence broken by snufflings lasted some minutes. The girl hung her head; Patricia's face, deeply trenched, reddened. Payne played bemused with a spoon.

'If that's what you think then it's no use arguing.' Mrs Payne forced herself back to her plate.

'I don't like that, Jess,' her father said, each word ugly. The daughter did not answer but quietened her distress. Her elders dealt with a few tortured mouthfuls.

'You can't love people to order.' The sentence burst out of her, but not clearly, an aside delivered away from the listeners, more sulky breath than meaning.

'We are not ordering anything,' Payne said, 'as well you know.'

'It sounds like it, then.'

'We're trying to help you as best we can.' Payne continued as his wife crumbled bread. 'God knows we can't undo what's done, but anything we can get for you, or say . . .'

'I don't want James Murren.'

'Then you shan't have him. That's easy.'

'We're not trying,' Patricia began, 'to foist him on to you. You don't see it, and we don't expect you to, but we're desperate. And when you suggest that we are pleased that Nigel's out of the way, then, then . . . .'

'I'm sorry,' the girl said, not lifting her eyes. 'I don't know what I'm doing. I . . . .' She howled in a squall of tears, pushing back her chair as if she'd run from the room. Patricia rose, slowly and awkwardly, smoothing the lap of her dress, then walked round the table to kneel by the girl's chair, to put an arm about her. For a moment it seemed Jessica was intent on resistance, but she leaned forward to allow her mother's arm more comfortable access.

'There, now.'

'I'm sorry, I'm sorry.' The crescendo of sobbing muffled itself on Patricia's shoulder, but still Jessica did not move arms or face in response; passively she allowed herself to be mothered. At the end of the table, Payne sniffed, got on with his tea, filled the others' half-emptied cups, put a manly face on it.

Next day, they reported, Jessica acted as if nothing had happened, in that she spoke pleasantly, lent a hand about the house, but had withdrawn into herself. No intimacies, verbal or by gesture, comforted the parents who talked the matter over. They let things ride, made no approach to Murren, until they decided they could offer him an explanation, as now, after his phone call. They seemed ashamed, and the plan, Murren decided, had been Patricia's. Father Payne would have used the phone when the girl was at work if it had been his choice, but his wife, or her troubles, had made up his mind for him, and he could not be bothered to argue.

'So you don't think she's any better?' Murren asked.

'We don't know.' Patricia.

'She must be, to some extent,' Payne objected. 'Time . . . .'

'I couldn't say that. I just couldn't say that.'

'And you want me to keep well out of her way?'

'That shouldn't be difficult.' As Patricia snapped, her husband grimaced behind her back.

Duty done, Mrs Payne marched her party off, refusing hospitality, and herself exuding a hostile aggression Murren felt to be undeserved.

He was surprised next Sunday, then, after evensong, to find Jessica waiting for him. The day had been fine, surprisingly, balmily mild, and now a warm wind moved in the darkness when Murren strolled from the south door with his assistant. As they descended the rounded steps from churchyard into street, he saw the dark figure, paid no attention.

She called out to him.

He stopped conversation with his companion as he recognized the voice, surprised at his bodily jolt. Pulling himself together he introduced her to John Pendleton, who, after a social word or two, and a quick clearing up of points about the next rehearsal, made off into the craggy half darkness of the narrow street.

'How are you?' Murren asked at loss. She nodded, acknowledging her health or sanity. Here, she appeared to be dressed in black, with a veiled hat or scarfed face so that only eyes, nose, mouth were distinct, and the outline of her features smudged unevenly. 'Were you at the service?' Nodding again. He waited, but she did not help him out.

The vicar shouted a geeting as he trotted down the steps, cassock billowing. They heard his footsteps, the fumble of his car door, the inefficient gulping engine of his departure. No words, silence in the warmth of spring darkness. 'Can I give you a lift home?' he managed.

'My parents don't know I'm here.'

'No.'

'They wouldn't mind.' She smiled, he thought. 'They might be surprised.'

'I see. Is there anything I can do?'

She did not reply immediately so that he wondered if he should stir her by walking towards his car.

'Well, no, not really. I hadn't seen you for, for some time.'

'Would you like to go somewhere for a drink?'

'If it doesn't . . . .'

Leaving the sentence incomplete, she moved as if to express relaxation, or a satisfactory outcome. He named several pubs, but she left the decision to him. Once in the car, he ordered her to fasten her seat-belt and they exchanged remarks about the clemency of the weather, in an awkwardness of embarrassment. He drove to the far side of the town, up a long hill to The Quorn, a place he had never patronized. They parked, then stood for some minutes in the unaccustomed warmth looking down the long slope and out to the lines of lights in the valley. Neither said a word.

The lounge was not yet full, but customers wore their Sunday best with the exception of a gin-drinking quartet of women who sat round two labradors and a man at the table next to where Murren directed Jessica. They spoke loudly, in public utterance, drawing attention to themselves.

'Did you ever get to Hong Kong, Jock?'

'No. Singapore, now,' the man did his best, 'that's . . .'

'It's fabulous,' the woman insisted. 'Another world. Magic.'

Murren raised his glass to Jessica, who had chosen orange juice. Her clothes, he noted, were not black, her coat, in fact, a light grey, and the gauzy scarf round her hair navy blue. As she sat neatly opposite, she had removed her headgear; she showed no indication of mourning, merely sabbath decorum, utterly suitable to her calm beauty.

'Your health.'

She shifted her glass formally to touch her lips. The women exploded into screeches of laughter at some reply from the man, who smirked complacently. The dogs lifted their noses.

'You comfortable?' he asked from behind his glass. She nodded. 'I haven't seen much of you lately.' She shook her head. 'Mark you, I've been busy.' He'd make it easy for her. 'You didn't go to either of Janet's recitals, did you?' She now looked blank, and he offered her a flat account at which she pinched her face into assumed interest. The women next door roared; they had acquired another balding man who put his arm across the check shirt of the urchin-cut female with her back to Murren. All refused, waving painted fingernails at fullish glasses and floating lemon-slices, the newcomer's offer of drinks. The big left paw awkwardly rubbed a shoulder-blade; she slapped his buttocks comically.

'Hands off my bum,' he ordered.

'Yes, please,' she replied. All squawked.

Murren smiled at Jessica.

'They're enjoying themselves,' he said.

'Bring a chair up if you're going to join us,' the woman advised.

'What will your husband say?'

'Sod-all, as usual, Where's he got to?'

'I didn't expect to see you,' Murren tried.

'You were going straight home? I'm sorry.'

'No. John Pendleton and I would probably have

dropped into the Robin Hood. He likes to get everything straight for rehearsals next week.'

'I'm sorry, then . . . .'

'Everything is straight,' Murren answered. 'He sees to that. He just likes to let me know.' That gave him opportunity to describe his assistant, to let his tongue wag; she smiled duly at Pendo's punctilious nature, his nagging mother, his tidy mind and its uses. Murren reached the bottom of his pot, waited for his companion, but she neither drank nor spoke.

'Sup up.' he said, mustering cheerfulness. She obeyed. 'How about something a shade stronger? Join the gin brigade.' She nodded absently, and he moved to the counter, where the service was good. He bought bags of crisps, but she did not respond to his jovial chat. Urchin-cut had stood up, in tapering jeans, and the man stroked the backs of her thighs before insisting that he'd now buy his round. Murren and Jessica smiled at the noisy knot, raised their glasses, but nothing came of it.

'Are you working tomorrow?' he asked. She was. 'What time do you have to be there?' Nine o'clock. 'Before the bank opens?' That was so. This conversation petered out so that he found himself reading the brewer's advertisements, the landlord's joky aphorisms: 'Every customer here gives pleasure, some when they come, some when they go', an upside-down folded copy of the *News of the World*. He forced himself to read slowly, a word at a time, so that he seemed to neglect his companion, but she gave no sign, concentrating perhaps a foot above his head.

'How are your mother and father?' he asked. They were well. 'Your mother's much better, then?' She was. 'I was a bit,' he floundered, 'concerned last time I saw her. She seemed,' awkward length, 'on edge.'

No answer vouchsafed, merely the raising of gin to lips. When Jessica replaced the glass, she stroked the surface of the table with the third finger of her right hand, most carefully, in minute diagonals. She still shaded in her three-quarter-inch lines as she spoke.

'They asked you not to see me, didn't they?' He admitted it. 'That was my fault. I blew my top at them. They liked you better than Nigel.' He could think of no answer to that. 'And you know what Patricia's like. She goes red in the face, gets hold of dad, and bundles him round to you.' Though the language had livened, the girl's face remained blank, her lips barely moving, the finger now tapping.

'It seemed understandable,' he said, lamely.

'And now I come bothering you.' Her words blocked easy comfort; an attempt at logic stirred under deadening sadness.

'Oh, that's all right. I'm glad to see you.'

She paused, resumed shading. Even the next table opted for silence.

'I don't know what to do. I stay in, and slouch round, and make currant-cakes. I know I should get about.'

'The weather's been rotten,' he said. 'When the spring comes, you'll feel more like . . . .'

'You talk like dad. He'll make any excuse for me. He doesn't know what's happening. Inside me.'

'No,' Murren answered. 'And I don't.'

'That's right. How can you?' The accusatory voice strengthened.

'Your father has lost two wives.' He'd be tough-minded.

'Yes, but there was some warning. He knew they were ill. He could prepare himself.' The fact that she had aroused herself to argument cheered him.

'But he knew them longer, had been married to them.'

'Do you think that makes a difference?'

'Must do.' He answered her blank voice with bluffness. She nodded, lugubriously, like a music-hall comic. 'But I don't suppose that's what you've come here to talk about.'

'Why have I come?' she asked.

'You tell me.' She did not. The next table created a diversion when the man who had not been to Hong Kong admitted ownership of the Volvo Estate with its lights still on. They ribbed him; he jangled his keys. Urchin-cut asked him to look out for Keith.

'What, in the car park', he asked. They roared innuendo. Jessica turned right round to enjoy the kerfuffle. The whole bar seemed livelier for the interlude. Keith returned to raucous jollity; Hong Kong came beaming back, still clinking his keys. Urchin-cut stretched her arms round the shoulders of husband and man-friend, and left for the ladies.

'I'm beginning to forget what Nigel's like,' Jessica said. Murren barely believed his ears.

'That's natural.'

'It's the pain because he's not there.'

Her eyes were brimming over, though she did not feel for her handkerchief. Murren braced himself for embarrassment and was suddenly surprised that she was normal again, straight lipped, her finger caressing the table in short, careful strokes. She finished her gin; he was not halfway down his pint, but he grabbed her glass, made for the bar, refilled.

'I've had enough,' she said.

'One orange, one gin?'

The next table noisily discussed a hand at bridge. The matter seemed important to a blonde matron who tugged one of the labradors nearer her feet as she asked, 'One heart, one spade, two hearts? What did I want? I mean, what did I want?'

'Drink this up,' Murren said. 'You needn't bother talking.'

'I don't mind.'

He asked again about her parents, learnt they were at home, that they had no idea where the daughter was. She, then, shyly, blushingly, admitted she had been to evensong the week before but had slipped away immediately the service ended.

'It was too cold to hang about.'

They settled to comfortable exchanges, she about a course she had volunteered for, he on the cost of repairs to the organ. Companionately each pressed the other with questions to lengthen the exchange. When Murren finally emptied his glass, she offered to buy him another.

'No thanks,' he said. 'That's my limit.'

'I'm enjoying this.'

'Let me get you another, then.'

She laid her hand flat across the top. On the next table tones had been reduced; the strong voice insisted, *con sordino*. Words like 'tragic' made solemn noise.

'How old was she, then?' Hong Kong.

'Thirty-four.'

Now the talk strengthened, swellings, mastectomy, second operation, just a skeleton.

'She was so beautiful,' Urchin-cut said. 'At the Henrys' wedding. She didn't look more than sixteen.'

'And those three children?'

'Who'll look after them?'

'Her mother, for the time being. But the father's a semi-invalid.' They all stared somewhere outwards, between the heads of those opposite, faces taut.

'It makes you think,' the balding man said.

Murren looked as Jessica, who was listening, her face expressionless as the other faces, her body held in the same stiff pose.

'That's something,' Keith said.

'What are you talking about?' his wife snapped.

'It made Jos think.'

They decided, it was touch and go, to laugh, and then they overdid it, slapping knees, emptying glasses, rocking buttocks. Jos led the laughter, most boisterous of the lot, a big man in body and soul. Their energy made Jessica smile, so that Keith winked at her, raised his glass in her direction, nodded friendly to Murren.

'Are you ready?' Murren asked soon. Standing-room only now. She nodded, sweetly enough. 'Home?' he inquired.

Outside the gates she thanked him, did not invite him in. As she wished him good night she placed a hand on his arm, briefly, but she did not look back as she shut the gate, walked to the front door. Immersed in her own concerns, she had immediately, he felt, forgotten him. He could not feel surprise.

14

The false spring did not last; March went out with cold, wind-driven rain.

Murren had heard nothing from Ashley about the London post and wrote, niggling to Stacey, the headmaster, who replied in four lines that the job was his but could not be offered officially. There was nothing either could do about it. This brought him no relief; he wrote again refusing the position in angry words, though he had sense to tear the thing up and burn it.

In March Prudence Mark had rung for an appointment.

She looked ill, drawn about eyes and mouth, and thinner. Now the paleness of hair and skin had been reduced to lack of colour, of health, so that she moved grudgingly, appeared nondescript, without beauty, ten years older.

'I wanted to see you,' she said. She made no attempt to touch or approach him. When he inquired after her health, she answered with a half-dozen well-rehearsed sentences, equally suitable for vicar, brother or greengrocer. 'I wanted to talk to you,' she continued, 'because I've decided not to go on with lessons.' He nodded, made sympathetic noises. 'I'm in no way dissatisfied with you, you understand. I've made tremendous progress. Everybody says so. Even Saint. And Maynard, he was dazzled. He was, honestly. But I've talked it over with Saint.' She had never called her husband that before. 'He thinks it's taking too much out of me, and that's why I've had such trouble with this flu.'

She talked on flatly about her thoughts, her husband's but never mentioned their affair. This woman had launched herself at him, and dragged him on top of her like a hungry navvy with his dinner, without finesse, in tasteless vigour, as if she answered some physical compulsion in her flesh that had little to do with the common courtesies or habits of everyday life. Now, perhaps, influenza had drained her of sexual energy; remembering, he could not believe that, though she sat now, hands clasped, as in a doctor's waiting room.

Her voice whined.

She would not complete this group of lessons, but she would pay for them. That was fair. It was no fault of his. Perhaps he'd be kind enough to make the bill out, and send it. She insisted. In a way she was sorry, and disappointed, that it had to end like this, but health came first, didn't it? She shook hands; now her glove was off, the palm struck clammily cold.

Murren stalked about his house after the interview.

What had happened typified his stay in this place: some success that must be dumped, and then lies, evasions, unmentions. God knows that he'd thought of Prudence Mark; in honest fact he'd not allowed himself to do so. He's taught her with steadily direct brilliance to make up for the unconcerned sexual exchange that would follow. As a human being Prudence was unseen; her moaning declarations of love for him he took as habit, acquired in liaisons, perhaps even in affection, but here groaned off almost muscularly. He had nothing to say in his own favour, but the fact that she had now withdrawn herself so sickly, so dully, left him down in the mouth, reduced, demeaned, a less than human consciousness cluttered and netted by a conscience he'd failed to ignore. Prudence Mark must be somebody. He'd employed her, as he'd play a good piano for practice, sexual scales and *arpeggios*. Who were his friends here? He had to stand aloof from his choirmen, his madrigalists or pupils for the good of music. But he could not understand or give a vaguely rational account of what had happened between him and Prudence. He'd used her, or been used by her, and that was the end; perhaps her admiration for his musicianship had led her to include him on her list, but there was no proof of that. She had happened like a blasphemous act of God, fire or flood, powerful, knocking him reeling. No truth there, as she had appeared each Wednesday for six weeks or thereabouts; not once. He was ashamed or would have been had he spare energy for morality.

Janet Bruce rang to talk about recitals, and he felt frustrated that he could not tell her he would not be here in a year's time to accompany her. She insisted that he came round to dinner, seemed over-pleased with herself. As soon as she opened the door to him, he saw the flashing of diamonds from her engagement ring, and his throat dried so that he said nothing. The Bruce parents purred, successful Scots, knowing what they were about, having it tied up, handing out pre-prandial sherry in glasses that stretched the fingers. Ten minutes later, no word yet said, the fiancé arrived, neatly grey of hair, eyes and suit, and then Janet made the announcement. Murren by this time was ready with his congratulations; Mother Bruce took him aside to explain how delighted they were, how happy Jan was with her Julian. No, they had not known him long, but his father had been a business acquaintaince of daddy's some time. Mrs Bruce crackled like a fire. Och, yaiss. They were a splendid family. Julian had been at Harrow, and was a stockbroker, a thoroughly good boy. 'And all of forty-five,' Murren decided. He had been married before, but, well, he knew how it was, it had come to grief, some years ago. There was a daughter of eighteen, who lived with the father; the mother, well, she was untrustworthy now, unstable. Murren considered Julian's elegantly crossed legs. The man did not smile as he talked to Janet and her father, but seemed preoccupied, intent on solving some problem they had set him. The expression suited him; he was well-preserved, handsome, sure of himself, perhaps even slightly contemptuous of his in-laws. Now, Murren had neither right nor reason in thinking that.

'Is he musical?' he asked Mrs Bruce.

'Well, no-o-o. Not in your sense. But he's interested.'

They sat to dinner, but Julian Talbot-Read ate sparingly, explaining to Murren that he needed to be careful. He drank one glass of white wine, and the hospitable Bruces pressed him to no more; he had trained them. He refused the delicious pudding, but exquisitely, in humorous politeness. When Janet pulled his leg about jogging, he made fun of himself, describing the University of California T-shirt his daughter had provided for wear under his claret track-suit.

'People don't even look at you these days,' he said. 'Everybody's at it.' Janet said she wasn't. Julian eyed her figure with mild irony, but kept quiet. George Bruce coughed out the obvious and pleased nobody.

At the end of the meal, Janet, Julian and Murren retired to the music room to discuss programmes.

'I'll let you smoke,' she said, fondling her fiancé's arm.

'Not in here. This is where you sing.'

'He has two cigars a day. Thin ones. Show him.' He produced a chased case which suited the silvery image of the man, self-deprecating. 'You be happy, Julian. You have your whiff.' He refused, adamant. They delighted each other.

Murren and Janet made a token show of choosing songs, in that she began to list her repertoire, and he to make suggestions of new things she might learn. Julian took third place, though once Jan stretched across to touch his hand for a moment, and he seemed satisfied, but at the end of twenty-five minutes, the girl suddenly stood, snapped shut a copy of Mahler's *Wer hat dies Liedlein erdacht?*, said, 'It's too depressing. I don't know anything.'

Julian slightly creased his forehead, uncrossed his legs.

'Let's go down,' she said. The men stood. She began to apologize to Murren who confessed that he understood what she meant. When he had been delivered to the parents and whisky, Janet and Julian disappeared.

'She's ideally suited,' Mrs Bruce confided. 'We were beginning to worry.' Half an hour of this and Murren slunk home, uncertain of his reaction, but feeling dizzy, pushed off the edge of the globe. His dog-in-manger attitude disgusted him; if he didn't want the woman, nobody else was to have her. He sat in his armchair, it was now ten o'clock, until the small hours, legs out, fidgeting, willing the phone to ring, Stacey, Jessica, the Paynes, Mrs McKie, some conscientious colleague; it crooked silent. The town locked its windows and doors against strangers.

On the next day returning from college he picked up Jessica, by chance, at a bus stop, asked if she knew about Janet's engagement. She did.

'He's been hanging around her for months now,' she said.

'You sound as if you don't approve.'

'They're rolling in money.'

'That's what counts, is it?' She said no more until he questioned her. Her parents were well, and she'd heard nothing of the Wisniewskis. At least she waved as she thanked him.

On the following morning, though he had no lectures he rose early, ate his breakfast in good time, was ready to leave at his usual hour. The weather seemed dull, under a uniformly grey sky, not warm. He waited until past nine when the traffic had thinned, called in at his petrol station and while hanging around in the forecourt decided to make for Derbyshire. He had to be back for a rehearsal at seven, but he could indulge himself, have lunch out in style, forget the world. The little hill towns on the border of the two counties were smoky, busy, garish with torn advertisements, shopping women, bungalow doors. Greyness did not suit these places; they smelt of soap-suds and chips. An ambulance flashed and howled its way through traffic; a policeman pointed at him when he stopped on a double yellow line.

Now the land rose, with fields dark green and the stone walls light, staggering almost cheerfully against the grey-black of the sky. He parked in Matlock to look at shops, bought a newspaper, Iris Murdoch's *The Fire and the Sun*, picture-postcards. It did him good, he thought, hopelessly, to change a five pound note, to be told by a grey-moustached shopkeeper that, appearances to the contrary, it wouldn't rain, to apologize to an old dear whose path he blocked. He sang out loud back in the car.

He drew up outside the pub at the misty head of Eskdale with not a soul in sight. Even the workmen who were enlarging the parking ground, building out on the hillside, were not to be seen. Machinery, heaps of sand and rubble, cement blocks under flapping plastic, scaffolding stood unused, discarded perhaps until better weather. Murren wrapped up, drew on Wellingtons, scarfed his head, crossed the stone stile.

The path was narrow, greasy, uninviting amongst bare twigs, damp boles. He stopped for a moment to stare at the viaduct below, which seemed as deserted as the land, before he stepped on. Now the track descended sharply, and once he slipped, skidded, saved himself by holding on to a tree. He had jarred his wrist, scratched his hand, but he laughed, kicked a great arc of water drops from the long grass. The river rustled below but unemphatically, while above the only noise was the occasional mad dash of a bird in the bushes; his own breathing, his clumping footsteps sounded powerfully. When the path widened with a gentler gradient he began to run, waving his arms in anorak and cagoule, until he reached the river level. Again he met nobody; last time he had been here, in the summer with Jessica, old ladies had stood on the bridge instructing each other, lovers had kissed, a father had larked about in the shallows with his shouting infants waving their fishing nets. Then people had torn paper from chocolates and biscuits, discarded their shoes, opened packets of sandwiches. Now a brown swollen river tumbled, and only wind disturbed the grass, but he enjoyed the dull chill; he knew nobody, and nobody asked him for anything.

He walked along the bank, checking his progress now and then to drop a twig or stone into the swirl of the current. Once he sat on a limestock block which had fallen down the hillside to his right, drumming his heels, picking at fossil forms with his fingernail. Diagonally he made out a patch of fallen rocks, nearly halfway up the slope, decided to climb to it. A dog barked. He began, crosswise, hanging on to grass or trees or outcrops of rock, sometimes able to take three or four steps upward without using his hands. He paused on a yard or two of flat ground by a little tree, ash, he thought, when a voice called.

'Good morning, sir.'

Turning he saw below a young man in anorak and

Wellingtons with a collie. Both lifted faces at the same angle comically, the dog's mouth panting open.

'Making for the top, then?'

'Not really.'

The man began to climb, using his stick, but not his hands, moving strongly upwards, each stride unbalanced, purposive. When he arrived at Murren's elbow he straightened without a sign of breathlessness, a smiling man with thick, wavy hair, who announced himself as warden.

'You have to be a bit careful in these places,' the man warned, 'specially at this time of the year. Over you go, break your leg and there's nobody about. Doesn't take many hours out here to do you in, not with the sort of weather we've been having.' The warden spoke in a friendly way, distantly, not laying down the law. 'There's an old quarry up there, bit of a thing, lot of it filled in, that's why there's so much of this about.' He gently toed a half-buried rock.

'Is it interesting?' Murren asked.

'Not really.'

Murren bent to pick up a polished piece of darkish rock.

'That's odd,' he said. 'Unusual.'

'Chert,' the warden answered. 'Are you interested in geology, then?' He didn't wait for an answer. 'Come on, I'll go up with you.'

Murren struggling, slipping, tearing at grass-clumps as he moved zigzag up the hill, paused for breath, watching the lazy progress of the other man. At the final moment, when Murren heaved himself alongside his companion on the edge of the quarry, his knees trembled, his chest thumped so that he stood, eyes closed on orange darkness, incapable of speech.

The quarry was small, had been abandoned early, and its outlines were disguised by earth and rock falls now covered with brambles, puny bent trees. At the side where they stood together the ground was littered with small irregular chunks of limestone, greasily wet, grass-patched.

'Plenty of holes in there,' the warden said, 'to fall in, and die in.' Murren asked questions. Yes, they'd had more than enough rescue work last winter, and a death. 'Exposure. Woman taking the dog for a walk. Local. Ought to have known better.'

Murren found comfort standing there, posing, one hand to a tree-trunk, listening to the Midland voice. The warden had been a regular soldier, an infantry sergeant, had served in Germany and Northern Ireland, and had applied for this job out in the wilds not quite certain what would come of it.

'We talked about it. My dad had been a farm-worker up here, but my wife was a townee, a London girl. We used to argue, that's not the word, about the solitude. There's social life galore in the forces if that's what you want. Mark you, I didn't think I stood an earthly; there were so many applying. The whole world wants to run away.'

'And how has it worked out?'

'This last three months has been bad, weather-wise, and yet the kids haven't missed one single day's school. I'd run 'em down in the Land-Rover to the bus pick-up point. It worked out a treat. They've enjoyed every minute.'

'And your wife?'

'She's been busy. She redecorated the house, done some carpentry. She's kept herself occupied. She's got her own little car once the weather picks up. It's next winter when the crunch comes.'

'You've enjoyed it?'

'I didn't know I was alive until I came up here.'

'Will it do, though, when you're fifty, sixty?'

'Don't see why not. There's no hurry in this job.' He turned, spoke authoritatively. 'Nothing much for us here, is there? Let's go down, shall we?'

They made for the road, Murren with some difficulty. On his arrival Murren blurted out, as if the physical exercise had forced the confession out of him, 'I've been lonely living in the middle of a town.'

The warden nodded, went through a series of brisk questions: job, happy, married, contacts, recreations; the father-sergeant's sympathetic routine. Murren answered, but rapport had vanished. Here a boring man did his duty and not well. The bold spirit who leapt from one dangerous life to another putting out, risking children, wife, peace of mind had altered himself into a barrack-trained administrator whose kindliness was as bogus as his square-bashing rant.

Murren wished him good-day.

'Don't go too far off the road, sir.' Murren promised. 'Spring's not here yet.' With a shrill whistle to the dog the warden made away, leaving Murren disappointed in himself in that he'd uttered his complaint. It was not the nature of the grouse that riled him, but rather the fact that the few minutes' clamber, the warden's obvious proficiency, the brief history of success had led him to come out with sentences which had been answered with banality, sincere banality. Wordsworth might have seen it differently, but Murren had demeaned himself. Five minutes' brisk walking lifted his spirit as the path rose from the river.

He did not wish to travel far, but the punch of his footsteps into the road seemed too cheerful to stop. When he finally halted, the river was perhaps fifty feet below hidden by the growth of trees and bushes on the steep bank. Murren did not waste time, but wheeled about, tracked off towards his car. Though he met no one and stopped twice at river level to trail a stick in the water and once to step on to a large stone above the bubbles, the road seemed shorter, less adventurous, even dull in its last uphill strait of slimy mud. As he turned to look back mist hung thinly round the trees of the valley. He picked at the muck on his Wellingtons with a stone, changed them, made his way into the pub.

The bar, a dun, sober, sombre place matched the weather; landlord and two customers looked him over. Murren asked for beer and beef sandwiches, dragged a stool under him, supped his ale, caught the eye of a man in a cloth cap, wished him good afternoon.

'Been down the dale, then?' the man said, and waved a hand at the clay marks on Murren's trousers above the line of his Wellington boots.

'I walked nearly to the other end and back.'

'Not many down there today?'

'No. I just saw the warden.'

'That's the new chap,' the second customer volunteered. 'They've done that little farmhouse at Outhwaite up for him.'

'Bit bleak out there.' Cloth cap. Three concentrated on beer. There was an interrogatory shout from elsewhere. 'It's you. Do you want mustard on, he wants to know?'

Murren called back, and they grinned. When the landlord returned with the food, it was thought worth while to mention that the young fellow had seen the warden.

'Bit off his track, in't he?' said the landlord.

'He said someone had died recently from exposure,' Murren answered. All perked up.

'That'd be that Mrs Taylor. Bit of an odd 'un, any road.'

'Wasn't down this end, either. Further up on the moors.'

'What's it like up there in winter?' Murren asked.

'Bloody grim, I'll tell you.' Cloth cap.

'His dad worked on a farm up there. Pretty well killed him in the end, didn't it, Bert?'

'That and one or two other things.'

The landlord, sauntering back from the second bar, joined in the laughter.

'You come up for the scenery?' Cloth cap asked. Murren agreed. 'You can never get used to it. Seems to change, radically,' he put his hand on the bar at the word, 'every five minutes. Of course, you're high up; you see clouds; they come down on you sometimes.' Bert made his way out to the lavatory. 'Warden's brother committed suicide,' Cloth cap said, lowering his voice though the door was closed. 'Disaster on disaster, and insurance inadequate. You need to be tough, but you need some capital to start.'

'Is there a living to be made up there?' Murren asked.

'I should say so. These days. Just about.' He appealed to the landlord.

'Well, yes. If you're prepared to work yourself silly.'

When Bert returned Murren bought drinks and talk blossomed. These two had worked in towns, one in Derby, one in Chesterfield, both were artisan-engineers, and had returned to their birthplace to potter in gardens or at lathes. Neither recommended village life for the uninitiated.

'Take this pub. On Bank Holiday in the summer

it's full to the doors, and the fields for miles about are littered with crisp-bags and lolly-sticks. It's like hell.'

'And not only at Bank Holidays. All through the good weather. Boy Scouts and Sunday school treats and geography outings and bangers that can just about make it here for the half day. The air's black with petrol fumes.'

'You haven't got a car, then?'

'You don't live in a village without a car if you can help it. Oh, no.'

'And nowadays there's the hang-gliding lot. A bit higher up from here, on Bealside, on the moors. Up there by the score. A bloody marvellous quick way of killing yourself. I was talking to a nurse down there at the hospital in Chesterfield, had to go down myself the other day, bit of chest trouble, and she said this brigade are brought in with broken legs and cracked pelvises and God knows what, but the one thing they all want to do is get well and up in the air again.'

'It must be a marvellous sensation,' Murren said.

'What, breaking your bloody neck?'

They inquired about Murren's work, and when they heard he was a musician, they immediately shouted for the landlord.

'Here's the gentleman for you,' they said, laughing.

The landlord pulled a wry face. There was a piano he'd acquired, if Murren had ten minutes to spare. The customers laughed again, as the landlord called out to his wife, asking her to take charge of the bar. Then the four men went upstairs. To Murren it was like walking off stage. The pub lounge was dull enough with its brown paint and smallish windows, but the lights, the mirrors, the glittering bottles were suddenly changed to austerity, uncarpeted treads, dusty objects in corners, walls with peeling paper, stretches of dull damp.

'We don't use this part much,' the landlord apologized. 'We've got a scheme to have a dining room, but it'll entail a hell of a lot of work, and that means outside labour, the wife and me can't do it ourselves, and an hell of an expenditure.'

'Won't the brewery help?' Murren.

'Well, yes. But they want a return for their money. Now neither me nor the wife's willing to give our life-blood to pay them back, that I can tell you. If I was younger, or my children had showed any interest, then I might. Now it's cloud-cuckoo land. We talk about it.' He laughed, and phlegm rattled. At most he'd be forty-five, but he spoke like an old man, suspicious and whacked. 'Here we are.' He fiddled at a door-knob and swore. 'It's the bloody wife. She'd lock the flamin' lavatories up if she had her way.' He cursed again, carrying his clump of keys over to a window. 'I keep telling her, and I waste my breath, "There's nowt in there anybody'll pinch", but it's no use. Wrong bloody thing.' He slouched back to the light, made another selection, tried them, succeeded. The four pressed into a room of a curious shape in that the side walls converged into a roughly vertical line. The end where they entered was spacious, and lit by a wide window by which stood a grand piano.

'Here it is.' The landlord slapped the top, fiddled with the lid. 'If she hasn't locked this bogger.' Again they all laughed as the search began amongst jangling keys.

Though the piano lay thick with dust, the surface shone a gingery colour beautifully mottled with a violence of grain, like smoke. 'Reminds me a bit of the fancy way they decorated doors when I was a lad,' Bert observed. The landlord laid back the lid from the slightly yellowed keyboard. An English piano, Edwardian. 'Give us a tune, then.'

Murren sat, stroked a chord of C major, which was out of tune, and flat from concert pitch. He continued with slow chords, a marching procession, together, bass, treble, rather metallic, the odd note missing. He rattled a scale or two, up, down, at speed, then a flight of major-minor *arpeggios*; the three watched him, intense as a male voice choir waiting for entries. Now he moved into the slow movement of the Mozart K 488, F sharp minor; sadness clanked from the old notes of the piano and he looked up at his audience. The landlord leaned on the lid; the others stood upright. Murren buckled, bustled with Brahms, the fourth Handel variation, until the room rocked with the flying octaves, cracked but fierce, knocking hell out of the cobwebbed corners.

'That's going some,' Bert said.

'Give us,' the other asked, grave as a chapel stewart at intimations, 'some Johann Sebastian Bach.' All four pulled faces; the pianist began on the D major, Book I, at speed, a divine sewing machine to which the men nodded their heads.

'Do you want the fugue?' he asked.

" 'Finished the soft preluding/And then the fugue began," ' Bert quoted, misquoted.

'How did you know that?' Murren was taken aback. He'd learnt the lines, correctly, years before, from his father.

' "S. S. Wesley Enters Heaven". The headmaster made us all learn it, didn't he, Horace?'

'Knocker Robinson. He did.'

'What's it like?' The landlord represented business,

without time to waste. Murren opened the lid, delighted with the Victorian poem, blew dust, peered inside.

'You'd need to spend a lot of money.' He pointed at worn felts, demonstrated the uncertainty of the action, flicked at broken and rusty wires.

'Is it worth it?'

'That's up to you.' Murren explained why he was not interested in this instrument as a piano, but remarked on the beauty of the case, the interest in auction rooms of pieces from this period. 'Make inquiries. Pay a pound or two to get the local music dealers up from Chesterfield or Buxton or Derby. They'll give you an estimate. They might even pay a bit to take it off your hands. Not much, mind you.'

The two companions touched the woodwork, lamented the demise of craftsmanship, diffident pensioners in a Christmas sketch, eyes down, thumbnails measuring. The landlord lowered the top, asked Murren's permission before closing the lid.

'You'd better lock it,' Horace said. They sniggered.

On the way downstairs the landlord gave an outline of the lifting of the piano from street to room. Back in the bar he pulled in their glasses, replenished them 'to wash t'dust out of your throat'.

'It belonged to some woman he was sweet on,' Bert whispered. 'In Sheffield. Knew her when he was younger. Left it him in her will. He told us all about it.'

'Why? Was he interested in music?'

They screwed their faces in their anxiety not to let the landlord know they talked about him.

'No. Don't think so. But a grand piano was unusual in their circumstances. It would pretty well fill, it did, he told us, the little front room it was in.'

'It cost him a packet to get it here. Wife wasn't pleased, but he made out it might be useful in one of the bars.'

'Sentiment, really,' Horace, face screwed. Murren was almost certain they were pulling his leg. 'Young love's dream.'

'How did the lady come to have the piano?' Murren asked.

'You have me there. Little terrace house. I know. I went with him. Probably come down in the world. You've heard what they say: clogs to clogs in three generations. My grandfather lived in just such a place, and there was a family next door to him had lorded it in a mansion, and blued the lot.'

'Wasn't the grand piano the first thing to go, though?' Bert asked.

'So they said. That's why I'd never have one.'

They roared at this, so that the landlord reappeared for an explanation. Murren refused more beer saying he had to drive.

'Where do you come from, then?' Bert asked him. 'What part of the world?' Murren, misunderstanding, mentioned Beechnall, St Botolph's College, but they pressed for his origins.

'Nowhere, really. London, I suppose.'

'That's nowhere if any place is.' Horace. When Murren explained his father lived and worked in France, the two talked of service in the Expeditionary Force, Dunkirk, holidays, the inevitably missing cup of tea. These were ordinary men.

'I've got no roots,' he complained.

'Makes not a ha'porth of difference. I could live anywhere,' Horace said.

'Why did you come back, then?'

'Chance. Visiting. Saw a house going cheap that I

liked. In his case here, his dad's cottage that he used for holidays. Wasn't the people.'

Murren left them, puzzled, drove out and parked on the moors at Bealside. Up there the wind blew keen. He wandered about, staggering from path to hillock, to rock face, to bleak heath, to deserted road, to cold crest. He could see little beyond, say, a hundred yards for in spite of the sharp breeze mist smothered the distant valleys. He crouched in a sheltering cleft, saw it was three-thirty and decided he'd had enough; thankfully he made for his civilization, the evening's rehearsal.

15

On Easter Saturday Murren listened to a concert in his own church, and took pleasure. Four young artists, ex-Royal Northern College, played the G major *Haydn* Quartet of Mozart, then the first Rasumovsky, and after the interval exploded into Verdi.

'Good? These players?' the vicar at the break. A big man, he seemed on the defensive about music, as if he were both enthusiastic and deaf. Murren had worked with him for eighteen months; they conferred at least once a week, had taken meals together, once had a holiday by the seaside with the choir under canvas, and yet the man was as unknown to him as one of the alabaster knights in the nave. 'What sort of living do they make?' That was the person, with a question for all seasons, but what he'd do with the answer set a second poser.

'They've had a success recently with a recording of

two of the Shostakovitch quartets, and that'll do them no harm. But they won't make much yet.'

'Even though they're so gifted?'

Murren looked down at the vicar's shoes, which were polished, thin-soled, black, hardly a support for so large a body.

'The second violin and the viola are married.'

'Ah, now. Is that an advantage, would you say?' The vicar's conversations were interrupted, as always, by his becks, smiles, hand-raisings to people he knew. Murren wondered if he liked the man, or trusted him. In spite of the southern standard accent, the good public school, Oxford, the clergyman seemed irrevocably provincial, bounded by small subscriptions, inconclusive meetings, inadequate heating; the pomp of Sunday services did not affect him. He preached his ten minutes of banality, flattened the prose of prayer-book or authorized version, but heartily shook hands with all.

Murren wondered what Sallis's reaction would be when he announced that he'd no longer be here after August. The fellow ought to guess that the town wouldn't hold a live-wire long; Murren grimaced at his self-description, wishing he believed it. The vicar's wife relieved her husband who abandoned his inattentive organist as he left his church, expecting it there, unchanged, when he returned. Mrs Sallis was different; beautiful still in middle age, she dressed well, private money about, and regarded Murren as valuable property. She knew that John Pendleton, the assistant, kept the choir happy, and Murren free from drudgery, but it was the organist who had regalized the services, kept contact with TV and radio, hung her church high on the map. Hilary Sallis understood business, kept the fabric in order, begged enough to keep the paint bright, the brass cleaned, the carpet-work respectable, but outside the town, St Michael and All Angels meant music. She approved, made a fuss of their celebrity.

'When are you leaving us, then?' she demanded now, taking him aback. He'd mentioned to no one the possibility of his return to London. He shrugged. She smiled, distantly. 'I met Penny Stacey at a party. She told me.' The headmaster's wife.

'They'd better get a move on, then, offering me the job.'

'They've not done so?'

'Not officially.'

'It's been mooted?' Ironic. 'She seemed certain.' Anger seethed mildly in his fingertips.

'You think I should have mentioned it to Hilary?'

'I have, if you haven't.' Short, this woman, sharp.

'Nothing may come of it,' he said. She sneered.

'You don't believe that any more than I do.'

Jean Sallis stared at him, with large, silvery grey eyes, despising him for a liar, he thought. She could please her bloody self.

'Congratulations,' she was saying, 'by the way, on your Easter anthem.'

'What about it?'

'It's on the radio twice next week. Tomorrow morning, Southwark Cathedral, Wednesday evensong, St George's, Windsor. Don't tell me you didn't know that, either.'

'I didn't.'

'It's in the *Radio Times*.' His mood had changed to irrational pleasure.

'Ashley must have handed copies round his friends.'

'He's influential, this Dr Ashley, Penny said.' They'd

given Murren a going over, clearly. 'Is it published yet?'

'Boosey's have accepted it.'

'You're a talented young man, aren't you?'

What she needed was a great thwack across her bottom. The audience shuffled back to seats for Verdi's operatic energies.

'Who are we going to get to replace you?' she asked.

'You'd do worse than John Pendleton.'

'He's a nice man,' she answered, cut-glass, turning her cold shoulder to leave him.

At the end of the concert the quartet decided against a drink with him; they seemed prickly as he felt, unable to grasp how well they'd done, anxious to be home.

'Like playing in the open air,' the cellist said. 'You need the Salvation Army in there.'

'The accoustics are superb,' Murren comforted. They did not know him, of him, and mooched northwards disgruntled.

Murren's spirits sagged. In the empty church some rearrangement was being made for the morrow's service, and humdrum voices laughed or queried, where only ten minutes earlier musical eloquence had ruled. That was music; an hour in delight, then people pushing chairs, finding buses, slamming doors. Over by the main door he noticed Walter Payne and Jessica, obviously waiting for him; he raised a hand to them.

At that moment the vicar came towards him, pushing through an untidy row of chairs. He stumbled, steadied himself, face red; though a big man, Sallis was by no means clumsy.

'Oh, James.' He used the first name, as one tries a word in a rusty language. His large left hand he held upwards; the right thumb was tucked into the belt of his cassock. 'I wanted a word. You're going to leave us, I hear.'

'It's by no means settled.' He offered succinct sentences about the position.

'I see. I see.' The vicar made remarkable shapes with his lips, shifted awkwardly from foot to foot, pulled hard at his belt with both hands. It was obvious to Murren that Mrs Sallis had insisted that her husband make some move this evening. 'When will you know?'

Murren shrugged, spoke sullenly. 'It it suits your book,' he said, 'you'd better have my resignation now.'

'Suppose you don't go?'

Murren waggled shoulders more grotesquely. 'You'll have a new organist. My presence or absence won't matter. I'm sorry if I'm upsetting your plans, but I've not even put an application in yet. Not that that makes any difference. Perhaps I should have warned you. I prefer certainties.'

'We don't want to lose you, James. Nor stand in your way. Not that we can.'

'Thank you.' Murren felt sorry, would have shaken hands.

'You've not been altogether happy here, have you?' Heavy breathing. 'I don't mean at St Michael's. In the city. You're always going back up to London. Not that I blame you.' This was true of the first six months, but not now.

'I haven't been to town since the beginning of October,' he answered.

'Oh.' A squeal; his wife's evidence needed support. 'Oh.' Back to clerical rationalism, to himself, 'Yes. Yes. You're the brightest adjunct to our diadem, you know.' The red face creased into a smile. 'We would not want to lose you.'

'Thanks. You've always got John Pendleton.'

'He's not you, James.' The vicar drew himself up tall. 'You'll let us know now, won't you? As soon as anything definite's settled?'

'Yes. And I'm sorry about this.' He did not blame Stacey, Mrs Stacey, Ashley, Mrs Sallis, God. 'This is a good place.'

The vicar nodded, solemnly, head wagging on huge shoulders. The squeal of moving chairs became audible again, the orders, the queries.

'Some people waiting. . . .' Murren began. Now the vicar apologized, glad to do so.

'I felt I had to have a word with you. We appreciate what you've done in this town. We shan't forget you.' He could continue like this for the next ten minutes.

As Murren marched the aisle, anxious not to delay the Paynes further, he felt anger; father and daughter looked pinched, piddling, to be swept by.

'Hello. Didn't realize you were waiting for me.'

'We thought you'd be here. We tried to ring you at home.' Father Payne.

'Easter Sunday tomorrow. There's a lot of last-minute work.'

'Are you doing your new anthem?' Jessica asked. 'We saw it in the *Radio Times*.' How anybody saw and remarked that small print presented problems.

'No. Not here.'

'Would you come back home with us?' Payne said.

'I'm a bit tired. I was up late last night, and I've a big day.'

'We shan't keep you long. There are two things.'

'Can't you tell them to me now?' They had not

moved outside the church yet. The old man glanced at his daughter.

'Mrs Wisniewski's dead,' Jessica stated. Then, it seemed louder. 'Mrs.'

'When?' Murren asked.

'Last week. Suddenly. She died of a stroke.'

'And what's happened to the old man?'

'They took him into hospital. I saw the daughter, and she says he won't last beyond a day or two.'

'I'm sorry.'

They paused there. Suddenly Walter Payne made a move, a scare-crow flap of arms to usher them outdoors. Jessica and Murren took to the path together, under the huge black shadow of the church, alongside the gravestones; the father brought up the dismal rear. Their footsteps clapped; voices were silent; the few guiding lamps darkened the sky. When they had reached the gate at the top of the steps, Murren asked, 'Do they want us to visit him?'

'No,' Jessica said, still descending, not looking back.

'By the way she spoke, he might very well be dead by now.' Payne seemed anxious to propitiate, but he reached the bottom of the steps before Murren, who had thrust his hands deep into his pockets. Why did these people wait about to hand him this information? And yet he could not shake off the sense that they were right, that it was his concern.

'Was it expected? Mrs Wisniewski's death?' He tiptoed the last three steps.

'No.' Jessica answered, a neat silhouette. 'The daughter found her in bed, when she went over. It must have happened in the night. She was dead. They had a post mortem.'

'Are you coming with us?' Payne asked.

'You said there were two things,' Murren answered, awkwardly.

'It's Pat,' he said. 'She's in trouble again.'

'It's about money,' Jessica added, voice near giggling.

'We thought you'd give us half an hour,' Payne said, 'talk to us. But it doesn't matter. Never mind. You've plenty of your own to think about.'

'Yes,' Murren answered. 'I might be leaving here, going to London.'

'When?' Jessica, sharply, startled.

'For September, if it happens.'

'What to do?'

'Back to St John's.'

'Isn't that where you came from?' Payne asked. 'What's the advantage in that?'

Murren did not reply but straightening his coat, looked about him.

'Where are you parked?' They showed him. 'All right. I'll follow you home.'

'Will you go in James's car?' Payne asked his daughter.

'It doesn't matter.' She shadowed her father.

Patricia appeared in the hall as they let themselves in. She looked untidy, flustered, ill-tempered, but quickly modified her attitude to suit the visitor. She did not, however, stay downstairs with them when they sat to coffee.

'How was Mrs McKie?' Murren asked.

'Calm, really. Just said what had to be said.'

'It puts a lot on her shoulders,' Payne spoke sociably, time-filling. 'But I'd think she'd manage, don't you, Jessica?'

'And there's nothing I can do?'

'What do you think you could?' Jessica, rudely.

'Visit her, offer sympathy, hand her a bunch of flowers.'

'You do that, then.' Acid.

Payne stirred his coffee vigorously, embarrassed perhaps at his daughter's sour sharpness. He poked at his short moustache, coughed, encouraged Murren towards the biscuit barrel.

'Patricia's other brother died, the oldest. It was expected; he's been a creaking gate. But he left my wife a thousand pounds, quite good that, because he'd children and grandchildren of his own to be provided for. But, and here's the snag, he'd left Mary Underwood her thousand. George's widow. Man you found dead.'

Jessica laughed, shifting her chair, scornfully dismissing the outcome.

'And, my word. She played pop about it. You'd think Mary had walked in here and stolen the money. Now I know she doesn't like the woman, and they had a row when she was over here, but it's no concern of hers if Jack leaves her a bit.'

'Did he know her, Mary?'

'Not except by name. So far as we know. But he altered his will recently, since George died, to include her.'

'Why should he do that?'

'You have me there. He'd perhaps met her, or been favourably impressed by something he'd heard. Perhaps didn't like to think of his brother's ex-wife living in poverty. Not that a thousand's anything. Wouldn't get you a decent second-hand car.'

'I'm sorry,' Murren said. 'Does she seem to be getting over it?'

'She never will.' Jessica said. 'She doesn't want to.'

'Come, Jess. That's not fair.' Her father spoke softly.

'It's nothing to do with money. She's looking round for excuses to blow her top because she's off her head.'

'She's having a difficult time.'

'I'll say. And she's seeing everybody else gets one with her.'

'Now, Jess.'

'Something happened to me,' the girl spoke quietly, but fierce, 'something tragic. But she's not, she's. . . .'

'Her brother committed suicide.'

'She had nothing to do with him. She didn't care.'

'You can't say that.'

'I can because it's true. Because she's got her nerves tangled, we all have to suffer. You most. I don't know why you put up with it.'

'That'll do,' the father ordered drily.

'You won't have a word against her. She can't go wrong, can she? She's as near mad as can be, but you won't see it, or say anything.'

'Mr Murren doesn't want to hear all this,' Payne said.

'You asked him up. To hear what was wrong with us. Well, I'll tell him. She's wrong with us.'

Jessica's face had paled almost to greenness, while her knuckles lumped into white. She was standing like one swept with a gust of hail-stones, shoulder foward. Payne, sighing, made a gesture towards Murren, a hand of surrender. Murren cringed back into his chair.

'Anybody for more coffee?' Payne said, in the end. His own cup was almost full. No one answered; Jessica sniffed, hugely, defying convention. Payne swigged his own, gallantly, raising the cup.

'Get me another, Jess, will you, please?'

The girl took a step towards him, then suddenly swung both arms, with fists clenched, outwards. Her face rumpled; she seemed stopped after the one social pace by a giant force of electricity that held her there, shattered but whole, in a killing current. Her mouth opened and shut, soundlessly, until she spoke in a thin howl, a squeal.

'Get your bloody own.'

Still she didn't shift, stood shaking there, before she wheeled, ran out, slamming the door with an intense violence that shook the walls, pained the eardrums. Payne sat with his hands on the table. After perhaps two long, barren minutes, Patricia opened the door.

'What was that crash?' she asked.

'Jessica. She's upset.'

'You've been at her again, have you? You might know what a state she's in. Now we all have to suffer again. Oh, Walter, I wish you'd think sometimes.' She heaved an immense theatrical sigh, and went out leaving the door slightly ajar. Both men looked in that direction, Murren with all sense blotted from his head, so that when he glanced back he was slightly startled to find Payne had deserted his chair. Only the coffee cup and dregs marked the place.

Murren had difficulty moving his head to locate Payne, but finally came on to him by the sideboard where the man stood, arms out against the doors, spider-fashion. His face was broken, a baked apple, something like that of his daughter a few moments before, and on one cheek, from the left eye, a huge tear blinked. Again, like Jessica, Payne did not move, was held by an immense force before a crack-up. He appeared neat, as always, except that his palms propped him by friction, did not allow of collapse. The creases in his trousers, the shine on his shoes, the fastened buttons of his coat signalled the man of substance, the retired manager, the ex-colonel. The twisted face and the bruised humps of his outline gently indicated his tragedy.

Murren, distressed, could not tell whether the other man was breathing. No sound broke from the open mouth. There in the frozen pain Nigel Brockless killed himself again, Patricia soured into madness, Jessica defied him in her despair. In this house, in this man, gall with sorrow seethed. Abashed, Murren dropped his eyes and hunched against the cold no radiator could dispel.

He was aroused by a flash of white, and, glancing up, found Walter Payne, still with his back to the sideboard, mopping his face with a clean handkerchief. Now the body was no longer crooked, but lithe, prepared to move, master of its own movements. Payne came forward, tucking the handkerchief away, and picked up his crock.

'We'll have that second round,' he said. His voice trembled. Murren swilled down his coffee, and stumbling up held out his cup.

'Do you want any help?' he asked.

'Leave it to me.'

Payne went out, glad to be away. Murren walked over to the polished walnut of the sideboard and touched it, exploring, found nothing but wood. He could hear no sound from the rest of the house. This was a beautiful room, with red velvet curtains, a flame-red carpet, warm chair- and settee-covers against white walls, dark wood, and the ornate, golden frame of a sombre Victorian woodland scene above the grey stone of hearth and fireplace. Someone had taken care, in choice, in maintenance. The bric-a-brac indicated liveliness, even mischievous taste; the other pictures startled, two Modigliani reproductions and a Chagall. No dust blurred; each piece of furniture was placed to advantage, to make room, to harmonise with the cleanly walls or the bright books. The owners did not go short of money, used it with judgement, got value.

The host marched in, with fresh coffee, different china. The men, smiling now if nervously, raised their cups facetiously, seriously wishing each other health. Payne obviously prepared himself to speak, fidgeting, watching for opportunity. Seeing none, he spoke, pushed his nose in.

'I ought not to have involved you in our difficulties,' he began. It sounded formal, a sentence from a Latin text-book, but it worked on the hearer, who sat forward in his chair. 'We're in trouble. You can see that. The house is divided against itself.' He looked up as if apologizing for melodrama. 'Sometimes it's unbearable, but a visitor cheers things for the moment. You see, it's. . . .' He crossed his legs, laced his fingers as he must have done often behind his manager's desk when he needed to explain why he could not recommend a loan or prolong an overdraft. 'To put it plainly, Jessica thinks my wife is as she is to get into the limelight. She thinks that Pat, seeing the sympathy that Jess attracted at the death of Nigel Brockless, became jealous and tried her own brand of disaster.'

Payne straightened legs and trouser-creases.

'Is there any truth in it?' Murren asked.

'Who's to say? Certainly my wife likes to be at the centre of affairs.'

'That sounds as if you believe Jessica?'

'Look,' Payne answered. 'Jess thinks it's deliberate,

put on, acted. I don't. But I wouldn't deny that that's perhaps how it started. But Pat is in a dangerously unstable state and was so well before this, the, the accident. That's why I've insisted she's spent time with the doctor.'

'Can he do anything?'

'He'll listen. He's very good. But he has only a limited time to give her. He prescribes sensibly, and now he's suggesting that she sees a psychiatrist. Privately.'

'Will she?'

'She's considering it. In Jess's language, she's tempted. It's like you and me, it's somebody to talk to. But there's hell between them. No holds barred. Pat will say straight out that Jess is well rid of Nigel, that he was useless. Oh, she'll add soft soap about pity if she remembers. Jess will listen, white-faced, and then she'll go for her. She's cruel-tongued, I'll tell you. Before long one or the other is in tears.'

'Can't you stop them?'

'Interfere or sit out, I'm in the wrong. It's blood they want.' Murren grimaced in surprise at the phrase. 'I can barely cope. I've seriously thought of suicide. Once, at least. There seemed nothing else at the time. But tonight I felt better, was convinced Jess did. That's why we turned out for the concert and asked you to come up. I was sure it would do good.' Payne shifted shoulderblades listlessly. 'I'd thought she'd shown signs of coming round just recently. Nothing much. But she's young, ought to be resilient. She'll get over it.'

'That's by no means certain.'

'No. But I can't work on any other assumption, can I? She's barely twenty-one. If she's not. . . . Oh, I know she'll be scarred.' He gave up, and the pair sat handling their cups. 'You'll be pleased to leave here, this town, will you?' He spoke flatly.

'Yes.'

'Ummh, ye', ye', suppose so. Is it you or the place?'

'Well, there'll be a lot more opportunities of the sort I want if I go back to London.'

'This is a backwater?' Payne stared down at his coffee, like an actor picking sense from a pronounced word.

'Yes, it is. People have been very good to me. . . .'

'But it's all going on up there?' Payne twinkled now.

'You don't come from this part of the world, do you?' Murren asked.

'No. Home counties. But I've been here over thirty years. Joanne, my second, was born up here. I've moved round the district. My army service stood me in good stead, sharpened my promotion. It's suited me.'

'And you like it here?'

'Yes. For my sort of life I'd say it was ideal. I don't feel a stranger. The status of a bank manager's changed, since I started, and his sort of responsibilities. But, no, this town's good enough for me.'

'That implies criticism of. . . .'

'It does not.' Payne spoke sharply. He'd a reputation for speaking his mind. 'I'm ordinary. I was lucky in the army, in the right place at the right time, and got bumped up to colonel. Did me no harm with the bank. You're a somebody, James, without accidents. Perhaps you need London, I don't know. You could have the best choir in the world up here, and nobody would hear about it. It's too far away from regular large audiences, is it? I don't know. I'm guessing.'

Payne now spoke with zest, as if conversation did him good. 'You go back there. Seize your chance with both hands while there's time.'

'I've not been offered the job yet.'

'Why's that?'

For a second time that night Murren outlined his predicament. Payne, now much at ease, hands deep in trouser pockets, legs outspread, listened sympathetically.

'Tell you what,' he said. 'You won't hear that anthem of yours tomorrow, will you? I'll put it on tape. I'm quite the expert.' Murren, touched, thanked him. That sentence filled in acres of soul-fen. 'Another thing. I can't help thinking about those Polish people. The mother came from a good family. Did you know that? Landowners. And we talk about being lost up here. Makes me ashamed.'

'You mean. . . .'

'I mean we're going wild over our troubles. But there's that woman, one of the landed gentry, stuck out in a country where she can't speak the language, knowing her husband's dying and her daughter married to an illiterate coal-miner. What must it have been like? She must have felt ill to go off like that all at once. They say you can only die for yourself. That's what she did. And in Polish in a country where nobody speaks the language.'

Payne seemed small, forceful, insistent, a colonel.

'Compared with that woman,' he continued, 'you and I have nothing to complain about.'

'Well, we don't know enough about her capability of feeling.'

'One gets used to pain, you mean, or degradation or change?'

'Roughly.' They laughed at the word and Payne

relaxed, determined to push the argument no further. When Murren said he must go, his host made no attempt to detain him.

With overcoat on in the hall, Murren asked,

'What will happen? Here? Next?'

'I shall lock up and go to bed. Too late for the workshop.'

'And Jessica, Patricia?'

'Pat'll come up before midnight. We shan't see Jess till the morning.'

'I'm sorry.'

'It's not your fault. And anyway, she's getting better. Don't you worry. I'll make a tape for you tomorrow.'

They shook solemn hands, and on his way home Murren went out of his way to pass the Wisniewskis' house, which stood dark. No one walked the street, this Saturday night. He felt worn out, hurried back to watch football on the television, found it over. Nothing surprised him; nothing was unbearable.

16

Murren, up with the lark, enjoyed Easter Day.

Nothing lifts better than cold, morning sunshine on pillars, on the lighted stone, under towering perpendicular arches. And below, in their dozens but dwarfed against the dazzling spaces of light alternating with bars of darkness, were the daffodils, smelling of spring, brought in and out of March winds to stand for a few days of resurrection before wilting in the wire litter-baskets. These flowers were alive, leaves deeply green, the heads sun-bright.

The choir pleased him; the boys' voices struck like arrows, shot straight, and at the last minute were bent by the curved stone, the echoing chambers above. The men sang fully, deeply, but the boys hammering Christian truths triumphed today, out-pierced the organ reeds, soared and reduced the pedals' ferocious rumble. Hymns, anthems shone, matched sunshine.

Before matins the vicar had insisted that the organist came home with him for lunch.

'We'll give you an armchair, and a radio, in a warm place and you can sleep all afternoon.'

'You must think I'm idle.'

'On the contrary. You need more rest than you allow yourself.'

Mrs Sallis had been at her husband again, almost certainly blaming him for discourtesy the night before. Murren felt sorry for the man. They drove away in the vicar's car, in the quiet of wind-brushed streets; the sun played brilliantly outside the dining-room windows on to the clumps of spring flowers in the lawn.

They ate well. Mrs Sallis said they had touched neither meat nor wine in Lent, surprising Murren who had thought them middle-of-the-road modernists, with more important concerns than these observations and penances. Sallis looked as if he'd been reared on beef-steak. Murren insisted on washing up, but was ordered into a panelled room, oak darkened, which for all its radiators and an electric fire seemed chilly. Perhaps he was catching a cold. In any case he could, would, not sleep in a stranger's house in spite of the red wine and heaped plates. He leafed through a pile of books, Hebrew psalms, *Emma*, Lawrence of Arabia,

Encyclopaedia of Garden Flowers, Larkin's *High Windows*, walked to the window to watch sparrows, stuck hands deep into pockets, whistled soundlessly. Not uncomfortable, not too warm, he found nothing of interest in books or room. He fidgeted for an hour until Mrs Sallis interrupted him.

'I wonder if you would look at Jane's harmony exercise?'

Daughter and manuscript book were produced. Murren corrected the obvious errors and then suggested improvements, was led to a piano so that the amateurs could hear what he'd written. Mrs Sallis grew effusive; Jane said nothing, preferring, he guessed, to pass or fail 'A'-level on her own. He played a snatch of Schubert before the doorbell interrupted them; the memsahib's parents, a sister, three nieces had arrived for tea and evensong.

The meal began at four-thirty at two tables, both in an uproar of conversation. The vicar romped, agile with tongue as with knife and fork, drawing delighted rebukes from his mother-in-law: 'Oh, Hilary, you are outrageous.' Murren next to the taciturn Jane found her younger sister pressing his leg with hers under the table, and sat still. One of the nieces dropped and smashed a plate; the older ladies were constantly on their feet pouring tea, fetching some forgotten item, noisily energetic.

After half-past six these would sit straight in church, occupying two pews solemn-faced while Sallis, robed, droned through his prayers, his sermon, his announcements. If such a tea party regularly occupied the vicar's Sunday afternoon, it was no wonder his evensong was so dull. Murren watched this outburst of family life with admiration as one watches a child in Budapest fluent in Hungarian. He'd never known such home-bred uproar, even when the ebullient Dorothea lived with or descended on them. His father's French servants, his mother's cautious occupations precluded noise at this level. It was like a classroom but without the constraints of learning. People, he felt, and admitted scepticism at the feeling, people loved, lifted each other in affection, enjoyed a warmth of fellow-feeling, of close relationship that burst into laughter, into word puns, mild mockery, exaggeration. A thin-booted parson pretended with graceful speed to drop a spoon into his niece's teacup, caught and flourished it. Oh, Hilary. Hilarious Hilary Sallis. His domineering wife cut rich fruitcake, and with no show, stroked the back of her father's head as she issued orders about division of trifle. Murren did not remember attending a children's party in his youth, but this had the energy, the home-bred levity of such functions without the splashed frocks, the spillages, the bellyache.

Murren went off with the vicar early, the rest following in two cars. Sallis sat silent now at the wheel, sobered but transformed in his passenger's mind by what he had been half an hour before.

'I've really enjoyed myself,' Murren said. The half-truth concealed a larger.

'We get on well. And we're rowdy. It was a bit of a send-off, really, for Mrs Leeper. She's due for hospital on Tuesday.' His wife's mother.

'Is it serious?'

'We don't know. Exploratory operation. We hope not.'

'But she seemed so lively. Full of vitality. Young, really.'

'She seems not afraid.' The vicar's voice, church-fashion, spoke from some distance, as through some mechanism, microphone or loud-hailer.

'She's very like your wife. The other way round, I mean.'

'In some ways, yes. They're like two sisters. Of course, my father-in-law's not an easy man. He's ill, and disappointed.' The vicar said no more but, when he drew up outside the black street-wall of the church, seemed in no hurry to get out as he tapped the wheel with his big, ugly red hand.

'I'm glad you enjoyed yourself,' he said, blowing his lips out. 'And I'm sorry you're leaving us. We knew you wouldn't stay long, of course. But we hoped for great things while you were here. You've done more than we could have expected. People come to hear you and the choir, and that's something. I've been here nearly ten years now, and I don't suppose I shall be shifted, except downwards. They might have made me a bishop, you know.'

'Did you want that?' Murren could not help his question.

'Yes, I think so. I'd admit to it. But I'm very ordinary.'

'I don't agree. Why, this afternoon. . . .'

'They don't promote in the Anglican Church because you're good at bunfights.'

'So much the worse for them, then,' Murren said.

The vicar consulted his watch.

'We've a minute or two to spare,' Sallis said. 'You're going to do well. You'll be heard of.'

'I've not been offered the St John's job yet.'

'Don't you worry. That's yours. I've never said this to you before, James. And I feel some embarrassment now, I can tell you. As if I'm getting into the act. You are a very talented man, but, and I hope you won't mind my saying this, and it will surprise you, I look on you as a son. So does Jean, in her different way. We've done little about it, but we've felt a responsibility. Not that you will have noticed. I hope not, at least. This probably has nothing to do with you, or you'll perhaps think not. And it's all to do with us. We have no son. Mind you, I don't complain. Those three girls of ours were, are a handful, I can tell you. And I'd be the first to admit that if we'd had a boy he'd be more like me than you, a nonentity or a mediocrity. Still, I have had this feeling, perhaps on account of your brilliant work. Another thing, I'd no idea that Jean felt the same, until I said something of the sort to her a month or two back. She was pleased I'd spoken, I could tell. Well, now.'

'Thanks,' Murren said, grimly, touched.

'Of course, that's my confession, and not the point. What I don't want you to do is to spend so much time on your music that the rest of your life seems, er, a, a parenthesis, er, a footnote. I'm not sure you'd agree with me. I don't want to preach, because I'm not much good at that either. You're living your life, your musical life to the full, but when you're my age, I'm fifty-three, you won't want to . . . no, you won't be able to do what seems to come so easy now. Then you need. . . .

'What do you suggest?' Murren asked, laughing, delighted with his companion. 'Marriage?'

'Why not? But it might be snooker, or reading or gardening or fretwork.'

'I see.' The last hobby fixed Sallis in time.

'I've a nerve to say this. It's not my place. But when I saw you at our table, at what Susan calls our jelly-splash, I knew I had to take this opportunity.' Now Sallis fumbled, grew awkward, mumbled a half-apology before shooing the young man from the car, and ushering him to the south porch where he patted his back ungainly and rolled off to his vestry.

Murren stood uncertainly.

His two years here seemed little to boast of; he guessed that in thirty years he'd barely retain a dozen memories of the time. And yet this awkward man of God had declared an affection, and in such a context that Murren was touched. This was worth while, no symbolic word, a truth. As soon as he began to frame words to the euphoria he felt, scepticism reasserted itself, doubt darkened. He did not wait for further decline but made for the choir-room where John Pendleton, already robed, was keeping order.

'Can I have a word?' Pendleton asked, pushing his superior into the organist's enclave.

'What's wrong?' He laughed at the frown of worry which dimpled the assistant's pale forehead.

'You're leaving, James? Is that right?'

'It's possible.' He explained once again, inquired the source of information. The vicar. 'If I do go, I hope they'll give you the job.'

'They won't.'

'They should. You've got your fellowship now.'

Pendleton moved towards the door, bent, looking older than his thin thirty-two years. One hand on latch, he said,

'You're a marvellous man to work with, James.'

'I don't think so. You and I complement each other. That's why we've done well. James and John.'

'When I say you're marvellous, you bloody are.' It was the first time he'd heard the man swear, and it impressed. This teacher, this organized man, this human computer, loved his art, cherished it keenly, swore by it. Murren thought himself so undeserving of such praise that he resented it. As he put on cassock, surplice, hood, Pendleton watched, hand up at the latch still; outside they could hear the screechy chatter of the choir boys.

'What are you playing tonight, James?'

'The G Major Fantasia for starters.'

'Do you like it?' Not a Pendletonian query.

'It's not the last piece I'd want to hear on earth, but it'll do.'

Pendleton went out, head down, shushed the boys. Murren said a word or two about the service, ran up the wooden stairs to the organ-loft, flashed bitingly into the Bach. Through the mirror he noted the arrival of the Sallis troupe, a full pew's worth.

Immersed in the service, he'd no leisure for himself. He conducted the anthem, decorated the hymn-tunes, kept the choir agog with his registration in the psalms. He played the congregation out, *pomposo*, at Mrs Sallis's request, with the Purcell Trumpet Tune and Air, a favourite with his men who hung about to listen. By the time he left his cell, the church was almost empty, the lights being dimmed; the vicar's wife called her thanks out from twenty yards off, and then there was nobody. He drove home, mildly excited, to a glass of whisky, a silent phone, an unknocked front door. Shrugging he prepared his schedule for the holiday on Easter Monday: a lie-in, practice at some new music, an hour or two with catalogues.

The day proved blank. He carried out his scheme, did a bit in the garden, but nobody called. Everywhere people set off to enjoy themselves, but nobody included him. Though he told himself that the lay-off did him good, he longed for the postman, the caller, even a pupil; perhaps Hilary Sallis had it right, that outside his music he was bored. He reminded himself of the rehearsals, festivals, meetings, concerts, an opera that he'd face in the summer term, and the even more hectic helter-skelter if the St John's job came off, but it did not fill in these blank minutes. Bored, he knew it.

He welcomed a telephone call on Tuesday evening from William McKie, guttural, aggressive, unsure.

'Hope you don't mind ma ringing. It's ma wife, Elisabeth. She wants to ask you to diew something for her.' Murren said it depended. Willy began an explanation, not easily followed, but at the end of five minutes Murren understood that Mrs McKie required his help to clear her parents' house. 'They're dead, y'know. Ay. Deid. It was tragic at the end. . . .' A further jam of clogged vowels, a phlegm of strong emotion, which Murren murmured out. McKie launched more fluent praised his listener, claimed the auld man regarded him highly. Murren, baffled, asked what he could do. 'She needs advice. Ah'm no guid to her. You respected the auld man, knaw the value o' articles. Naw, not just financial, either.' Finally, after more hedging, he said that his wife dared not approach Murren.

'So she asked you to.'

'She did not. She'll play hell. But it's what she wants. An' if you can get it for her, wull. She's worth it.' The 'r' rattled triumphantly clear. They agreed on the next morning, when McKie would be able to care for the child. Ten o'clock. The man muttered thanks, his praise like imprecations.

Murren, not pleased, knocked at the Wisniewski door on time.

Elzbieta's footsteps echoed hollowly, for the house was almost empty. Another case like Patricia Payne's, without necessity, a mere sham, an appearance to no purpose.

'The house is pretty well cleared,' Elzbieta apologized, 'but I'm having Foulds's in to take the rest, and I'd like someone to see that I'm not leaving any valuables.'

Murren nodded solemnly in the damp of the house, then followed her about. There was neither anything of worth nor anything Polish; the bits and pieces left, even the bric-a-brac, were post-war rubbish, from the time of austerity when presumably the newlyweds set up together.

'Did they always live here?'

'No. I was born in Basford. They had a little house there, but they sold it and came here, oh, twenty years ago.'

From room to carpetless room in empty, stale tramping. Ten minutes saw them back in the kitchen where the woman turned on the gas jet under a kettle.

'You'll have a cup of coffee,' she said, and marched out. He looked out of the window at the litter in the yard, but she was back inside a minute. 'Would you have this?' she said, holding out a Co-op plastic bag folded round a rectangular object.

'What is it?'

'Look.'

He took, unwrapped the parcel and found a book of music. The title page was in gilt Polish, brown-stained at the edges.

'They're folk-songs,' she said, 'from Poland.' He opened the book at random and whistled the tune he turned up in embarrassment; she immediately named it. 'I think my father would have liked you to have it. He took a fancy. The musician, that was his name for you.'

'But you. . . . It will be. . . .'

'I have plenty of mementos, don't you bother.'

He thanked her, turning the pages. She stood waiting for the kettle, dull in brown coat, finger-ends red. This was the naked woman Payne saw, but this morning incipient middle age, working clothes, fatigue reduced her to a shopper passing in the street. Here was the grand-daughter of a Polish landowner, daughter of an officer; drab as the dark doors, the stained wallpapers with disfiguring squares of pristine cleanliness where pictures had hung, she spooned instant coffee from a small jar into mugs.

They sat, he on the corner of a table, she on the one rickety stool.

'You're not moving here, then,' he asked to make conversation.

'No. We're buying our house. Jock earns a good wage; he's regular at work.' She lowered her coffee, understanding that further explanation was necessary. 'I couldn't move in here. It's their place, not mine. I disappointed them, I know. Perhaps they expected a miracle that somehow I would lift them back nearer where they belonged, that I would marry well, or. . . . I can't say. They were Polish, to the last. You wouldn't understand this. You English have never moved, or you have always had the chance to return. They lived strangers in strange country.' Her accent became Slavonic, tight-lipped.

Murren did not speak, thought vaguely of his father's residence in France. 'Their end came quickly, and I am sorry. My father was desperately ill, but my mother seemed all right.' The flat English words were grotesque. 'She always complained, but she seemed healthy. And then she died. Brain haemorrhage, they said. I found her, in her bed. She had twisted over. She must have known something was happening. And then I had to break it to my father. Can you imagine that? He was ill, but he must have heard the footsteps and the voices, the ambulance men. And she had not been in to see him, though this sometimes happened, so that I was over first. My mother was human; she overslept; she was no saint. Not very often, you understand. But, here she was now. I had gone into his room first, made him comfortable, didn't give my mother a call. I thought I would let her have a few minutes longer. I took them tea. I never expected anything. . . . There she was, as if she was trying to scramble out of bed, or reach for the light, half twisted over. I went downstairs on tiptoe, not to alarm him, and into the neighbour's to phone. Then I went back to the bedroom, his. I said, "My mother's not very well." He didn't answer, didn't understand. He was very ill, and drinking his tea was a great struggle for him. I took his cup and told him about the ambulance, and then I tucked him up. The men were very quick, but they saw she was . . . was dead. They made the arrangements; she was taken. I went into the kitchen, down here.' She looked round the place wildly, at taps, the gap left by a stove, the discoloured green and white walls. 'Half an hour later, perhaps, I do not know, I did not go with her, with the body, I took my father his porridge, helped him to eat it, what little he could. He was very weak.' Elzbieta sipped, scratched a knee. ' "How is your mother?" he asked. His eyes seemed so wide; the whites had turned yellow, but they were large and so intelligent, as if he saw through me, and my . . . trick, my deception. I did not answer, until I lied, told him she had gone to hospital. "It is serious, then?" he asked.' She repeated the words in Polish, *ipsissima verba*. ' "Eat your porridge," I said. "We can't do anything." Jock had come across. He'd put Christina next door. I had to go down to the hospital; I had said I would. But I told my husband, "I have to break it to daddy." He said he wouldn't. He's a kind man. I did not. I went; the hospital is not far, to see the officials. They said they could not issue a certificate, asked questions. But that was nothing, did not worry me. I told them about my father. They said they would attend to him, but it did not happen that day. My husband had to take time off and see our doctor, and look after our daughter. It seems like a nightmare now, as if I didn't know what happened. I don't.' She cried, but her tears neither staunched nor slowed the fluency of her words.

Murren, cup in both hands, knew why he had been invited. He saw Payne again, back to the sideboard, hands out, crucified with knowledge. He snatched the kettle up, waved it about.

'Coffee? Would you like more coffee?' he asked.

Elzbieta's mouth opened, her eyes cloudily on the wall behind.

'When I came back,' she said, stopping her tears, 'I had to tell him. I went up, and Jock with me. My father had slipped down the bed, and we heaved him back and arranged his pillows. Before, he was half asleep, but now his eyes opened wider and black. "How is she?" he asked. "How is your mother?" And I thought we'd woken him up and straightened him to break him in two. I shook my head at him, to try to tell him without speaking. Somehow he pushed himself up straighter, "What do you mean?" I put my hand on him. "She's dead." He shook himself free of me, and gave a kind of small shriek and began to cry.' She wept, herself, again, now, silently, in big tears. ' "Don't, daddy," I said, but he paid no attention. He had lived a brave life; the king decorated him in the air force; he never complained of his dull work, his poverty. I could not stand it. I ran out of the room, into the place where she had died, and out again to the landing. I am ashamed now. My husband stayed with him, saying something, wiping his face, giving him a drink. I ran downstairs, threw myself on the sofa. I dared not move. When Jockie called down, I could hear, but I did not answer. He came after me, and found me, and put a cushion under my head, and lit the gas-fire. "You lie there, girl," he said. "Lie there for a bit and I'll see to the both of you." '

She stood up, angrily, dabbed at her face and then with violence rinsed her cup under the tap. As she turned for his, he saw that her face had grown obstinate again, fixed, wooden against tears.

'It don't bear thinking about,' she said.

She spoke again about the book of folk-songs, of her father's affection for him, even of the old man's death, but all calmly enough. She packed up the crockery, the packet of biscuits, the tea-towel into her shopping bag, and stood buttoning her coat, defying him to make something of it. He felt totally at a loss, as if her character had taken one metamorphosis too many for credibility. She looked about, tore two days off the calendar to bring it up to date; the useless action seemed as reasonable as any.

'We'll go then,' she said, and thanked him.

'Is there nothing I can do?'

She shook her head, but took the book from him, opening it to its cream title-page.

'That's my father's name,' she said. 'In his handwriting. That means Henry in Polish.'

He thanked her as she stared at the book before she snapped it to and handed it back.

'Look at the time,' she said. 'This'll never buy the baby a new bonnet.' She laughed, quite loud, unless the empty place magnified the sound, and preceded him into the bare passage. 'The house agents are sending a man this afternoon. It's all made a lot of work.'

Murren looked along the corridor; at the sides the linoleum still showed signs of polish, but was dulled with footmarks up the middle. The walls were shabby, not dirty, but unevenly clean, and the curtain against draught, a red and yellow, speckled, oriental, exotic thing had been removed, leaving its discoloured tube of rail, its awkward wooden rings. Above, the fanlight shone, so that the door was darkened and the ceiling's unevenness revealed. No picture or mirror brightened the place; it stretched towards that rectangle of light, cold, already smelling of damp.

In a month or two the new tenants would have freshened the surfaces with a coat of paint. No traces of the Wisniewskis remained, except for the wooden rings, peasant-large. This stood well-constructed, an English house, built 1908, ready for the next family, from the Caribbean, Pakistan, Singapore, Galway or the council estate not a half-mile away. In sixteen years of Polish cooking and voluble relatives, the growing Elzbieta had disappeared into thin lines of accumulated dust under picture frames, a cobweb high in a corner, a rusty, dropped nail.

'We'll go then,' she said.

He had been standing, he did not know for how long, keeping her waiting.

'Right,' he said.

She opened the door, flooding the passage with dull daylight. He'd never cross that threshold again; he tried to examine himself to see if he minded, but failed to come up with an answer. The song-book was held under his arm.

Man and woman shook hands in the street.

'Thanks for the book,' he said.

'Thanks to you.' Ordinary, worn as the paving-stones, she swayed, turned, paddled off, not looking back. Perhaps she had shut the door for the last time, leaving the calendar leaves to curl or brown. An occasional letter would slot through the box, addressed to Mr H. I. Z. Wisniewski, gather dust on the lino-leum, present a problem for the next occupier.

Murren hitched his book, marched.

17

'Mr Murren? Ah, Julian Talbot-Read, here.' Who in hell? 'We have met. At Janet Bruce's. You remember?'

'Yes.'

'Good. Janet is worried, Mr Murren.' The voice cracked, energetically flicked. 'About her recitals next October. She's heard you're leaving, and wonders if you'll be able to come back to accompany her.' Julian waited; Murren mumbled an explanation of why he could give no answer. Julian, toothily, it sounded, understood. 'She wouldn't ring you herself, Mr Murren. She'd wait. "Until such time as James tells me himself" is how she put it. I knew you wouldn't mind my ringing. But it's unlikely, is it, if you go that you'll be able to help her out?' Again, Murren said why he did not know. Talbot-Read clattered vocables into his mouthpiece, smiling, rang off abruptly. Murren could imagine the modern, squared phone, one of three, the shining area of desk, manicured nails inspected, the cuffs adjusted, the next task attended to, the financial fiancé.

The following day Janet appeared replete with apologies.

'I'm cross with Julian. He had no right to interrupt you. I really am angry.' She looked it.

'No, Janet. He acted properly.'

'He had better not do it again, I tell you.'

'Let's have a sing now,' he said.

Pergolesi, Schubert, Brahms, folk-songs. They enjoyed the hour. At the end of Britten's spiky bird-song in the 'Ash Grove', she bent down and kissed him full on the mouth.

'You do me good,' she said, kneeling, head on his lap.

'You have a husband-to-be,' he said, mocking her, 'who'll do pretty well anything for you.'

'He can't play the piano.' She fondled him, intimately, without compunction. 'I'd drop him like a hot cake. And you know it.'

Murren had the sense not to argue, but stroked her back. After a time she settled, sprang to her feet, walked across to a mirror.

'I could kill you,' she said.

'Don't.'

'Julian's worth ten of you.'

'Agreed.'

She tore her small square of lace-edged handkerchief across, violently, but concentrated on the face in the mirror. After a few moments, she asked,

'Do you want to sing any more?'

'Up to you.'

'Bugger you, then.'

He closed his piano, stood, straight.

'Get your coat on, Jan,' he said. 'We're not doing much good.'

'You know how it is,' she said. 'At least you know that.'

'Yes. Let's get your coat.'

She fastened it, fine lady, led the way to the door.

'I expect we shall meet again before you go,' she said.

'We're certain to.'

'I don't know that I want. . . .'

He patted her back; she bridled, but took to smiling. He understood the soreness of her heart, but felt disinclined to act generously, if that were possible. While the world roughed him up, he'd not succour a soul; his emotions pecked at crumbs of comfort in conflict like winter starlings.

A day later, on a mild evening Alan Mark pushed across a crowded pub to speak to him. Murren, listening half-heartedly to his choir-men, wasn't averse to standing, moving off a step or two, which was what the man seemed to want.

'I'm glad I've met you.' That was the truth to judge by the vigorous pumping of the hand. 'I keep saying to Prue that I ought to go round to see you. But you know how it is.'

'Is she well?'

'Yes. She is. And she's pregnant.'

'Are you glad?'

'I'll say. We both are. You'd be surprised at the difference in her. Another woman altogether. She's only a couple of months gone, but you should see her.' Mark leaned over; confidentiality is as difficult as handshaking in a crowded bar. The man's face gleamed with healthy sweat; eyebrows and moustache grew in rich, pale culture.

Murren buried his face in his glass.

Who was the father, then? Was he? He doubted that; Prudence had taken on too many men. He remembered her without warmth, a beautiful, dominating but pliable woman, or rather, machine. That was more like it, a well-oiled mechanism, performing with an exigent exactness to his wishes, but without depth of feeling, a mere powerful reaction to the touch on erogenous accelerator or brakes. There could not be truth in that; human machines might suit a moment's thought as a metaphor, but such did not exist. She had called out to him, he feared, with her body, demonstrated her need, but had stilled it for a brief hour before she flung her sex at the next eligible partner. Now she was a mother, and perhaps glandular miracles would transform her, still her, warm her for milk and comfort, night-waking, responsibility.

'Is she with you?' he asked.

'Oh, no. She won't go out much, at night. I'm just here for an hour. She sends me off.' He spoke in innocence. 'She's taken to the piano again, and that's good. Perhaps his nibs'll be a musician.'

'His nibs might be a girl.'

'I don't mind that.' Mark insisted that Murren drained his beer, then shouldered a way to the bar. Murren thought of blonde Prudence, at home, at the keyboard, skittling through Chopin, or serious at the Beethoven he'd done with her. He wanted to remember her as a woman, as a talented woman, but again and again, lips slobbering on lips, they fell to the carpet, wild, animal enough, but uncouth, no, wrong that, nor mad, performing with fervour and great delicacy what should have been the culmination of a deep attachment. The hymn sang, 'Emptied Himself of all but Love', but they emptied, violated themselves of everything but. And yet she was beautiful, and a real musician. Sexual lust touched his loins even in his regret.

Back with beer, Murren wished health.

'You might have a new pupil in a few years' time,' Mark said, colour heightened. He should have been in a scrum or line-out. 'She can play, can Prue.' Murren reassured him, was invited to visit the Mark household. 'We'll have him, her, christened at your place. How about that?'

Murren said nothing about leaving.

'I'll give you a ring,' he said. 'To congratulate her.'

'She'd like that. She really would. She looked up to you, y'know. Man in a thousand.' The gingery hair gleamed, and the healthy fist round the pint pot paled at the knuckles. They gripped hands like brothers, in satisfaction, in the ale-washed bar.

Murren kept his word, in anticlimax.

Prudence Mark answered the phone primly, distantly, made him aware that at two or three months congratulations were premature. Murren, not to be beaten, pressed her.

'Alan seemed over the moon with it,' he said.

'He's boyish,' she managed, 'for a man of thirty-eight.'

'He doesn't look anything like that.'

'That's what he is.'

She spoke as if she rebuked him unenthusiastically, like a schoolma'am doing her duty. Perhaps she was afraid of what she'd undertaken, now it was no longer private between her and her husband; the public knew, and had its expectations to which she, however shudderingly, must conform. Taken aback, Murren asked about her piano playing, but she answered as slightingly. He outlined his summer concert, his serenata at the college, and described the progress of the Harmonic Society, which he'd taken over to prepare for a one-off B Minor Mass, to be done twice in June. Suddenly she was talking, about her mother who was in the Harmonic, her brilliant sister who'd been sent to South Africa for two months, a neighbour's troubles with an expensive stereo, a recital in Lincoln Cathedral by Timothy Gelsthorpe she'd driven over to, his Easter sonnet she'd heard on the radio. This free, casual talk she offered in a friendly bundle, without sense of provocation, and he in his turn drummed up capping anecdotes. For ten minutes they laughed, giggled even, and after he had again wished her well he left the phone elated. They had never talked so before, face to face; now they had liked each other uninhibited by lust.

He stuck his chest out, whistled all the morning.

Shortly afterwards, on a rainy Saturday, Stacey's letter arrived offering him the St John's job. The merest note expressed intense satisfaction, as if obstacles had been overcome, but the headmaster gave no details. A letter from General Lord Arthur Tallent, chairman of the governing body, made the offer official. Bill Ashley had sent the enormous programme of next year's engagements, terrifyingly long and complicated, and offered to come up for discussion. The fourth envelope was from Myra Friedlander's agent; she was to do a five-day mini-tour, Newark, York, Manchester, Edinburgh next month, playing the Brahms and Bach again at each concert, and wanted him as accompanist. Reply at once; they'd arrange a rehearsal in London. Peremptory, without explanations, the demand delighted him. He disturbed the leisure of the principal of his college who gave him guarded permission to absent himself for a week, and declared himself sorry indeed, ah, um, sorry, that Murren was leaving in the summer.

He caught the Saturday morning post in reply to the agent, but Stacey and Co. could wait until Monday. They'd been long enough. Now they'd assured his future, he felt no excitement; he was grateful for the Friedlander venture, and puzzled. Why had she called on him? There must be a dozen, a score, of professional accompanists in London who wouldn't sniff at a week's work with so distinguished an artist. On the cheap? He hardly thought so, for she would have no truck, he guessed, with economies that would spoil her work. He'd impressed her, perhaps? He enjoyed the thought, and in elation spent an hour practising the Brahms. He studied without show, making sure of himself, with humility, elbows and crashing wrists under constraint.

On the Sunday services he announced his departure officially to the vicar, to Mrs Sallis, to John Pendleton and the choir. It quietened the men, who'd heard rumours, anyway, but they muttered, looked askance. He told them that he hoped the powers-that-be had the sense to elect John to the post, but in his own mind he feared the worst. To see that good man blush at his word of confidence would be enough to sink him in the eyes of Jean Sallis and other arbiters of local taste who'd be instructing their husbands what was required.

After the service Walter Payne waited.

Murren, not sorry to see him, drove him home

where Patricia, dressed in flowing silks with a wide cummerbund, lacking only a hat for Buckingham Palace garden party elegance, welcomed, swept him into the drawing-room. She asked him about his leaving, and he now explained to both exactly what would happen.

'And are you sorry to be deserting us?' she asked.

'Not really.' He felt he could speak honestly.

'He's a metropolitan,' Payne said.

'I've learned a good deal here,' Murren said.

'Such as?'

'I got away from Bill Ashley, for a start. I've made some good music, without him on my back. I've made some good friends.'

'A sojourner,' Payne said, solemnly, 'dwelling in tabernacles. For he looked for a city which hath foundations.'

Patricia eyed him as she would a recalcitrant infant who failed to deposit his milk-bottle top in the basket.

'Epistle to the Hebrews,' her husband answered grinning, and went out to provide hospitality. Patricia immediately began to speak about herself, to describe her trouble, her recovery.

'It's come with the spring, like a miracle,' she explained. She had feared through the winter months that she would be driven, like her brother, to suicide. 'Walter and I used to argue. He said George had always been unstable, that he and I were temperamentally quite different, but he could not convince me. During that cold weather I knew that some small setback would be enough, and I should be over the edge. I'd lock my bottles away, make Walter hold the key. This Nigel Brockless business didn't help things; Jessica's a brave girl in some ways, but she's what my mother would have called a "madam". You know she's there.'

Mrs Payne talked of her school, the snags and small upsets, of her embarrassment to find herself in a violent fit of trembling, with tears, after a minor tiff with some argumentative young miss on the staff.

'That's not me, you know. I had to hide myself in the lavatory. So long, in fact, that the secretary got worried. I made out I'd tummy trouble. Another thing, about the same time, if you remember, I took you with me up to George's flat. I'd cleared that, or had it cleared, but I could not make the final break on my own. I kept the rent on for some weeks, until you could go with me. It's irrational; it cost money; but it seemed exactly sensible, what I had to do.'

'And if you hadn't?'

'I don't know. Some catastrophe. That did happen. With Nigel.'

'Has she got over it?'

'Who can say?' If Patricia could not, who indeed? 'I don't fathom the girl. She's her father's child.'

Payne stayed out so long that it seemed by pre-arrangement. Patricia needed confession, to announce her regeneration. This constituted weakness in itself, though she exuded confidence, bossed both men when the drinks and titbits appeared. Jessica looked in at ten-thirty, calling out that she'd been in a pub. When her step-mother mentioned Murren's new job, she said,

'That's good. That's what you wanted. You didn't belong here.'

'Epistle to the Hebrews,' Murren answered.

'What the hell does that mean?'

She frowned furiously at the laughter of the other three, snatched up her gin, to hide her face. Payne, sympathetic, fetched out the two recordings of Murren's *Easter Sonnet*. He'd made beautiful tapes; magnificent sounds of hammering voices, the snarl of giant reeds, the huge tremor of pedals.

'Which is better?'

'Two different buildings.'

'It must be the most satisfying thing on earth to hear somebody else perform what you have composed,' Patricia said, in her assembly voice. This led to a discussion on her nativity play compiled on summer holiday. 'I know exactly how you must feel,' she pronounced. They listened. Payne hurried diplomatically to play the tape again. Patricia held forth at length that the music somehow expressed her own recovery.

'I know Walter will laugh at me, and Jessica always thinks I exaggerate, but that's how I am, a glorious shout, a riot of triumphant pleasure.'

It sounded hysterical. Payne coughed drily. Jessica patted her step-mother on the shoulder with bitter irony. 'Congratulations, ma,' she said, and left the room.

'You see what I mean.' Patricia loudly, invulnerable, crowing.

Murren stayed until past midnight, elated, yet part frightened. Payne skulked behind his whisky, as if he expected his wife's manic power, her laying down of the law, to switch off into foggy depression. He squinted at her, at Murren, ready to feint when the blow was delivered. The celebratory, noisy shaking of hands in the hall moved all three down to steps on to the drive.

Night wind warmly moved in the branches; the moon, odd-shaped, three-quarters full, humped its back over a blue, cloud-patterned sky.

'You have done us good,' Patricia said, shouted, and kissed him. He smelt gin, breath, powder, overpowering scent in the spring air. 'Hasn't he, Walter?'

Murren wondered what Jessica did. No lights broke in the front windows.

> 'From far, from eve and morning
> And you twelve-winded sky
> The stuff of life to knit me
> Blew hither; here am I,'

he quoted as to himself.

Patricia laughed wildly strong.

'Are you sober enough to drive?' Payne asked.

'And if I'm not?'

18

Ashley spent a day with Murren who found the professor-elect less daunting.

They worked through next year's programme, but Ashley's head was already in America, reorganizing his department. He made suggestions; he damned or praised; he outlined what he had intended, but he obviously expected his successor to scrap and change. It amused Murren, for he remembered the Ashley whose decisions were the word of God, unalterable law.

'There's one thing I want you to do for me,' Ashley said. Now he waited, black eyes, hook nose, balding head intense.

'Go on.'

Ashley felt in his pocket, drew out a typescript.

'Another bit of Housman. I heard your last. I want you to set it for baritone. Possible?'

'Well. . . .'

'In the next fortnight.'

Murren read the poem: 'Far in a western brookland', pulled doubtful faces. 'Must be set already,' he said. 'How about Vaughan Williams?' He sang the last two lines in parody.

'My soul that lingers sighing
About the glimmering weirs.'

'I don't want your bloody Vaughan Williams. You. Get it to me in a fortnight.' He explained that his last engagement in England was a musical festival, and they'd demanded some original works. Murren scowled at the words. 'You'd be amazed at the excuses people make. If I went to Haydn and asked him to set words, he'd do it in the lunch hour. But not now with our bloody costive un-composers. Any student could, should do it, why can't they? So I thought, "Jim Murren'll manage it." So. Get going.'

'I'm the last resort?'

'Yes, but what's that matter?'

'Elgar wouldn't have stood for it.'

'You're not Elgar, mister.'

'Only Haydn, eh? Come on, Bill. Do better than that.'

'You're getting to be an impertinent young sod, my friend. Will you do it? I'm begging.'

'I'll see.'

'I want it. You understand that. I want it.'

'Write it yourself.'

'I need something better than that, as well you know.'

Murren enjoyed the passage of arms with his mentor. He flashed his new independence, but Ashley's confidence strengthened him; Ashley knew how to trust. Murren re-read the poem while the other sat silent. Already the parody was transforming itself into music.

'Don't like Housman,' Ashley said, after a pause. 'But it has possibilities. And they asked for it. Didn't allow me to choose.'

'They didn't? And you put up with it?'

'Age. Time. Defeats us all. Ah, boy, boy.'

Ashley knew exactly when to relax, when to whip. The two drank beer together, not a great deal, and Ashley muttered about America. He was already used to two-day trips to the States. Murren remembered his aunt's house, the funeral parlor, the concert. It seemed a country of great light, dry heat, bright eyes and handshakes. He asked why St John's had taken so long with its official offer.

'Because they'd made their minds up. They wanted you. There was no hurry.'

Murren expressed his displeasure.

'I told Stacey it would upset you. He said not. J. T. P. Murren the cool customer was the line he took. He should have known. And I should have pushed him. Usual selfish pursuit of our own ends, eh, boy?' He apologized. Murren saw why Ashley was a great leader. Moderately talented, he had the tact to use his overbounding energy with exactitude.

A week with Dr Ashley would have maddened him, but this day encouraged him, strong, warm, cheering. Murren, twice the man, considered his future, lived out his present commitments, dashed down the Housman song in a muddle of confident strength.

Twice he rang Jessica Payne, and twice she refused to meet him, politely, apologizing that her leisure did not fit with his few free days. He could not believe this, but did not know how to arrange his thoughts. He might ring her father, or Patricia, for a report, and did so once but was glad, surprising himself, to find the phone unanswered. He wondered what event had taken the whole family out and decided it would be an evening at Madam's school, into which Walter had been forced in some subsidiary role, tea-maker, caretaker's mate, flex-and-fuse-box-man, and from which Jessica had organized herself a visit to a disco, theatre, friend's house to keep well out of the way.

He spent a day in London with the Friedlander, which he enjoyed masochistically.

This time she acted the pedagogue, making demands, marking his copy, insisting that he repeated passages until he had them right. This spurred him, even when he disagreed with the interpretation, so that at the end of the two sessions he felt exhausted, and then she turned him out, with no fancywork about entertainment, hospitality, friendship. She had provided brand-new copies of all the works for him, and had marked them heavily in thick pencil. He was so knocked about by her treatment, no equality here, that he kept his spirits by impudently suggesting to himself that she'd examine the copies for fingermarks next time they met to discover how much practice he'd done.

When he asked about the next rehearsal, she said brusquely, 'Newark. On the day of the recital. We'll have an hour.'

'Will that be enough?' he asked, bruised.

She looked for no ironies. Unattractive, sallow, ruffle-bummed in her navy trousers, she answered, 'You're musician enough to know what's wanted. Do it on your own.'

He barely took it as praise.

Exactly one week before the first Friedlander recital, he called on the Paynes. Walter answered the door, in a white rib-apron, twisting a wood-shaving abstractedly in his fingers. Yes, they were all well. Yes, his wife flourished, had gone to the Education Centre to hear some H.M.I. pronounce on the teaching of reading. Yes, Jessica was at home; he'd fetch her down and then he hoped Murren would excuse him. He bawled upstairs; the girl appeared, smiling, face almost plump.

Murren made his excuses. He'd called on the off-chance, with nothing in mind, really, but would she come out for a drink. She would if he'd give her five minutes.

He waited fifteen, but she had transmogrified herself, even to hair-style. She walked smartly smart in a scarlet coat with gilt buttons, a small comical hat, also golden buttoned, big-buckled shoes, figure rounded and stiff as a dummy, eyes delighted.

'My word,' he said, admiring. She took no obvious notice.

'We'll tell dad.' He did not follow. 'Come on. We'll go out at the back.' He fell in. 'Down here.' They went down well-lighted steps, with new substantial banisters fixed to both walls. Below there were three cellar doors, all freshly painted. She made for the one on the right, pulling it back, flooding the already illuminated foyer with a glare of light.

'We're going out,' she called from the threshold.

'Oh, yes.' Mumbled, tacks-in-mouth. 'Is James there? Come on in for a moment. This is my kingdom.'

The cellar, brilliant with bar-lights, walls damp-free, heated and ventilated, was fitted out as a workshop. A bench, with vice, occupied the middle space; Payne, beaming stood over one of two lathes, a half-worked wooden fruit-bowl between his hands. Behind him, regimentally neat, in racks, were rows of shining tools, shelves of labelled tins. Only the litter of wood-shavings on the floor was disordered, and brushes, pans, baskets, a bin were lined, ready in their place to recreate discipline.

Payne's head shone, as did the curls above his ears, the nape of his neck. Murren expressed admiring surprise.

'My den.' He pointed to one corner where Murren moved towards a magnificent rocking-horse, capable of seating three on its red brass-studded seats; it stretched out huge, with its head high and fierce, its flaring nostrils bright crimson, the sheen of its flanks grey and black, the great rockers jazz-striped like barber poles, the handles leather-covered, the eyes staring brown with lashes curly as question marks.

Murren began his praises.

'For my wife's school,' Payne said.

'How long has it taken you?'

'Six months, on and off. One last touching-up with the paint brush and he's away.' Proud fingers pointed out alleged defects. 'I wanted to make something that would last, solid and Victorian, that her young rips wouldn't kick to pieces in five minutes.' One hand swung the horse effortlessly, noiselessly. 'Moving parts are the snag.' He closed his lips on a smile as one who'd solved the problem.

He led them on a mini-tour, fetching out a half-finished lute, detailing the next three projects, extracting from a chest of designed drawers scaled plans.

'I'd no idea.' Murren was cheered, if reduced to clichés, but these flat words were what Payne required of him. 'It's marvellous.'

'Mustn't keep you hanging about here.' The lieutenant-colonel ordered them out, stiff inside his apron. Jessica led up the stairs, out through a door into the back-yard, and thus round the house. Murren felt exhilarated, whistled a line of 'Far in a Western Brookland', tripped over a badly set paving slab, righted himself, laughed out loud.

In the car, with the girl still, her perfume strong, too strong, he expressed his delight.

'It's marvellous,' he said. 'It beats cock-fighting.'

'What's that mean?' Encouragingly.

'A saw from my grandfather, apparently.'

'He must have lived way back.'

'Born 1880. Where are we going now? The Albany?'

'If you like.'

'To suit your get-up.'

'It's your money,' she said, catching his mood.

They drank in one of the huge bars, brightly carpeted, rich with silver fittings and black glass. A few middle-aged men and their sober ladies occupied tables as by right. Jessica sipped Martini and iced lemonade from a long glass, excited in a subdued way, much at home here, dressed for the part but unable to conceal her pleasure at the opportunity.

For ten minutes they talked about Walter Payne's hobby, his disappearances for hours on end into the workshop, the projects Patricia set him and then her impatience at his slow, methodical approach, his drawings, consultations, insistence on matching grains, tight joints, high-gloss finish.

'Patty wants it out of the way,' she said, laughing. 'The kitchen took months, but he's not to be hurried. He spends as much time there cooking as she does.'

'They get on well?'

'Oh, yes. For them. He's a bit of a sly-boots, because when she asks him to do something, he does his bank manager act and explains exactly how long it will last and what precise degree of upset he'll cause.'

'How does she take that?'

'A bit like a child. She wants the improvements desperately. But she complains all the way through the completion.'

'He doesn't slow it down to annoy her?'

'No. Why should he? He works at the pace that suits him.'

She described her father with fondness, but said she was glad she did not work in his bank because he'd be a stickler. Her present man was bad enough, though Payne would look on him as slapdash. The young people giggled together, temperately in accordance with the surroundings, began to talk about Elzbieta McKie as she encouraged him to describe the last visit to the Wisniewskis' empty house. Jessica had seen nothing of the woman lately, spoke dismissively, even of the visits to the old man's bedside – 'it gave me the creeps' – and the trip to the Lincolnshire aerodrome. Murren felt surprise and disappointment, because he had expected the death of Nigel Brockless, so far unmentioned, to have made Jessica look more seriously on these other bereavements. It did not seem to have happened so. Her dealings with the Polish household had been unusual, but not especially interesting, and to be spoken of later with frivolity if at all. Details of the dark house, the smell, the mother's barbarous English, the bedroom curtains were remembered, but as slightly foreign, comic, worthy of a shrug rather than sympathetic scrutiny.

'Are you ready for London?' she asked, changing the subject.

'I shall be by the summer. I shall have to be.'

'Will you be glad to go?'

'I think so.'

'There's more going on there.' Her voice making the statement a half question. 'Don't you think?'

'I expect so,' he replied. He did not want to talk to her about what he had to face. At one time, when he wanted to impress, he'd have tried, but now he guessed she'd half listen, if that, and follow with some silliness. He picked up her glass and without asking her permission advanced on the bar, eyed by the matrons there and back. Jessica thanked him pertly.

'I'm going,' she said when he'd settled.

'Where?'

'To London. To work.'

'When?'

'The end of next week.'

She had applied soon after Nigel's death, she called it 'accident', and she'd learnt the date of the move a fortnight ago. The bank had found her temporary lodgings, from where she'd look round when she arrived; it would mean a rise in salary, and a more interesting job. She spoke with force; this explained her excitement, and certainly he'd never seen her so animated, as she was describing the work she'd do. When he questioned her about leisure activities, she'd no set ideas, but from the energy of the voice she expected equal advancement. She ventured smiling clichés about living too long in one place.

'What do your parents say?'

'What can they? Patty keeps running into her good advice act. Daddy'll miss me, but he won't say anything. He thinks he's lost me, anyway.'

'And has he?'

'Yes. I'm going my own way.'

Jessica spoke with bright-eyed modesty, not boasting, that small segment of the human condition clear in her mind. She mentioned Nigel again without too much distress, and told how his mother had insisted she had one or two keepsakes, a St Christopher on a chain, and a heavy man's wristlet-watch.

'She wanted,' the girl said, 'to make a thing of it, but I've just dropped them in a drawer, and that's that. I can't promise that I'll never forget him, can I?'

'I don't imagine you will.'

'But I can't promise. That's what she wanted.' Jessica's voice quickened, breathily, a Cordelia.

'Is there a father?' Murren asked.

'Oh, yes. He's something to do with telephones. And there are two other brothers.' Mrs Brockless stood condemned. 'She's quite nice, really.'

Soon Jessica spoke of other young men; one had taken her to the greyhound track, one to a football match. Another, a post-graduate student of American literature at the university, had written her some poems.

'Were they good?'

'I couldn't tell. I couldn't understand them. But he's had some published because he showed them to me in a quarterly magazine.'

'Were they about you?'

She poked an ironical finger straight at him, began to wag it. Both laughed, self-consciously, uncomfortably. Not long afterwards she thanked him, drained her glass, said she must go home.

'We've got into the habit, just the last week or so, of having a cup of something together about ten o'clock.'

'That's good,' he said.

'It's as much as I can do.'

Outside the gate of her home, she leaned across him in the car, kissed him, said, 'Probably shan't see you again. Not for a bit, anyhow. Look after yourself.' She wriggled out, closed the door, but relented and bent to wiggle fingers. He wound the window down.

'Let me take you out to dinner,' he said. 'Our last fling.'

'No, thanks. Thanks very much, but there's nothing in it for you, you know.'

'I should enjoy it, your company.'

She shook her head.

'I don't think so.'

'Is that because I don't write you poems?'

'Something like that. I've enjoyed going about with you, but I'm off now, away somewhere else. Another thing, I was always a bit frightened of you. I didn't like that much.'

'Why?'

'Everybody praised you,' she said. 'You were a marvel, and I thought to myself that I was nobody out of the ordinary. It didn't fit.' She looked up and down the empty street. 'I tried to tell you often enough, but you wouldn't listen. When you go back to London and make a big name there'll be plenty of people talking about the time you were here.'

'But not you?'

'Oh, I shall remember you. Patty won't let me

forget, for one thing. But you and I are different, and it's no use arguing otherwise.'

'You puzzle me,' he said, smiling.

'Because you're looking for what's not there. You'll get on all right without me; better in fact. It's time I went in.'

'The cocoa cups are rattling, are they?'

He could see her, under the street lamp, as a neat shape, with the face a mere blur, a vague pallor to which he must add, as he did, any beauty or distinction.

'Bye,' she said, swung about, dashed at the gate. He drove off without closing the window, but stopped three streets away to rectify this. He sat shocked for a moment, in that he had no doubt that he'd make progress without Jessica, but her dismissal of him was too complete. It was as if he'd been allowed to look into some building or garden, and then, just as interest quickened, had been bundled off, competently and without explanation. He felt he had not finished with her, that something significant remained to be shared, that the relationship, if not permanent, still held promise. She clearly had no such illusion; he was sure that she found him now a dead man.

He bit his lip, wristily flicked at his ignition key.

Perhaps her youth allowed her this certainty of action, or her immaturity, her shallowness. He could flash rude words about, just as he could accuse her, as he remembered, of mere clichés, but the girl herself, for whatever reason or lack of it, had thrown him over without regret because he presented nothing of much interest to her now. She might quote encomia, but she treated him like a nonentity. Payne's daughter. That funny quizzical ill-tempered individualist had bequeathed a double portion of his independent spirit to his beautiful child. She'd squander it, no doubt, and the Murrens, the sensitives, would bitterly regret as she stepped off to the next pair of broad shoulders or manly eyebrows. What would she be like at thirty? That was a question he did not want to answer. She had dismissed him, peremptorily, this year, not ten hence.

He started his engine, roared off. Stars winked between clouds.

> He hears: no more remembered
> In fields where I was known
> Here I lie down in London
> And turn to rest alone.

God, garbage. He had set it, made a fair copy, and tomorrow it would go off in its envelope to Ashley. The bloody, bloody woman. He slammed the garage doors, stood in the warm breeze, cursing himself.

For a fortnight the dismissal galled him; even at some interesting task, choir or college or piano, he'd stop and know a hollowness behind all the activity, a sense that whatever the importance of his present occupation it did little but scab over the festering lesion that left him weakly uncertain of himself. He worked; bullied pupils, was pleased when the Friedlander sent him a copy of the Brahms A major, op. 100 to prepare. 'We might need it.' He needed something. Until that final evening the book of his attachment to Jessica had never been closed. Now she was in London, at a counter doing arithmetic, warming sausages and baked beans, being jostled in the Tube, feeling homesick, as ordinary as a supermarket tin. But he could not help reflecting that in a month or two she'd pounce, be seen with her choice, unexpected as plague, be he married man, musician, pimply bank-clerk. No one would ever make her out, catch up with her, latch on to her. The bright would accuse her of flat language, the dull of vacillation or arbitrary choice, but she'd be just out of reach, not because she did much, but because that was the way they decided to interpret the delicate face, the eyes, the dark curls, the body, the gait. Murren kicked stones from his garden path, and was ashamed of himself.

Myra Friedlander instructed him by telephone to take an early train to Newark on the day of the first recital, and to report at the hotel for eleven o'clock. Her husband drove them in her limousine to the concert hall, and they practised there for an hour and a half, at the end of which she expressed herself satisfied, but in a noncommittal way as if she now regretted her invitation, handed him two short pieces to look at, saying that they might play them, but 'not tonight'. She offered him a lift back to the hotel on her way to lunch with friends at some manor, hall, in the county. He refused, was instructed to be ready at her room in the hotel just before seven, and watched the car glide away like a hearse. Down in the mouth, he ate a solid lunch in a tudor-style restaurant, went back to the hall and practised for an hour before slouching into a book shop where he bought a biography of Alexander the Great, and made for his bed. He could not read, or understand what he read; twice he checked his evening wear, decided to walk round the streets again, but now it drizzled heavily. Flat on his back, fighting to keep his paperback open, he fell asleep until nearly five, when he coaxed a pot of tea, bread and butter, quite delicious scones out of a middle-aged woman grotesquely dressed in black with lace apron and head-frill. She made it clear she did him a favour, but talked to him, sitting down in his corner, about her son who was studying science in London. When she learnt Murren's occupation in the town, she talked about Myra Friedlander, who had arrived the night before.

'She can be a terror. She and her husband went out last night. Dinner at Lord Parinder's. But she wouldn't put up there. Has to have her place here. Didn't get back till the early hours.' Explained her off-hand behaviour, he thought. She'd had all her violins locked away by the manager; four, they reckoned, all worth fortunes. 'But she's such a funny little body, in't she? A bit like an animal.' The woman talked on, pouring his tea. Nobody interrupted them, nor called her to duties behind the panelled, dark-oak doors. It was odd; she might have been serving her scientific son his tea at home. No, she was not responsible for the scones, but she'd say this: they did some things well here, she'd give 'em that. She looked him up and down and instructed him to get a bath, and relax.

'I shall need one when I come back tonight.'

'That's the beauty,' she answered, 'of staying in a decent hotel. Hot water, any time of day or night.'

She cleared his china, swept the crumbs with a small machine, and watched him upstairs before retiring from the dining room.

Back in his room he carefully checked his music, made himself read some school-book pages about Philip of Macedon, kept a close eye on the clock. He bathed, donned his concert clothes, awkwardly examined his reflection, walking round the room touching objects, trying switches, until he reported exactly on time at the Friedlanders' room.

Myra, in tight trousers, lay in an armchair, a sherry in hand. She pursed her lips, barely greeted him, committed herself to some self-examination in which he, and other people, had no part. Her husband produced the evening's printed programme, which, it seemed, Murren was expected to admire, and then asked to go through the music. Hugo, the husband, managed this genially, but made his companion turn over every single page.

'We've had some idiots,' he confided. Murren wondered whose back-sliding had given rise to his own invitation.

Myra got out of the chair and room, purposefully but silent. A young man entered, was introduced as Donald Archer, shook hands heartily. A toilet flushed, Myra returned struggling into a fur coat and instructing Archer to take two prepared portmanteaux, and her husband three violins to the car. Murren offered assistance, was snubbed.

'You keep your fingers supple,' she said.

They filed downstairs.

In the small room backstage notables milled about, reported a full house, a queue for standing room in the foyer-aisle. Myra opened a case, tuned a violin, ran over some exercise to the silent astonishment of the strangers and then retired elsewhere to dress for the concert. Murren sat on the edge of his chair; she had hardly offered him a word; nobody else bothered to talk in his direction. She returned robed, twice the height, her hair pinned up with a circular, jewelled comb. Again she snatched at her violin-case, briefly rubbed rosin, flashed through some rapid passages touching the strings merely with the point of the bow. They all watched, but she paid no attention. Her husband cleared the room.

'Right, James Murren,' she said fiercely.

Three minutes late, they advanced across the platform.

The concert blazed, a magnificent success. Her tone in this place seemed huge, hitting back from ceiling and walls, richly romantic, and Murren after a moment or two of uncertainty lost himself in the rewarding labour of matching her. They played the same programme as at her first concert, and in the interval she thanked him, not at length but warmly, laying that brilliant left hand for a moment on his upper arm. After the second half the audience would not let her go; she gave them Kreisler, Wienawski's 'Scherzo-Tarantella', and row on row thumped the floor, cheering. She expressed her pleasure in savage little bows, her eyes black. In the storm of applause she came across, asked Murren if he had the Brahms A major there. He nodded.

'Last movement, then.' She bowed deeply at the front of the stage, stretched her white arms, fiddle-and-bow-tipped, wide, silenced them with a finger, said, 'We will play once again for you. The last. But we will play seriously. No lollipop. We will do the Rondo of the Brahms Sonata in A, Opus 100.' She curtseyed, kept her head down. Standing she touched her A, made sure that Murren had found the copy, and swung eloquently on the lowest string into Brahms's flowing tune. She was superb.

Again in the back room, now crowded, she thanked him, rather laconically, as if nothing mattered, as if she were tired. That might be true, Murren thought; he was exhausted, sitting with his legs out, plucking at his cuffs for want of occupation. Archer came across with congratulatory noises; one or two locals nodded and smiled. A small pile of programmes came in for

Friedlander's autograph; she left her circle of pressing admirers, borrowed a pen, sat at the table to sign and then insisted that Murren sign under his printed name. He did so rather neatly, modestly, compared with her flamboyant scrawl.

'That's made 'em really worth something,' her husband said, gathering them up, and taking them to the door. Myra stood, gorgeously, a white shawl over her shoulders among the men, in a bright mist of cigar smoke. In the deafening chatter Archer and Hugo stood guard over the fiddles, and Myra slipped out to change.

'Have they told you the programme for tomorrow?' Hugo asked, handing himself down on to the creaking chair next to Murren's. 'No, they haven't. Because that's my job. Be ready and packed to leave at eleven. Pay your own room, will you? You'll get that back from the agent. Is that all right? Then it's train to York. There'll be time in the afternoon for you to have a look at the piano. We'll be going back very soon to the hotel. My wife never whoops it up on the first night of a tour. We'll sit half an hour and drink and be in bed by midnight. Suit you?'

'How do you think it went?'

'You don't need to ask me. It was bloody good. You saw the audience. Not that you can trust them; some would shout their heads loose if I played to 'em, provided it said the right name on the programme.'

'Do you play?'

'A bit. Chamber music. Amateur status.' The man grinned; he spoke with a far-back accent. 'I'm a retired paper-manufacturer.' He tapped Murren's sleeve as if this confession explained something. 'She's pleased with you. "He's a musician", she says; that's her line.

"Sometimes it might almost be the young Brahms playing." '

'The sonatas are late works,' Murren answered, embarrassed, grudging.

'Oh, yes. I know that.' As if that capped it all. 'Oh, yes.' He laid a hand on Murren's forearm, squeezed, and rose, as Myra, trousered and in fur coat, bridled in, signalling.

'Bed,' she called to Murren. 'We've done enough for tonight.'

It took a further half-hour to escape from the celebrations, load the taxis, but once back at the hotel, Murren was dismissed. Myra thanked him, kissed his cheek, but stepped away.

'Eleven, sharp,' Hugo warned.

Back in his bedroom, Murren could not sleep in his excitement, wished he'd provided himself with drink, decided against ringing the night-porter. He tiptoed downstairs and bought, after key-clanking and eye-closing, a miniature whisky. No glass was provided, even though the porter reacted less churlishly to his tip. Upstairs, Murren sipped, longed for a keyboard to work his bounding high spirits nearer a temperance. He heard the audience again thumping their feet, the Friedlander lacing into Brahms, his own chordal temerities beneath her. He had no doubt that she differed from ordinary people, from him. Whatever he had, she had fiftyfold. The comparison was unfair; piano playing was not his first accomplishment, but it did him good to measure himself against this powerful woman whose early talents had been developed into a violence of art. He wondered what she was doing at this minute: sitting, drinking? What? Sex? What did she and her husband discuss? Did he, Murren, get a mention?

The hotel bedroom was like nothing, nondescript, its curtains faded oatmeal, its carpet repetitious orange lozenges. Lights gleamed, over washstand, mantelpiece, the centre of the room, by the bed, over the bed, in the furthest empty corner, but merely to display the characterless walls, the standard smart bed, the lack of a picture. He turned on the TV set, watched, with the sound turned down almost to inaudibility, a film of Italian youths gathering menacingly, wild-haired, grimy-faced, while behind them squat housewives and pairs of nuns waddled and walked. He closed his eyes. Something must happen. Some explosion of joy to match their evening's attainment, but all was quiet, reduced like the telly to a murmur. He had not realized how the strength of the voices, the thuds, the plangent bursts of music affected one's viewing. Did Myra see this?

As he sat, sipping watered whisky, he realized, staring beyond the television to a metal tea-pot and jug, a cup and a saucer, that Myra Friedlander spent many evenings in such places, often after a jet flight, jagged into exotic languages, comestibles, diseases; and expected to lift hundreds of foreign faces with Bach or Mozart, Bruch, Britten, Bartók. How shall I sing the Lord's song in a strange land? She had a home in London, but how long she stayed there, wished even to do so, he did not know. Perhaps she lounged, disciplining herself, to thrive only by these wanderings, only when she changed these Slavonic or American or Asian features with the power of her music. For him this was a foreign experience, but to her the everyday means of earning a living. She belonged nowhere but on the flower-banked concert platforms, and the hotel rooms with their civilities and anonymous comfort. He finished his drink, but sat long enough, legs out straight, too excited for bed and, later, for sleep.

They travelled by train to York, and the four, Archer included, called in at the hall. Myra took a turn or two, about the platform, instructed Murren to have 'an hour with the piano' and Donald to see the instrument was tuned again and her accompanist picked up and returned to the hotel. Her violins remained encased, though she said there were one or two passages she must look at in the hotel.

'We'll perhaps have a little re-think together in Manchester,' she said, patting his bicep. 'We'll see.'

'Have you told James what we propose there?' Hugo asked.

'No. You can tell him.'

The Friedlander strutted off, to poke into the dressing rooms.

'We're staying an extra day in Manchester,' Hugo said, 'to go to a concert. Same hall; next night.'

'By whom?'

'Jasio Matyszczyk, the Polish pianist. Myra has been told for two years now that this boy is extraordinary. He won the Chopin at eighteen, the Tchaikowsky a year later. Cynosure at the Warsaw and Moscow Conservatoires. Then to Richter for lessons. He's said to be extraordinary. There's only been one record yet over here, and this is his first visit.'

'How old is he?'

'Twenty-five now, and in no hurry. The great classical executant. That's what they say, Myra's friends behind the Iron Curtain. And they don't enthuse. So she must hear him.'

'She doesn't get bored with recitals?' Murren asked.

'She doesn't go often enough. She's little time. But

when she hears of anybody like this of outstanding talent, she must make the effort to judge for herself.'

'To test herself against him?'

'Who knows? To learn, perhaps. She is not too far gone. To revive what custom has made stale?'

'Has she met Matyszczyk?'

'No. This is his first visit. He plays on Thursday in Manchester, then twice in London next week, and straight back home to think about it.'

Hugo shook his head, as if he'd said something he didn't understand or relish; he acted Myra's messenger, in outlandish tongue. Murren expressed his pleasure.

Both York and Manchester recitals went well. After the first Myra expressed one or two criticisms, and they spent an hour together. She merely sketched her part at rehearsal, but exacted enormous concentration from her pianist. He listened, learnt, for after all she'd performed these works with world-famous figures. When, occasionally, he disagreed, she heard him with courteous impatience, tried out his suggestions, but by and large disregarded them.

'You are capable of change,' she said, foreign accent strong. 'I am an old dog. I cannot learn these new tricks. Maybe yours is as good. But.'

She played the concerts with enormous warmth, with a nervous zest that was almost palpable, lifting him, directing him. Sometimes he shook at a passage like a model in a wind-tunnel, barely resisting the natural, splendid element that flowed, thrashed, whirled about him; he retained his balance with difficulty and the conflict, his edginess added brilliance to the music. After each concert again, there was early bed, no celebration.

'I have to preserve my strength,' she said. 'I am old.'

'You don't believe that,' he told her, laughing.

No reply; the black eyes rested momentarily on him, as on a goldfish or a dull bibelot or a plate about to be filled.

On the Thursday of Matyszczyk's recital, Murren was summoned to Friedlander's room to be shown what *The Times* critic said of the York concert, and the *Guardian* of the Manchester.

'They like you,' she said. Certainly he had his two or three lines of conventional praise after the celebration of her art.

'She likes you,' Hugo interpreted. Myra had no time for flippancy, but invited him to lunch at the house of some friend. He was to take his music, because they might well do an hour's practice.

'We do not play again till Saturday,' she said. 'It will be useful, and it will please the Lassmans.'

The meal, enormous and leisurely, did not begin until two o'clock, and it was four when he sat down at the Steinway. Hugo chose to snooze elsewhere, but their hosts, small, intelligent people in their sixties, sat in silence. Now and then Myra made a corrective or appreciative remark, but not seriously, though she played with élan. The two listeners sat together, round-faced Jews, in love with their ears. Myra ended with a Bach partita, saying, though straight-faced, that she must not tire her partner. Her violin sang with such potency as if it sounded inside his head, bursting out, huge in impact.

As they padded out of the room into a panelled corridor Mrs Lassman murmured, but clearly, to Murren,

'It is a privilege. Bach. A giant.'

She talked to herself, perhaps, but perfectly.

They played with a light collation; when the ladies

had changed, all stepped into the chauffeur-driven Rolls-Royce for the concert.

On the way there Mr Lassman asked if they knew what Matyszczyk was playing, hinting that it had been impossible to find out even from the ticket office. Myra laughed. 'I'll tell you something,' she said. 'This boy is beginning his programme with the last two Beethoven sonatas.'

They argued about such foolishness, keeping good wine until last, young men's arrogance. Murren sat silently, watching unfamiliar buildings, lights and shadows, in air-conditioned warmth.

'It will be a miracle if he brings it off,' Fay Lassman hazarded.

'That is what we have paid to see,' Myra answered. 'He has good hands, but playing notes is not Beethoven.'

They disembarked, not far from the hall, travelled the last few yards under umbrellas as it now drizzled. Myra had become silent, like a punter, as if she'd invested her good name on this young man's performance. Once or twice they were stopped with brief introductions made; several times they were recognized, whispered about, stared at. Murren caught the eye of a young woman who gaped at him, and grinned at her in enjoyment. As far as he could make out the audience was not so large as theirs of the previous evening; he recognized nobody, wondered if enthusiasts turned out twice in two nights. As they reached their seats, two minutes before the half-hour, a dowager smiled at him, bowing her head, quite deeply, as he passed her.

The flowers on the stage looked much the same, as far as he could tell from this side, but they had changed the piano. The one he had used was tucked away, under covers, at the far corner of the platform. He read the programme note on the A flat sonata, looked about him, felt mildly annoyed at late-comers who did not hasten as they handed in their tickets or clinked money for programmes. Matyszczyk himself was in no hurry. The audience occupied itself coughing, rustling, shifting coats. Seven minutes late the pianist arrived.

He walked quickly, nervously across the stage, a tall, pale young man with large hands. His fair hair was cut short and plastered flat, and his expression, as far as one could judge from this distance, seemed politely puckered round his mouth. Evening clothes make dummies of us all. From the middle of the stage, his great black instrument behind him, he bowed twice, leisurely enough, without affectation, then stood to let them see him before he patted his hair and moved back to his stool. There, before he sat, with one hand on the piano, he bowed again to the students in the cheap seats at the back of the platform.

With chin down, thin face sad or non-committal, he contemplated his keyboard. There was no fiddling with the stool, no reorganizing of cuffs; his tails already lay neatly in place. He looked down, a pale, strong young man, praying perhaps, making some decision, but without trouble, unfidgeting, neither relaxed nor wooden. He breathed in, lifted his hands.

The first chords spoke with a sweetness, a simplicity, an amiability that touched and appealed. Every note called clear and unforced, with a singing beauty of sound, an orderly delight in order. Matyszczyk did not play to impress; his range was subtle between temperate extremities; one was drawn forward, made to listen, at home. One did not think of his technique for he did not stagger at any difficulty or obstacle; he could, one knew, have doubled his pace without alarming himself, but he played, sitting mildly still, as if that great, rough, deaf and lonely master sat with him, listening, yes, listening to this young man reveal the unusual sweetness and clarity of his composer's mind. Tears pricked, filled Murren's eyes. Heart warmed, he lost himself. If this was not great music, it was urged from a great man, renewed into quietness, after illness perhaps, on Christmas Day, but smiling now, unequivocally cured, but surprised, uncertain still. Matyszczyk concluded, slipped into the second mischievous movement, dodging between *forte* and *piano*, but never over-violent. This, Beethoven indicated, is music; chords, notes and rhythms to liven you in a formality before I speak of myself. Enjoy this bagatelle, this little savagery, but its dodging, its dig in the ribs, its caprice will introduce my serious voice; vagaries are controlled, because soon, soon I shall stumble into eloquence, and lift myself fugally free.

Matyszczyk's face nodded down, unlined, un- and in- tense as he began the recitative, reached the *arioso*. Here his hands were sovereign; closed eyes, pallor and the awareness in his barely moving shoulder demonstrated that he, his self watched as his fingers grieved, sighing and immoderate. Here one called from a sick-bed, from the border of death, but with an eloquent lament, each note poignant of itself and for the next, beautiful with the agony of lifted hands in a pietà. The pianist neither emphasised nor exaggerated; what these fingers drew from wood and wire needed no histrionics. Pain etched its own landscape, and the composer's spirit, withered inside dehumanizing weakness, torture of bone and nerve, could yet claim its home, a human being, cared for by others, tended in its despair, preparing for a recovery or a quietus.

In the interval between the two sonatas, Murren the musician tried to account for his amazement that so great an effect had been called up by so ordinary means. To say each note lasted its length, had its proper volume or resonance was pleonasm. This *arioso*, this exhausted song lacked formal order, perhaps. No, it did not. It had spoken to him, through the music to the reality behind, the loneliness. But, again, it was no black, sodden body on a cold pond, no Wisniewski, yellow-faced with cancer, passing five minutes with two young people in an alien place, no Patricia stripped of her brazen confidence, no Nigel smashed bleeding into a gutter puddle. Beethoven knew these in his own exhausted weakness, but demonstrated his strength to say a word; that was the difference. He had, for a short respite, come through so that he suffered his song rather than acted it. Beethoven looked with the eyes of Wisniewski, but his voice was a master's. Ermattet, exhausted.

Three days later Murren on his return from Edinburgh and the final, marvellous concert had found a letter from Ashley briefly announcing that Tim Gelsthorpe the organist had turned his car over on the motorway, was not expected to live. That brilliant young man had died next day, and Murren was overwhelmed with the icy frenzy of grief that unmanned him at his mother's death. He tried to play, then, through this Beethoven, but it lay empty on the page. Gelsthorpe's dazzling fingers were smashed; the nerve, the miraculous muscular control broken, crushed in a dead body. Timothy Arnold Gelsthorpe, the extrovert, the virtuoso of huge sounds, the bobby-dazzler who whirled dervish brilliance up at cathedral roofs and crashed thunder between pillar and arch, was gone, done in; one small error, mismanagement, misjudgement, fluff, had put him beyond all correction; one slip, one wrong note, dead.

Murren remembered a poem his father often quoted. The old chap was interested in music, with a good voice, but a nobody between the Peterson sisters and his son; just now and again, perhaps once a year, deliberately or not, he'd come out, settle scores with this his bit of Victoriana, the Organist in Heaven. Father Murren knew nobody approved; and his face registered an ironical rejection of their disdain. The last time he'd said it was in France, back to his fire, hands in trouser pocket, a man unknown to his son, double-chinned, in a strange land, smirking.

> And likest to a soft dove brooding
>   The innocent figure ran;
> So breathed the breath of his preluding
>   And then his fugue began.

Jasio Matyszczyk stepped into Beethoven's fugue, *con calma*, his fingers calling out the certainty of rising fourths, which spoke the order of health, the end of illness, the knowledge that art, that old-fashioned mastery of controlled flight, could resume life after the most desperate of smashes. The hands were at their work of healing, lifting this audience, reassuring, reasserting the spring, the warmth of resurrection, the revitalizing of broken tissue. This was the composer's gift. It could not, remembered, bring back Gelsthorpe; not Nigel Brockless; it settled nothing of Prudence Mark's saddening sexuality; it did not shift shadows from the bedrooms of the dying Wisniewskis. Patricia Payne severed connection with sanity for tethered hours; her brother faced the icy pond in spite of it; Jessica took death full in the face. This fugue did not prevent, nor prohibit; it could not. But it asserted life; someone spoke in these measured, unbullying tones and we were comforted for minutes on end. That eloquent lament would claw again, tear grief out of Beethoven's bleeding side, but he would rise, invert his fugue and reinvent, '*wieder auflebend*', not in a banging paean of joy, but with strong and measurable certainty, counterpoint devoured, its work gloriously done, into a pleasure, a sturdy delight of melody.

Matyszczyk played with eloquence, with this touch, this sovereign understanding, all through the recital, although his tumult or heavenly serenity in the great op. 111 or the Chopin B flat, the Liszt, Rachmaninov and Scriabin of his second half did not move Murren as the last pages of his wide-eyed Beethoven. Music did what it could. What warm hearth or bleak landscape this young man knew for his home did not count; what foreign language here flitted in his brain; behind the artificial leaves in this city he led Murren temporarily homewards, to where the spirit lifted, to where Beethoven smiled friendly, where snow melted, the quickest way out of Manchester into Manchester the Golden.

Matyszczyk rose, and bowed. Myra Friedlander signalled with a finger, almost minutely, her intense satisfaction. The audience clapped, but would soon fall to talking between items, reassuming the decent world of shops and advertisements, meals and everyday humdrum. 'And thou shalt remember that thou wast a bondman in the land of Egypt,' the piano stood dumb, polished and unresponsive, 'and the Lord Thy God redeemed thee.'

Matyszczyk bowed.